THE
PAEGONAEAN
STORY

David Blair

Grosvenor House
Publishing Limited

This book is published by
Grosvenor House Publishing Ltd
28-30 High Street, Guildford, Surrey, GU1 3HY.
www.grosvenorhousepublishing.co.uk

A CIP record for this book
is available from the British Library

ISBN 978-1-908105-62-2

For Angela

The sky calls to us. If we do not destroy ourselves, we will one day venture to the stars.

~ Carl Sagan ~

– Prologue –

Three Tales from the Wastelands

Once upon a time, Earth was a deeply divided and unenlightened world, and it is towards the end of this dark age that our story begins. The colonisation of its solar system had yet to begin and this little planet stood all alone amidst an infinite ocean of untold mystery. All they knew was war and aggression, and it seemed that this new and struggling race would promptly extinguish themselves once they developed the necessary technology.

It was there that the ingredients for life were stirred together, and where their primitive ancestors first crawled upon the land from the watery cauldrons in which they were formed. These creatures began walking upright and grew more intelligent, eventually evolving into consciously thinking beings. Through this emerging consciousness, the people of Earth connected with the Cosmos; an ancient and omniscient spirit that bestowed upon their minds the first test of universal existence. Mankind was then filled with a powerful and inexplicable desire to conquer and unite; for all worlds must be as one before they can unlock the second of the universal tests. It was this very quest that made almost all of the burgeoning civilisations across the cosmic plain rush headlong towards self-destruction, only a few ever surviving to become vast galactic systems, armed with inter-stellar travel and rich with the wisdom of the Universe.

The Empires of Earth rose and fell through the centuries thereafter; territories contested by the might of their armies as the battle for this planet was fought. But it was the people of the Paegonaean Empire, who arose just before the close of their twenty-first century a.d., who defeated all opposition and finally united the continents and oceans of Earth under one system.

Their conquest lasted twelve years, and saw the victorious new regime install an unrivalled worldwide dominion with only a scrap of the old world yet to conquer. All that stood between them and final victory was this last pocket of shattered resistance, and the Paegonaeans built a wall as high as the sky itself around this land, as they prepared for its annihilation.

Those contained within this great wall had their worst fears realised when the Paegonaeans' powerful defence grid began encroaching upon them from all sides, gathering the four million of this forsaken land within its tightening and inescapable grasp. All surrounding towns and villages were reduced to a desert of red dust by this awesome weapon as it slowly closed in around the capital city of the last rebel stronghold. These people took to the basements and cellars of this city in the hope that this apocalypse would somehow pass them by. Buildings began to crack and crumble as the surrounding horizon darkened and filled with a wrathful element. Some of those brave enough to look likened the destructive force of this weapon to a relentless shower of meteors crashing down from above and scoring deeply into the land beyond. Others claimed to see houses and farmlands being tore from the ground and vaporised as its front line edged closer towards them. Those underground heard ireful shrieks mixed with thunderous groans of unimaginable destruction, growing louder and louder and shaking all that it had besieged with its terrible promise. The people closed their eyes and solemnly awaited their fate, praying to their Gods for salvation.

Three days and nights passed in these dark and trembling bunkers before the furious clamour began to subside, and those who had survived emerged to the new reality of their little world. Though much of the infrastructure and many of the city's buildings had collapsed as a result of the shockwaves, the Paegonaeans' defence grid had not passed overhead as expected, but had retreated back from the edge of their city across the settling dust beyond. The city now stood however, as though an island, surrounded on all sides by a red and barren wilderness that would soon become known as the wastelands.

A group of scouts were assembled in the central city, and set off from points in the north, south, east and west, to travel through the newly-formed wastelands, to the great surrounding wall and bring back what information they could. When none of these scouts returned, teams were dispatched to find out why, and found that their enemy's powerful defence grid had not retreated fully, but held an impenetrable line of defence, twenty kilometres before the great wall that contained them. Those who strayed into this protected area were vaporised on the spot, and a wire fence was erected just before it and encircled the periphery of their little world.

Back in the forgotten city, the people looked out to the dull and reddened horizon around them for any sign of the Paegonaeans' final onslaught... but it never came. With neither the capability of attack nor hope of salvation through surrender, their forlorn position in this new world was clear, and the people pondered with unease the cruel twist of absurdity in the mercy they had been shown. Just why had they been spared and left abandoned within this wall?

Nevertheless, life must always go on, and these forsaken people had first to rebuild their city and establish some kind of working civilisation. Memories of the Paegonaeans and the global Empire beyond their protected wall grew distant and forgotten through the years that followed. The leadership of the old resistance were the first to claim control of the city and its surrounding desert. They set up all manner of defensive measures along the periphery of their little world, but with the threat of invasion diminishing with time, this leadership soon crumbled and the city descended into anarchy. Many fled to the vast new plains of the wastelands to escape the ensuing chaos, populating the arid wilderness with a growing network of small communes and encampments.

Rival gangs contested bitterly for the streets of the unclaimed city, and through the violence and bloodshed in the years that followed, it was a group known only as the Company who eventually rose to a position of governmental power. They had amassed wealth and resources through the profitable trade of weaponry and had armed all sides of the city's brutal struggle. Once in a position of power themselves, they began manufacturing defence systems and equipping the struggling neighbourhoods with all they needed to protect themselves. Through the growth of the

Company's security network, stability and order were gradually restored under their management. It would be many years before they again heard from the Paegonaeans, and the Company were free to resurrect a system of government similar to that of their old world.

Citizens of this renewed society were to be registered onto a database alongside their individual retinal identity, and this was at the centre of everything. Credit accounts were set up for each of them in the Company's new monetary system, and this little world began to flourish, revived by a growing cycle of consumerism. Those who refused registration soon found themselves exiled by the emerging technology, as they were now unable to buy or sell and had very limited access to the newly fortified city around them. This new system meant that the Company were able to monitor the whereabouts of each and every citizen through the transactions they logged and the buildings they accessed. Having achieved incontestable and irrevocable control of what was to be known henceforth as Fortress city, the Company turned their attention to the communes in the surrounding wasteland.

Life was never easy in the wastelands, and in every commune there were tales of woe and desperation. The Company's proposition in the twentieth year since the war was seen as a lifeline to the people of the wastelands. Though some maintained a wariness of their institution, most accepted with only a hint of reluctance. Every wastelander was to be registered onto their database and, thereafter, they would receive monthly supplies of all they needed and their communes updated with the technology necessary for the new system.

In the year that followed, technicians from the Company installed their computers in ninety percent of these communes and educated their people on how it all worked. A mechanical beast of unparalleled ambition called the Trade-convoy was constructed for the purpose of delivering much-needed supplies throughout the newly-registered wastelands, for a small but rising fee, and set off on its maiden voyage shortly after. But it was in a quiet and unassuming little commune in the very depths of the wastelands that they were to receive a more permanent resolution to their problem.

~ The Greenery ~

A shabby watchtower stood at each of the commune's corners and looked out above its battle-scarred walls to the endless desert of red dust beyond. There was little of life out there but for those small and twisted red nubs that poked from its surface here and there and stretched out their gnarled limbs. Only those most desperate souls travelled so far south through the wastelands to this purgatorial refuge, and did what was asked of them for sanctuary.

One night, during a particularly notable windstorm, a small shrouded figure appeared through the dusty mist and banged on its gates with one final gust of energy. The young woman then collapsed; almost perished from the journey she had just endured and was carried inside by the people of the commune. Her recovery was made comfortable by the attention she received and was soon strong enough to explore her new surroundings. The people welcomed her with mild curiosity and watched with interest as she wandered through the rugged commune with serene detachment.

She was put to work in the kitchen, and each evening the young Miss Carver would quietly retire to her small lodging alone and remain there until morning. The mundane lives of those there resumed in much the same way they had until the stagnant air of the commune was stirred one morning with a shout from one of its watchtowers. Armed guards took their positions and the crowd that had gathered watched with tense apprehension as the gates of their commune opened and a weather-beaten truck entered. Each and every one of them was confounded when it dumped a load of soil right there, and they slowly approached to investigate. It had been so long since any of them had seen the natural brown substance, and the children of the commune chased one another with handfuls of it, not really knowing what it was. Miss Carver appeared through the bewildered crowd and explained in her gentle manner that she had ordered it with the intention of testing some of the poisoned dust in the hope that it would some day be able to sustain a small garden. A stir of murmurs arose around her and she was suddenly the debate of her neighbours, many of whom were quick to praise such a novel pursuit and offered their support right there and then. The rest just nodded and walked away, allowing that it would at least keep them occupied until something else came along.

There was little success to talk about in the first year, though support for her endeavour grew and grew. Friends and neighbours claimed that it was the young woman's knowledge and infinite faith that they admired most, whereas others claimed it to be her seemingly endless funds. Failed plots of reddened soil were carted away and replaced by more, supplied by a steady stream of deliveries from the unscathed reaches of Fortress city. Her small lodging became a laboratory, where mysterious chemicals with unpronounceable names were mixed and tested, and where she schooled all those willing to learn. The decision was then made by the commune's chiefs to relieve her of her post in the kitchen so that she could apply herself more fully on what she had invested. Soon, plots of soil were popping up everywhere within the walls of that little commune and everyone was becoming interested in this new science.

It took until the following Spring for the first rewards of their labour to show and an excitement filled the commune. Miss Carver and a group of her most loyal workers gathered around their original patch of soil to witness the thin mist of green as the first of the shoots breached its surface. The successful method was noted and replicated and several more plots blossomed in the weeks that followed.

News travelled through neighbouring encampments to the larger communes further north, and from there it made its way into the most secluded reaches of the wastelands, bringing people from all over to come and see. Security around the commune was tightened and only a handful of the travelling masses were permitted entry at any one time. Those outside waited eagerly through harsh and unprotected windstorms and wallowed in the mud that followed the heavy rain. But what they beheld once inside filled their hearts with the same primal joy that their ancestors felt as they gathered around the first fires. They asked how much a small portion to have for themselves would cost or perhaps even to know its secret. It was then that the more enterprising of those in the commune pondered how best to exploit this discovery using the Company's new monetary system. They closed their doors to the public and reopened several months later as a place of business.

The little commune, which, before this time, never had a reason to be called anything, took the Greenery for its name, and became the first marketplace in those barren depths. No longer a shelter for the outcasts of Fortress city, wastelanders gathered there each day to purchase DIY garden-kits and equipment, as well as fresh produce from a growing range of stock.

Before long, grass was again working its way through the red dust all over the wastelands. Though the process of purchasing and maintaining a garden out there was expensive and complicated, it was no longer uncommon to find a patch of green framing some lonely abode or a large open square being shared by a small community. The increasing availability of this technology brought business and competition, which in turn brought a level of prosperity and restoration to the wastelands, reminding those simple folk who lived there what their world had once been like.

By the Greenery's third year of trading, the men of the commune were sowing seeds in the empty drills of huge fields well beyond their fortified outer wall. Stalks of corn and wheat rose from those around them and in others cattle and sheep grazed upon luscious green grass. A state of the art defence system was installed to protect the commune's growing perimeter. During the years that followed, the Greenery lost much of the garden-kit market to the larger companies in Fortress city, who revolutionised the industry with mass production and cheaper kits. However, the Greenery's line of fresh produce had already grown to become a brand familiar throughout the wastelands, with twelve acres of quality-assured land now to farm.

Central to all was the hallowed original belonging to Miss Carver, now enclosed with adequate security so the passing tourists could enjoy without touching. They travelled there from every corner of their tiny world; even those from Fortress city came to see the rare and beautiful mix of flowers on display there. Though now an old woman in her eightieth year, the legendary Miss Carver could still be seen plucking weeds and wild flowers from her award-winning garden and sharing a few secrets with those who passed by.

On that particular day, the elderly Miss Carver was busy preparing her garden for the rush of tourists that would resume again at two. She took a satisfied glance around her once she had finished her chores and returned to her kitchen to prepare some lunch. The weather was hot that day and she sat down on her celebrated little meadow with a plate of boiled eggs and ham while proudly surveying her creation. Every year, the colour returned with more vibrancy and the fragrance more intense and passionate. There were other gardens in the wastelands, one or two perhaps in the Greenery that could have rivalled hers for aesthetic beauty and imagination, but this was her art, and she reckoned it among the best.

The clock struck one as Miss Carver swallowed her last bite of lunch and she leaned back upon her manicured lawn. She watched the clouds pass by overhead and pushed the level of her hearing-aid up several notches, listening to the sounds of the world around her. She could hear the buzz of the insects going about their business, having somehow just appeared one day when her flowers began to blossom and had clung to her garden since like a shipwrecked crew upon an island. She could hear the soft wind caress all it touched and rustle the leaves of the baby oak tree beside her. She could hear the gentle hum of the filtration system beneath the soil and her eyelids began to grow heavy. She lay back fully upon the grass and drew a deep breath and held the symphony of fragrances, as sleep beckoned with one lazy finger.

Then something happened in the world around her and she startled from the brink of slumber. 'What was that?' she asked aloud.

The door of a house in the distance shot open and a large woman in a pink nightgown burst from it and made her way sternly towards some boys playing football on a small patch of grass nearby. The boys lifted their ball and shuffled close together. She approached them with a hand raised towards an aerial that hung slightly crooked above her house and asked angrily. 'Who hit that?'

The boys looked at each other and shook their heads in unison. 'Wasn't any of us,' answered the tallest of them.

'If I don't get a name from one of you, I will have footballs banned. Gardens are not meant for sport,' said the woman in a cool even tone, striking fear more earnestly in the hearts of the boys. 'Now tell me, who hit the aerial?'

The boys responded with awkward movements and dismissed their accuser gladly when her attention snagged on someone in the distance.

'I hope these boys aren't disturbing you, my dear,' the woman shouted.

'Not at all,' replied Miss Carver, peeping above the wall that surrounded her garden. 'Is there a problem?'

'No problem. I was just watching television when, all of a sudden, the picture turned as clear as life. Every channel. No fuzz. I've never seen such a reception. Did you notice anyone near the aerials?'

Miss Carver looked up to the sky and found herself uttering the words. 'Something strange is drawing near.'

~ The Junkyard ~

Earl had worked at the junkyard since he was a boy and had come of age in the days when such establishments out there in the wastelands had to protect themselves. Armed with moderate weaponry and light armour, the changing face of the junkyard crew had fought back endless waves of bandits through the years, while at the same time trading with those wishing to do business. All this was to end some years ago however when the Company began subcontracting the protection of the registered territories to local security firms. With the Company claiming one percent of every credit spent on their monetary system as tax, it proved very profitable to introduce another level of expenditure above the daily transactions of the people, and competition amongst the prospective firms was encouraged. The security firms that arose under the Company's summoning hand armed all such establishments under their jurisdictions with expensive and elaborate defence systems. This resulted in the creation of a highly fortified new wasteland, in which the only invaders were those who did so from their computers, hoping to impress their local security firm or even the Company with their hacking skills.

Earl arrived there around ten that morning and began the day with the usual routines; arming certain parts of the defence system while resting others and luring the dogs back to their enclosure. With these out of the way, there was little else to do but sit back and take the rest of the day at his leisure. Business had slowed steadily through the years and his diminishing workforce had reflected this. No longer did he need guards to watch over the desert outside or a team of mechanics to restore the old and rusted vehicles of an underprivileged community. However, business had slightly improved since they first heard of this recession four years ago, and people were being more cautious with their credit. Earl chose not to understand the perplexities of the Company's financial system, but stated simply that he failed to see how there could be less credit in circulation today than there had been before all this chat began. A winding down of the monetary system, he had heard his nephew call it. Not that it really bothered him; as long as it brought customers from the manufacturers' showrooms in Fortress city to the junkyard looking for parts, a recession was a good thing.

Earl reclined into his soft and inviting chair and turned on a television, flicking through the channels before finally settling upon the Hexlon Security judicial page. It was there that the people of the southern wastelands came to view the news from their province and vote on the punishment of the criminals they had listed there. All they had today however was an exhaustive inventory of those with warrants for unpaid bills and those who had fallen into debt. Earl turned off the television with a disdainful grunt and threw his feet upon the defence console and closed his eyes for a nap.

Suddenly, the dogs began to bark...

Earl awoke and rose hurriedly from his chair and walked towards a window overlooking the yard. Something had spooked the dogs and their barking pierced an eerie silence. He returned to his station and flexed his fingers before setting to work. At the touch of a single button, a bank of screens illuminated around him and, through the silent corridors of the junkyard, heat and motion sensors began to roam. He watched intently for movement or a glimpse of something somewhere. But there was nothing.

Earl leaned back into his chair to muse the dilemma. Had it been an alarm there would be protocol to follow, but in the case of barking dogs there was nothing. Even dogs had been made redundant in this golden age, though Earl kept them around should the technology ever falter. With the touch of another button, the door to their enclosure swung open, but instead of watching them race across the junkyard and search hungrily through the aisles of stacked cars, they remained on their hind legs, howling wildly into the air. Earl paced the control room with long thoughtful strides. Fearful that an invading force had somehow bypassed the defence system and was slowly infiltrating the ranks of the junkyard, he turned towards the control panel and lifted the switch for the mosquito system. The mosquito was the primary measure against an attack and deafened everyone beyond the control room with a high frequency siren. As he hit it, the barking stopped. He looked out the window and saw that the dogs had returned to all fours, somehow appeased by the frequency of the mosquito, though they anxiously paced their enclosure with obvious unease. This only served to further the dilemma and Earl scratched his clueless head. He picked up the phone and dialled the emergency number for the first time in as long as he could remember. It rang several times and was answered by a sprightly, youthful voice. 'Hexlon Security.'

Earl explained the situation

'Dogs barking?' said the guard, before taking some time to ponder it himself. 'Strange, but probably nothing. I will see what we have down there and send them over your way. Please switch off all defensive measures and await their arrival. You have a nice day, sir.'

Earl hung up the phone and turned off the mosquito system. As he did, the barking erupted again. He closed his eyes and just sat there, letting his mind wander far from that place until an alarm brought him back again. Eleven vehicles had just appeared on radar, racing towards the junkyard from all directions. Screens jumped to life all around him, showing different angles of each approaching vehicle while flicking through an alphabet of colours. Others brought up the official registration of each occupant and compiled comprehensive lists of useless information. The vehicles were all registered to Hexlon Security and Earl looked no further than that. He pressed the button for the main gate and, after several warnings that he had not prepped the inner defence system, they swung open to accept the oncoming guards.

The vehicles skidded to a halt in a rough V formation just inside the main gates. Their doors burst open and the first wave of guards jumped from them, venturing through the aisles of the junkyard with their weapons held high. The second wave emerged less hurriedly and began setting up equipment here and there. With all engaged in their tasks, a tall thin man stepped out from the head vehicle and wandered leisurely towards Earl with both hands held behind his back, taking all in with a contented smile. On either side of the path he walked were plots of reddened soil that Earl had bought for a considerable fee from the nearby Greenery in the hope of brightening the dull façade of his workplace with a few flowers. Though the guard who approached seemed quite young, he was obviously more senior than his colleagues, wearing attire more ceremonial than practical.

'Dogs barking?' said the guard. 'Nothing on radar or any other alarms going off?'

Earl shook his head and then looked around him more thoughtfully. 'Something is up… I can feel it in my bones.'

'Don't get so excited just yet. Have you run thermal scans of the area and taken measures against an attack?'

Earl shook his head. 'Only the mosquito.'

'There are ways of passing through a mosquito system,' he responded, but added quickly. 'No matter. My boys are running every manner of scan at the moment. I wouldn't expect it to be anything sinister, but it will give the boys some training.' He then turned towards his men combing the junkyard. 'Sure would be special if we found something.'

'How do you mean?'

'Well… Things have been mighty slow lately. Computers are the new domain for crime. Another year or two and there'll be no Hexlon guards left, just technicians and analysts. For every one of us that gets the boot, one of those boys get elected.' He shrugged his shoulders. 'Progress.'

Another guard approached. 'Nothing here, boss,' he said, looking in the direction of the barking dogs. 'Could be the scent of a pack of desert dogs nearby. Could be fleas. Whatever it is, it is none of our business.'

The guards packed up and left after some final checks, leaving Earl all alone with the dogs still barking. He stamped up the steps to the control room, where the final shreds of his patience wore ragged and thin, and picked up the phone once more.

The call was answered by a flustered and fatigued voice with an unmistakeable chorus of dogs barking in the background.

'Your dogs are barking, too?' said Earl.

'Sure are. Can't shut them up. I take it that's why you're calling. People from all around have been ringing me since one o clock with the same problem. You registering anything strange on your computers?'

'Nothing. It seems the dogs know something they don't.'

~ The Outpost ~

In the very depths of the southern wastelands, beyond Miss Carver and her garden-filled commune and beyond Earl's junkyard of barking dogs, along the perimeter that stretched before the invisible barrier of the Paegonaeans' dormant defence grid, sat a small and solitary outpost. It was owned by a scientific department of the Company, who used the small hut as a dust-testing facility. Though the method of preparing the poisoned ground of the wastelands for nature to again flourish through it had already been developed, it had yet to be made economically viable for widespread implementation, and this pursuit was the purpose of this facility. A team of three scientists would stay there for a month at a time; digging up old probes and recording their results before planting others elsewhere in the treated dust. There was usually little to do after the first week but sit around, see to the occasional flashing light and maintain a general presence around the expensive equipment.

A seasoned scientist called John sat on the porch of the small outpost, listening to some music through headphones while his two younger colleagues kicked a ball about in the lifeless dust. Fifty yards beyond them was the wire fence that marked the perimeter of their little world, with a sign on every post warning that the land beyond was protected by the Paegonaeans; their great wall only visible on the clearest of days from this distance.

The clock struck one and John sighed quietly. Just another three days of this scorching sun and merciless desert, he thought, and he'd be back by his swimming pool in Fortress city. As his mind began to settle and dip beneath the waken world, a buzzer sounded from inside the outpost. Before he could gather his thoughts from the depths of his snooze, another buzzer began to chime, quickly followed by another.

Bob and Marcus, his young colleagues, came running when they heard the commotion and entered the outpost to find John running reams of data through his hands, shaking his head as he read. 'Something has happened,' he announced. 'All our recordings have just dropped.'

'All of them?' asked Marcus with an incredulous frown. He pulled out a drawer from the filing cabinet and searched for the recordings of the previous week. When he found them, he snapped the ream of data from John and set both on the table next to each other. His head swayed back and forth, from one to the other and then back.

'Well?'

'The readings have indeed dropped, John. But it seems that those closer to the perimeter are more affected than those we planted further back. Pod 3165 is planted eight kilometres inland and shows a drop of only one percent while pod 3127 is planted just before the wire fence and shows a drop of fifteen percent. Pod 3144 is somewhere between and shows a drop of seven percent. Make sense of that, if you will?'

John nodded to himself. 'At least it's a place to start.'

The three men walked outside and looked around, pointing roughly in the direction of each pod and checking its new reading, scratching their heads at the conundrum.

'There is one explanation,' said Bob, the junior of the three. 'In fact, it would explain all this quite neatly.'

'And what would that be?'

Bob turned and looked in the direction of the wire fence and beyond. 'The Paegonaeans' defence grid is down.'

John and Marcus turned to one another and laughed at what they thought was a joke, but were checked when its implications dawned on them. The dormant defence grid gave off so much energy that it affected the pods. There was a formula they used before assessing the readings and one of the variables was distance from the wire fence. It had been so ingrained in their logic that they had accepted it as one would the effect of oxygen in the air. Then John shook his head and waved his hands before him. 'No... no, no, no. You mean that after eighty years or so, it has just gone off? And that it was the three of us that made this discovery?'

'There's only one way to find out for sure,' said Marcus, nominating Bob with a pat on the back.

John drew a long reminiscent breath before speaking. 'I was out here years ago, back when I had just started with the Company. We kept hearing a dog at night when we had gone to bed, but there was never any sight of it the next day. Then one morning I went outside earlier than usual and there it stood, starved and beaten. I went back in and got some meat to take out to it. The dog saw me approach and bolted. It found a spot under the wire fence and crawled underneath. There was a noise like thunder and a sudden gust of wind blew me back against the outpost. The dust eventually settled and there was a crater the size of a house just beyond the fence. The dog was nowhere to be seen.'

Again there was silence until Marcus spoke with an eerie realisation. 'Does this mean that the Paegonaeans are coming? Their army could be heading this way right now to finish us all off! We'd be rabbits to them; sport before the fight! We need to call someone!'

'Who?'

'Hexlon Security... The Company. I don't know. Someone!'

'We need something more than our pods failing for them to send someone all the way down here,' said John.

The three men walked to the wire fence and peered into the distance for any sign of an advancing army when a strange noise could be heard from the sky behind them. They turned and looked up and saw a small flock of birds fly overhead and into the protected area.

... 'Get headquarters on the phone,' said John. 'They can take it from here.'

The Journey Begins

The mayhem unfolded in the early hours of the following morning with the arrival of the media and the hordes following close behind. What was once the desolate and forgotten periphery of their little world was now the playground for everyone's hopes and fears, and many travelled out there to join in the fused celebration of this mysterious event. Some came waving huge colourful banners and singing loudly while others proclaimed the end of things to come. Vehicles from every security firm were scattered amidst the eclectic mix of pilgrims and their personnel were setting up makeshift outposts along the perimeter. Of course, such a gathering would not have been complete without those preachers who had spent their lives arguing one way or the other, and now here it was before them. Stages were erected for these men and women, and people flocked around them to hear what they had to say.

'The time has come, my brethren!' shouted one fiery preacher. 'We have repented for the sins of our fathers and those who stood against the Paegonaeans, and now their doors are opening and acceptance finally upon us! From crushed resistance we have returned, strong and harmonious, so that we may become the final and unifying jigsaw piece that will complete this great

Empire of Earth! No longer do they need the wall that surrounds us nor the defence grid they have just turned off! This world of ours shall be united at last!'

'That man is a fool, and so too are those who listen to him!' shouted another from a neighbouring stage. 'How easy we forget! How easy we forget the brutality of their conquest! How easy we forget that they have forsaken us here upon this tiny piece of land and blasted our border to dust with their defence grid so that we could never rise against them! We call ourselves the Free world, but we are no freer than the cattle that graze their fields! Through the ashes of our towns and cities we crawled to make pilgrimages of surrender and found that they are protected by this needless defence grid! And we are to fall to our knees and praise them now it has been turned off! Do not listen to that man or his fantasies of glorious redemption! He would have you bend your neck before their axe and thank them for the honour! This defence grid will awaken once more and repeat what it did eighty years ago! Only this time they'll leave nothing and complete their Empire without us!'

'Maybe they're coming to surrender!' shouted someone from the crowd, and laughter arose all around.

Such interchanges went on without resolve throughout the bewildered little state of the Free world, and its media had given themselves entirely to the debate. An official statement from the Company was released later that morning in which they called for calm, and for everyone to remain behind the perimeter and not to approach the wall. They then went on to confirm that they had consolidated all security firms under their command and were implementing a defence strategy designed for such an occasion. Outposts were being erected at points all along the perimeter, concentrating mainly along the east and west. They called upon all men, naming those in the north and south especially, to remain vigilant and, where possible, set up checkpoints of their own and report anything suspicious to their nearest security firm. They ended by reiterating their official policy regarding the Paegonaeans. 'We will keep our distance if they keep theirs.' It was clear that the Company did not need this right now, and hoped that it would simply go away if they continued on as normal.

News indeed for those villages that dotted the south, most of which had grown from encampments when justice and order had been maintained with the help of bounty hunters. It was twenty years ago when Jeb Williams and Colt Riderson followed the trail of the Carson gang down there after Hexlon Security put one thousand credits on each of their heads. With the trail growing cold amid rumours that the gang had met with an ambush set by Hexlon themselves, the men were left with the decision to make the long journey home empty-handed or set up camp and see what else came their way. They had remained there ever since, with a village grown up around them, built from the bounties of those they had brought in.

Jeb Williams retired to the den in the attic of his house, where memories of the old days lived most prominently. His friends and he would play cards up there twice a week with the youngsters of the village in the background quietly listening to their banter. But today old Jeb sat alone, puffing on a ventilator with the knowledge that his end was coming near. His breathing had deteriorated steadily in the last few years and on warm days like this he suffered most.

The door creaked open and his wife peeked in from behind it.

Jeb did not say a word but motioned for her to sit.

She shook her head. 'The Riderson boys are here.'

'Is it important?' he asked between blasts of oxygen.

'I don't know,' she replied. 'They have maps. I heard them mention something about news from the front.'

Jeb nodded with a sudden glint of interest and began packing away his breathing apparatus. 'Tell the boys I'm in the bathroom and send them up in five minutes.'

There was a knock at the door five minutes later and the three Riderson boys entered to find old Jeb facing an empty sofa, towards which he nodded for them to sit. In frames all around the den were newspaper cut-outs and photographs, most of which included a youthful Jeb and the boys' father, Colt, with some unfortunate bounty trussed like a turkey by their feet.

'What news do you bring?'

The Ridersons informed old Jeb of the statement the Company had just issued and implored him that they act.

'If the rumours are true and we are to be invaded, it is very likely that they will be coming this way,' said the eldest, pulling out a map and laying it across the table between them. 'We can assume that Fortress city is their target, at the very centre of our world. But the distance between Fortress city and the wall they built around us is great. A march through the wastelands would severely weaken an invading army and give the Company and her security forces ample opportunity to repel them. Therefore, it would be advantageous for them to capture a base within our land, from where they could advance more readily upon their ultimate target. There are many towns and large communes in the surrounding wastelands, but none that equal the might of Hexlon city, in the midst of the southern wastelands. This would prove to be an invaluable base, halfway between their wall and Fortress city. With the Company using three quarters of their resources towards the east and the west, this leaves this path relatively unguarded.'

Old Jeb nodded for the boys to continue their brief.

The second eldest leaned forward with a more detailed and localised map and set it on top of the other. He pointed to a position not far from their village and ran his finger behind the wire fence into the grey area beyond that had until yesterday been protected by the Paegonaeans' defence grid. 'These highlands offer many advantages. Neither heat nor motion sensors will pick them up from that height. There are only a handful of other places that offer that kind of natural protection along the perimeter. An army could easily move through here undetected until they were well on their way to Hexlon city.'

Old Jeb nodded. 'You boys have learned well. Your father would have been proud of you.' He leaned back into his chair and glanced around the walls of his den. 'Go round up the troops.'

A group of the village's most eager young men were assembled and vehicles loaded with old and dusty equipment. The awakening spirit of combat stirred in each of them as they travelled to the proposed site and set up checkpoints at the bottom of each of the three descents from the highland beyond. Jeb selected two of the young men to help him set up and maintain a command post further back, where he could survey their entire operation. They nailed pegs into the soft dust and erected tents, in which they set up computers, equipment and beds should they need to spend the night out there. It took just under thirty minutes to set everything up and relay the feeds to the equipment inside the tents. The newly-ordained guards watched the screens all about them and the paths they guarded in silence. Campfires were lit and food prepared for the long evening ahead. But what they all failed to notice was that it was *they* who were being watched.

Beyond the wire fence, where the land began to rise more steeply, there was a cliff that jutted out from that around it, where a solitary figure shuffled close to the edge on his elbows. He held a small pair of binoculars to his eyes, watching the checkpoints at the bottom of each descent before him and the more central command post further back. A tear would occasionally trickle from his eyes, as his every movement roused the fine dust on which he lay. As he watched the men before him, the stranger sneezed without warning and its echo reverberated through the hollows below.

The youngest of the Ridersons lifted his head from the campfire and turned his eyes towards the highland. 'What was that?' he asked, as he rose to his feet.

Though it was not the marching feet of an approaching army nor the distinct whoomph of mortar fire on their position, the boy had heard something. He walked to the wire fence and stood there motionless and silent as his eyes darted about the peaks. After the other members of his team assured him that they had heard nothing, he decided that it must have been his imagination and returned to his checkpoint after one final glance.

Once the boy had sat down and engaged himself in the conversation of those around the campfire, the stranger returned to his cruiser some distance back. With its bulky and deep-treaded tyres and moderate defence capabilities, it could have been a vehicle from any security firm in the wastelands. The stranger hoped that he would not have to rely on either of these features on his journey. When the on-board computer of his vehicle flickered on, the digital-layout of the surrounding area confirmed that there were no other ways down from this height. Five heat signatures clustered at the base of each of the descents with three more further back, where his vehicle's sensors had detected some heavy artillery. His armoured cruiser could battle its way through the checkpoints, but this command post would first have to be silenced. The trunk yawned open and he lifted a rifle from it and returned to his position at the cliff's edge.

The shutter of its scope flipped open and the stranger found old Jeb, now scouring through the bands of a radio for any scrap of information that may have been of use to them. His finger stiffened along the trigger when the stranger suddenly lowered his weapon and looked thoughtfully on the scene before him. He unhooked a small walkie-talkie from his belt and tuned it to the Company's secured line and spoke in an accentless voice. 'Company outpost G – 54386. Emergency broadcast. Reporting contact four kilometres south of our position. One of our vehicles has been found burning after a team failed to check in. Assistance required. Hostiles likely.'

Watching the old man through the telescopic sight of his rifle, he repeated the broadcast over and over until Jeb jumped from his seat and into the air as though he had just heard all six of his numbers on the Free world lottery. His young colleagues looked stunned as they received their new directives and then whooped and cheered and fired shots into the air as they took off to rendezvous with their leader, leaving their posts unattended.

The stranger rose from the ground as the trails of dust disappeared into the distance, and looked out upon the featureless desert of red dust. What a sight to behold! There were other vehicles out there on the vast landscape, coming this way and that, and some small encampments here and there, but for the most part, the path ahead was clear. He scanned the horizon with focussed and determined eyes and saw a glint of sunlight reflecting from its very edge. Through the binoculars, he found the large satellite dish in the distance, under which huddled the small town of Galleagh. He returned to his cruiser and prepared to move out.

The ground gave slightly as he rolled towards the edge and down the steep descent. At the bottom, he approached the wire fence slowly and pressed the wheels of his cruiser against its flimsy frame and forced the metal poles that held it to the floor. With a final reassurance from his vehicle's digital-layout that the checkpoints ahead had been fully vacated, the stranger pulled forward on his thrusters and took off with a whoosh through the lowlands.

The digital-layout flashed with the encampments that dotted the vast wilderness, and though it did not detect any threatening weaponry in the immediate vicinity, the vehicle's defence system remained at its highest alert. Its weapons idly scanned the surroundings when a sudden warning sounded and they sprung to life with purpose. A cluster of heat signatures had appeared from nowhere to his left and the stranger looked out to see a pack of desert dogs emerge from an underground tunnel where they had escaped his sensors. He immediately aborted the automatic response and savoured the sight of these wild and unusual creatures. As the cruiser bounced along on the endless waves of dust, the huge satellite emerged slowly from the horizon, and below it, the walled town of Galleagh.

A paved path rose from beneath the dust and the stranger pulled back on his thrusters and continued along with more modesty. The digital-layout showed a large crowd of people gathered outside the walls of this town, though what lay within had been protected for defence purposes. A sign hung overhead, held by a metal post on either side, reading HEXLON SECURED AREA, below which, it thanked those approaching for turning off their defence systems and all on-board computers.

A well-tended green encased the town, where families and friends sat on benches and chatted with those around them. Smoke rose from barbecues and filled the air with the aroma of sizzling meat. Large screens had been mounted around the town's wall so that the people there could share in the excitement of the times. On one of these screens, a young male presenter wearing a brightly coloured shirt talked loudly into a microphone with one finger in his ear as the crowd behind sang merrily. On the screen next to it, a more serious female newscaster was recycling the events since it all began. Between them was a small gateway, and the crowd took little interest as the cruiser passed through into their town.

The town of Galleagh had once been a Hexlon outpost, with a row of ten houses along each of the four sides of the Company-owned satellite they were charged with protecting. As the importance of the satellite grew, and with the guards stationed there starting families, a second, longer row of houses was built around them, followed by another and another until it had become the town it was today with a wall built around the final product. The turreted weaponry that once lined its streets had been replaced, for the most part, with channels of fresh flowing water and stretches of garden and flowers. But it was a primitive and forced form of society that could go no further than where it now stood, like considering the evolutionary path of apes when placed alongside the progress of his cousin man. The hints of their demise were evident in the unnatural hierarchy and disconnected nature of these people. Those in positions of power within this town looked upon the rest with a cold and usurious eye and grew rich through their extortion while others struggled to survive. Their imaginations had been bridled by the religious effigies of the old world that lined its streets, and the infinite wonder and glory of our universe supplanted by their kingdoms. Such a world would never know true and everlasting peace, nor would its people evolve with any meaningful progression.

The stranger proceeded slowly through the avenues of the town, looking all around with great interest, and approached the archway leading onto the town's inner square. Above this archway, there was a large stone angel, almost eight metres tall with smaller stone men, women and children huddling behind her protection. Written in the steps leading up to it were the names of those who had given their lives in the war against the Paegonaeans and in the concluding sweep of their defence grid. A group of children sat around the feet of this monument, listening to the tale of a local storyteller. With the sound of the approaching vehicle, the storyteller's voice faltered and his attention broke. He arose from the midst of his audience to watch the cruiser pass beneath in silence. A wind began to blow and he looked out upon the empty street with a wistful air while the children begged him to continue. He took his place amongst them again and began afresh with a new and wonderful tale.

There was an audible hum from the huge satellite as the stranger entered into its presence and passed alongside the wire fence that hemmed it. This was the only connection to the Company's mainframe computer in the southern wasteland until Hexlon city, and all the transactions and communication of the surrounding area passed through here. The fortified area was now relatively empty, as almost all of the guards who lived there had been appropriated by the Company and were setting up outposts along the perimeter. Those who had remained played football in the shade of the satellite while the rest watched from the sidelines. All were too engrossed in the game to acknowledge the presence of the stranger, who silently passed them by.

A recharging station lay beyond the wall at the far edge of the town, overlooking the wasteland beyond, and with the cruiser's fuel cells depleting fast, the stranger pulled into its grand and empty forecourt. There were twenty charging-ports, stretching the entire length of the town, for the purpose of recharging the Company's great Trade-convoy on its monthly rounds, delivering produce to the registered wastelands. The stranger noticed huge tracks leading out from the forecourt and into the dust beyond, and he searched the horizon in the hope of glimpsing the monstrous machine.

A sharp and caustic wind blew as he stepped out of the cruiser and his nose began to run with blood. He looked up from his handkerchief and saw that several cameras were now watching him from a variety of angles. They followed his every step as he approached the small building at the head of the forecourt. The building itself looked like an old and stubborn bomb shelter with a line of windows along the top, too small for anyone to break and climb through. Signs warned patrons that the building had installed a B5 defence system that was connected directly to Hexlon Security. The stranger noted, however, that the hinges on which it all pivoted were old and rusted and had not been tested in years. Beside the shuttered door was a retinal scanner, which the stranger placed his eye against. A light above flashed red with each attempt and, upon the third and final time, the shutters rolled up slowly from the bottom.

The depository had recently been stocked with meats that now lay stacked in its refrigerators and with cordials and other luxuries that stocked its shelves. Their deliveries were not as large as they once had been however, as those in the town were feeling the increasing pinch of this recession. The keeper himself sat behind three inches of glass and communicated through a small intercom system. He looked the stranger up and down as he walked towards him and then back to his computer screen. 'I'm having some difficulty locating your file on the system. Are you from around here?'

'You won't find me on the system,' said the stranger. 'I was born and raised in a small encampment in the very depths of the wastelands. Our people have never been registered and we sustain ourselves. We usually don't venture this far from camp.'

'I take it grass grows there.'

The stranger looked at the shopkeeper warily. 'Some,' he answered finally.

The shopkeeper nodded. 'You look like a man who eats fresh fruit and vegetables regularly. Well... if you're not on the system, you'll have something to trade?'

The stranger pulled a small sack from his pocket and from it took three translucent stones and placed them in the tray between them. The shopkeeper pulled them towards him and poked them about the palm of his hand. 'Fancy stones,' he said flatly. 'These won't get you far.' He threw two of them back into the tray and held one up to a thin sliver of light to observe it more closely. As the light touched this stone, the shopkeeper's dank little booth was illuminated by a spectrum of colour. His mouth opened and his eyes widened at the little stone's command of light. 'I have never seen anything like it before. Where did you find these?'

'Will you accept them in trade?' asked the stranger, pushing the tray back to his side.

The shopkeeper took a deep breath and looked at the other two resting in the tray. Glorified stones or not, they were exceptional, and were the kind of thing that his wife enjoyed. There was a jeweller in town who could make earrings of two of them and perhaps a ring with the third. He smiled at the thought of her face as she opened such a gift and then nodded towards the stranger. 'Sure.'

They shared a silence as the cruiser outside charged when finally the shopkeeper asked. 'So where are you heading, if it is not too bold a question?'

'Hexlon,' replied the stranger. 'My people have some business there. I have heard many stories of the great city and wished to see it with my own eyes.'

The shopkeeper nodded. 'Well, we're the last beacon of civilisation until Hexlon… lot of nothing in between, of course.'

A buzzer sounded when the cruiser had fully charged and the shopkeeper, now captivated by the power of the stones and the rainbows they created, offered only a grunt as the stranger bid him farewell. The shuttered door opened as the stranger walked towards it and a young man of the town entered and greeted him in the customary manner. The young man glanced over his shoulder as the stranger exited and then lifted a strip of meat from the refrigerator. His attention then turned to the shopkeeper, now holding each stone in turn against the light.

'Who was he?'

'Don't know,' said the shopkeeper unconcernedly. 'He wasn't registered. Strange looking chap. Good skin. Anyhow, I didn't ask.'

'Shouldn't you report that kind of thing to Hexlon?'

'If I reported all the people who came through here not wanting to be found, we wouldn't do very much business, would we? Besides, he gave me these stones in trade.'

'Stones?' said the young man quickly, enquiring over the partition with his eyes. 'They look like diamonds?'

'Diamonds?'

'Precious stones,' the young man explained.

'What's so precious about them?'

A sudden frown fell upon the young man's face and he demanded that the shopkeeper hand them over. 'If these are what I think they are, they are worth a fortune. There are only a few of them in the Free world, and they are in a museum in Fortress city.' His eyes widened at a dawning realisation and he turned on his heels without a word and ran out onto the forecourt just in time to see the thrusters of the cruiser fire up and disappear in a cloud of dust. The shopkeeper came running out behind him. 'What's wrong?'

'Have you any idea what's going on, Norman? The Paegonaeans' defence grid goes down and you get an unregistered stranger who gives you rare stones! He could be one of them, and you just charged his vehicle and sent him off towards Fortress city! He could be carrying a bomb! Did he say anything, where he was going, where he was coming from…? Anything?'

'Nothing… just that his people had some business in Hexlon city.'

– II –

Welcome to Hexlon

The story of Hexlon begins in the fortieth year of this forsaken world with the rise of a mysterious vigilante. His myth was a whirlwind of hearsay and gossip that had captured the imagination of the people at a time when their new civilisation seemed most fragile. Attempts by the Company to build a railroad through the wastelands to link the constituent jurisdictions of its security firms and consolidate their control were being continually thwarted by bandits. The Company were losing the battle for the vast wasteland beyond their city, and there were many who sought to supplant them with their own form of power in its depths.

The legend of the vigilante himself began in a small commune that had been besieged by a band of desperate nomads for some weeks. Those inside had fought their attackers back with everything they had, but were growing weaker by the day without fresh supplies. Then one starry night, just as all seemed lost, there was a fierce exchange of gunfire beyond their outer wall and the sun arose the next morning upon the bloodied corpses of their tormentors, scattered lifelessly amidst the surrounding dust. Whatever semblance of media existed back then was contacted by the people of this commune and told the curious tale of a lone warrior, vanishing just as he appeared.

Headlines came thick and fast thereafter. A criminal gang would be found by a member of the public on a leisurely stroll in some remote location, bound and gagged, without so much as a note in explanation. Days later, a tyrannous organisation would crumble after being dealt a debilitating blow by an unknown source in the night.

The Company offered a bounty of one thousand credits, a substantial sum in those days, for information leading to the capture of the vigilante. But there was never any hint of him at any of the scenes nor a trail one could follow leading from them. Many argued that the feats attributed to the unknown crusader were impossible for one man to have achieved alone, and followed that it had to be the work of a clandestine crew of hunters. Others believed that he worked directly for the Company, despite their outward show of opposition, taking down those who challenged or disrupted their authority. And then all news of the vigilante simply disappeared from the public domain, with some suggesting that he had never existed at all. An invention of the media, they would say.

Tales of his exploits were soon forgotten in the years that followed and were replaced with reports of huge trucks making their way south through the wastelands to the Red mountain; where the city of Hexlon now stands. Communes around the base of the mountain reported strange happenings such as sunlight reflecting from its peaks and curious echoes at night. Taverns overflowed with gossip, while villains sat in their darkened corners, idly listening for some slipped secret that may sate their greed. One by one, the rumours that surrounded this mystery withered until all agreed that the vigilante was somehow involved. But what did he want with the peaks of Red mountain? Whispers circulated through the underbelly of the wastelands that members of the thief and assassin guilds had joined forces and were raising an army to climb the mountain and take what was up there.

A motley crew of criminals gathered at an encampment near the base of the mountain on the evening of the summer's longest day. A man named Whitebeard stood before a ragged army of one hundred and cast his eye across them before he spoke. 'Welcome all. I see friends from long ago and some who would have called me an enemy before this day. But we gather here not as members of our respective guilds, but as one. Up in that mountain's peaks await riches, and an equal share for every man here that makes it there. The path ahead will be treacherous, no doubt, and a battle awaits us at the top. But no guts no glory, and I see before me a batch of the finest warriors there has ever been. We will take the peaks, my brothers, and some day this new army of ours shall rule all the wastelands!'

They set off the following morning into the lower reaches of the mountain and by nightfall reached a cave where they set up camp. Fires were lit and food slowly cooked while the men relaxed after their long trek and forgotten muscles whined. When all had eaten, most lay down to rest or sat by the edge looking out upon the darkness. Whitebeard and four others huddled around a map, illuminated by a burning torch that flickered in the night's soft wind.

'It's steep, to be sure,' said Whitebeard, 'but we can expect less resistance. The path you speak of shall surely be guarded and we would lose the element of surprise. No... we climb the rock face and take them while they sleep.'

The men awoke the following morning and geared up for the long ascent to the top. A scorching sun scalded their skin as it rose high above them and, as it set that evening, a fierce and howling wind blew. As evening turned to night, each man could sense the summit drawing near and they continued with their minds full of riches.

As the first man placed his hand on the edge of the summit and pulled himself upon it, he whispered back to those behind that they had made it. He rose to his feet and dusted himself down, observing the obstacle ahead in the dying shards of twilight. A great metal wall, reaching ten metres high, stretched from one end of rock to the other. Several cameras sat atop it and watched the men gather silently.

'Get a rope,' shouted one man, while another called out for explosives.

About twenty men had gathered upon the small pockmarked plateau when a high-pitched noise rose from between their whispers, and they quietened down and searched for its source. It grew louder and louder until it almost pierced their eardrums and what sounded like thunder began to stir. In an instant of immeasurable wrath, each man who stood upon that plateau was blasted into an unrecognisable pulp. The mountain seemed to resonate afterwards and there was a haunting sound that lingered in the air. The immediate instinct to retreat was gradually replaced by the confusion of what had happened and there was little talk amongst those who remained as they descended the mountain and regrouped in the cave.

'What was that?' said one man, deep in shock. 'I saw them… just turn into a mist of red. I heard the splash of their bodies. I…'

'I blame Whitebeard!' shouted another, with a small dissenting faction roaring their agreement. 'Take the impossible path and find at the top a wall that cannot be breached! You couldn't lead your finger up your ass, Whitebeard!'

'Shut your jabber!' the man in charge returned. 'What we encountered there today will be tenfold on the other side. Men were lost, but in exchange for knowing what it is we face. Better a few sacrificed than the whole troupe. What can be up there so important that it should merit such a defence system? Get some food and rest. We shall approach by the main path tomorrow.'

The morning sun arose to find that the dissenting faction had left in the night. Those who remained crowded around Whitebeard and listened as he spoke. 'The element of surprise has gone, and so, we no longer need to climb the steep rock. There is a path to the top and, no doubt, an entrance, though I fear it will be justly protected. We will approach with caution and better assess our situation once there. Those of you who wish to leave may do so now, and for those who stay, a larger share in this fortune.'

Each man looked to his neighbour and then to the group and everyone nodded their allegiance to Whitebeard's plan; their hopes now galvanised more than ever. Whitebeard jumped down from the rock on which he preached and shuffled through his men to lead them into battle once more for the peaks of Red mountain.

The winding path to the top had been modified and trodden and there were hints of goings-on up ahead. Forward they marched in single file and, high above them, they could see more of the metal walls they had come upon the night before. Around midday, news trickled from the front, where one of the crew had climbed upon a rock to look beyond the compound's lower walls. The thief sat there in amazement for some time before speaking in an excited manner about endless rows of green. It was, however, the realisation that these rows of green were stretches of marijuana plants that befuddled his avaricious mind and spluttered the flow of his words. He then looked to the mountain's peaks and thought what reward awaited if the entire compound held the same. Such a bounty would indeed raise those who possessed it into power.

Later that day, on their advance to the peaks, those in front noticed something up ahead and their monotonous march was slowed so they could investigate. A scout was dispatched and used the surroundings to advance stealthily on what he found to be a small village. It consisted of thirty houses, with fifteen on each side of the path they travelled. There were no visible signs of life from any of these houses nor any hint that anyone had ever lived there. The scout turned and motioned for those behind to approach and they took positions up along each side silently and waited for the battle cry from their leader. With a blow from Whitebeard's whistle, thirty doors were kicked in simultaneously and a jagged chorus of shots rang out. Whitebeard stood at the base of the village and watched as his men entered back onto the path, each shaking their head that they had found nothing or no one inside.

'An empty village?' said Whitebeard. 'We can assume they are hard at work in the fields. We now know their number and will need some alive if we are to take control swiftly. Onwards.'

They encountered many more empty villages belonging to these mountainfolk on their long and winding ascent and their number must have been close to a thousand. But this did not deter the men. As Whitebeard explained, many would be women and children and the men would be farmers, not soldiers. They could all be used to work the land.

It was late evening when the mischievous crew reached the summit and they peeked from their concealed positions and marvelled at what they found. A beautiful stone Palace with magnificent spires crowned the jagged peaks and sat some distance behind a wall, much larger than those they had seen before. A large plateau stretched between them and this wall, where the huge doors of its gateway lay invitingly open. Though there were many boulders and rocks to use as shelter, the plateau was more heavily pockmarked than that at the far side. They took thermal scans of the area and set up observation posts along the path they had just trekked to gather what information they could.

'I'm only picking up one person inside the compound,' said one of the thieves.

'Are you sure?'

'Unless they have some way of deceiving us. I can find only one heat signature and that person is in the Palace.'

Whitebeard rose to his feet and motioned for everyone to fall in around him. 'We should find no cheer in there being only one man. It took only one man to cut those upon the plateau to pieces last night... I did not bring you all the way up here to blow smoke... Some will not make it. It is every man for himself from here on in. Five will remain further back with the job of taking out the cameras upon the wall while the rest storm the compound. Spread out and make sure you are covered at all times. Once beyond those gates all is ours.'

Each man took his position at the edge of the plateau and eyed its rocky complexion for cover. The five Whitebeard had chosen, renowned for their aim, took elevated positions further back and set up their weapons. All fell silent and a soft wind carried the faint aroma of their prize. The rattle of gunfire erupted above the heads of the eager force and cameras sparked with injuries and fell broken to the floor. More appeared to replace those that had been damaged and the team above took them out with remarkable precision. At Whitebeard's whistle, his men stormed the plateau with a unified roar.

The high pitched scream they had heard the night before rose more sharply this time, as though to match the invaders' haste. Some found shelter as the thunder began to rattle while others floundered before it. It roared so loud that those five left behind dropped their weapons and it subsided seconds later as a wave of dust rolled in on top of them. They rose from their positions when it cleared and found the deserted plateau red with clumps of their comrades. As they stood looking on in a daze of dismay, a rifle shot ripped through the air, and then another, and another, until one of the five shooters found himself all alone. His eyes searched the peaks all around him, but could find nothing but jagged rock. He threw his weapon to the floor, followed by a blade that he removed from a sheath in his boot. When no one appeared, he ripped off his shirt and stepped out of his trousers and turned three-sixty in his underwear with his hands behind his head.

A man in his late twenties, known only as the vigilante before that day, appeared from a cliff to his left and followed a small passage down through the rocks towards the plateau. The tattered rags he wore served only to protect his skin from the sun, and two bright blue eyes shone from beneath his straggly blonde hair and unkempt beard. He maintained the aim of his rifle on the last of the motley crew and walked to within a few feet of him. 'You will leave this place with your life,' he told him. 'In exchange for your life, you will tell everyone you meet of what you have seen up here this day. The empty houses and villages along the route have been built for the people below and, once I am accepted as their King, all are welcome. What you have seen is just the beginning. My defence system can protect the entire upper reaches of the mountain and will only grow in the years to come.'

The criminal nodded his shaking head and did not turn his back while the vigilante still stood. Instead, he watched him return through the gateway of the compound, and only when the huge doors closed after him did he gather his clothes and scarper.

News of the proposition spread quickly, and the people came in droves up the mountainside to settle in this new and protected environment. Through the years that followed, the King grew increasingly reclusive, and the fields that surrounded his Palace were replaced with gardens of paradisal beauty that were forbidden to the people below. It was there that the King lived in absolute solitude, giving his orders through a small network of Generals. A city was built for the people at the base of the mountain and was protected by a level three fortress installed in its lower regions. The prophesised Kingdom of Hexlon was complete.

Upon his death, twenty-four years ago, the reclusive King was entombed in a Temple built by the people in his honour, and was replaced by an equally shadowy figure known only as the Priest. Very little was known about their new leader and many rumours abounded, shrouding the Palace of Hexlon and its forbidden surroundings in myth and folklore. There were whispers of the King having had a son before his untimely death, who the Priest now raised in the seclusion of the peaks until the day he was ready to assume his father's crown. But, despite this mystery, life in their city went on as normal and the people went about their business as they had before, never really knowing the true design of their Kingdom.

On the day that followed the mysterious deactivation of the Paegonaeans' defence grid, an incredible sense of ceremony had befallen Hexlon city. People lined the streets to watch the huge parade of trucks carry an endless procession of cannons and artillery to the fortress that watched over them. The Company's permission to upgrade Hexlon from a level three to a level one security installation had invoked a mixed response from the people of the Free world, but inside the city walls there was only an atmosphere of celebration and occasion. Truck after truck rolled through its streets, laden with level one, short, medium and long range missile defence systems with all the paraphernalia that went with it; serenaded by the men, women and children of the city. History was being written, and there they were to see it for it themselves.

Reserves had been drafted from the people of the city to maintain order amongst the growing crowd, as people scrambled as best they could for a glimpse of the goings-on up and down the mountain. Gigantic cranes hoisted artillery high into the air under the direction of men below waving them this way and that. Sirens echoed from every sector as the old equipment was taken off-line to be replaced by the new, making Hexlon's fortress the first level one security installation in the wastelands and only the third in all of the Free world.

The bottom floors of Hexlon's fortress had also requested extra help to deal with the huge influx of calls from people all over their jurisdiction and beyond. The embers of fantasy and paranoia were being fanned by the silence that surrounded the mystery of the Paegonaeans' defence grid, and many rang to report strange happenings. They ranged from a list of ominous portents to strange lights zipping through the sky.

'They were like fireflies, two of them. Too fast to be from here,' explained one farmer. 'Beings from another planet, I would say. Beings who the Paegonaeans have allied themselves with and are here to blast us from existence.'

'Human beings from the future,' explained one housewife excitedly. 'They've travelled back in time to see this momentous event in their history. Does that mean there is going to be a war?'

Those phonecalls containing a modicum of value were put through to the floors higher up and those deemed important enough made it to the top. There, one hundred men and women sat in rows of ten, communicating with the outside world through headsets while tapping feverishly on their keyboards or searching through cameras all over the wastelands. Before them stood a huge digital-layout mapping clearly those areas they protected. Any registered person could be located at the touch of a button and even the majority of their conversations could be replayed in this room.

General Luther Banderos walked amongst them as fast as his prosthetic leg would allow, through the tight aisles, collecting report after report amidst the melee of action.

'Sir,' shouted a young guard with a hand raised in the air. 'I may have something.'

The General winced as he strode towards the guard's station and placed a load-bearing hand upon his shoulder. 'Well, what might you have?'

'We just received a phonecall from a depository in the deep south claiming that a man unregistered on the system charged his vehicle there fifteen minutes ago.'

'We have thirty-seven other reports of unregistered people to be investigated,' answered Banderos. 'Put it on the list and someone will get to it. Were you told what this person used to barter with?'

'That's just it, he said it was precious stones of some kind... two of them.'

The General stood upright and his eyes narrowed into an abyss of thought. 'Where exactly did this take place?'

The guard tapped on his keyboard and then looked towards the large digital-layout. 'There,' he said, as it blipped on the screen. 'How would you like me to proceed?'

'It is almost certainly nothing,' he answered. 'I shall look into it myself.' Banderos then walked towards the exit with a brisk stride, regarding none of the guards who had raised their hand for his attention, and down the long corridor to his private office. Once the door closed behind him, he picked up the phone and dialled a three digit number and waited for a response. 'This is Banderos,' he said. 'Get me the Priest.'

The Priest's private chamber was a small circular room in the Palace's highest turret and contained only a small bed and a desk from where he oversaw the Kingdom. There were few areas in the city that their cameras could not reach and, though he had very little to do with its daily administration, the Priest enjoyed watching the people go about their lives. Recent events had sharpened his interest in the world below and he flicked through shots of barren wasteland and busy streets in the hope of catching something out of the ordinary. The phone beside him began to ring. A flicker of excitement tempered the intensity of his face as he listened to what his General had to say. 'Good,' he replied, before setting down the receiver.

A moment passed where all before him unveiled in his mind and the Priest then lifted the receiver again. 'Bring the boy to the study. Tell him there will be no training today.'

A set of spiralling stone steps led the Priest from his quarters and out onto the western annexe of the Palace. Shadows of every colour resided there as the midday light strained through the stained glass windows that ran overhead. The study lay some way near the end of the annexe and housed a comprehensive collection of books that would have rivalled any other in the Free world. There were many old and dusty books there, printed long before the war and many were unique to this collection. It was there that the Priest taught the boy all he needed to know and edified him in the arts of the world below.

He opened the door to the study to find a maid sobbing with her head buried in her hands. She looked up as he approached and wiped the tears from her cheeks. 'I'm sorry, sir. He does not listen to me. He is the King, after all.'

The Priest dismissed the tearful maid and sat down at the table with the wealth of books all around him and gently stroked his long grey beard. The boy had been growing increasingly restless for some time now and he knew that the Palace would not hold him much longer. But was he ready to face the world below all alone? Knowledge would only take him so far and the Priest was haunted by a lingering concern, now that the time was upon them, that the boy was not yet ready.

The young King's private chamber was a vast and open space situated at the very back of the Palace. Much of his twenty-four years had been spent there between those walls. At one end was a small library and an arrangement of soft chairs, where he would often relax with a book from his personal collection or work on the riddles set by the Priest. At the other end was his sleeping quarters, and between them were all those things that kept him amused through the years. The curtains had been pulled shut and the Priest descended the small flight of stairs into the darkened and silent chamber with a watchful tension. He sensed a lurking presence somewhere nearby and his eyes scanned the shadows and rafters. 'Come out, boy. I have news from the lower reaches.'

There was a sudden creak, followed by the fleeting patter of nimble feet along the beams overhead. 'Boy!' shouted the Priest with sheer exasperation.

'I was to have an exercise this day,' came a voice, steady and unquavering, from the darkness at the far end of the long chamber. Again the wooden beams creaked as the King took off across them.

'There is no time for these games! The day is upon us! You must prepare for the arrival of our guest!'

With that, the King emerged from behind him, running down the banister of the steps the Priest had just descended and almost toppled him at the bottom as he dived up into the rafters and vanished once more. Only the boy could evoke such hostile emotions in a character so calm and composed, and the Priest, now enraged at his insolence, lifted a long wooden stick they used to train with and threatened him more vehemently. 'Show yourself at once!'

A soft mocking laugh rang out in the distance. 'Or you will do what?'

All hint of the boy above him had gone, and the Priest circled the centre of the silent room with the wooden stick held out in defence, listening intently for the betrayal of his footsteps. There was not a sound this time as the boy descended from the rafters and connected with the Priest more forcefully, sending him crashing to the floor. The wooden stick fell from his grip and the Priest watched it roll from his reach.

'I was to have an exercise today,' repeated the King, now standing over the Priest's felled body. 'What will you do with the prisoner you have been training for the last forty days? You cannot let him go now that he has seen our world. Allow me this exercise and I will then do as you say.'

The Priest waved away the boy's threatening stance and rose to his feet with a measure of regained authority. 'Make it quick. There is much to do.'

They walked along a narrow passageway, which opened onto a small domed arena made almost entirely from marble; a commodity which had become a rarity since the Paegonaeans erected the protected barrier around them. Displays of new and antique weaponry hung around its walls with several doors leading off into smaller rooms beyond. In the centre was a circular sand pit with three steps leading down to it between marble columns at each corner.

A young maid entered the room carrying a large jug of water, which she poured slowly into a bowl while watching the King prepare. She then took some lemon halves and assorted herbs and threw all into the bowl and stirred the mixture before carrying it to a table near the pit. Her name was Aloa, and she was one of three girls brought to the Palace as personal maids to the King. Though she had beautiful dark eyes and flowing hair, there was a plainness in everything else about her, and the Priest found her to be the most troublesome of the three. She raised a hand in the King's direction before the Priest sharply dismissed her, scolding her impudence as he escorted her brusquely from the room. Once he closed the door behind her, he walked to the edge of the arena and clapped his hands twice. 'Release the prisoner!'

The doors to the holding room opened, and a man in rags was led in by two guards. This man was then summoned by the Priest to the top of the steps leading down to the pit and he looked all around and marvelled at the awesome sight. Where was this place and what did they want with him? His eyes turned towards the impressive designs on the roof and then to the array of weapons that lined the wall. 'Where am I?'

'You are in the inner sanctum of the Palace of Hexlon,' answered the Priest. 'You have been found guilty of crimes against our system and now have the opportunity to fight for your freedom.'

'The Palace of Hexlon?' he repeated airily, forgetting his situation momentarily, before asking more fearfully. 'What do you mean by fight for my freedom?'

He had been there for over a month now with little explanation as to why he had been taken from his family and friends. He remembered walking home from the blacksmith when a van halted abruptly on the red dust beside him and being bundled into the back of it by men who seemed to come from everywhere. He awoke the next morning in a modestly furnished apartment, which he eventually found to be a cell. He was brought a cooked breakfast and told to prepare for his training. He exercised harder than he ever had before that day and trained with a variety of weapons under the tutelage of the old man who now offered him this chance of freedom.

'Who must I fight?' he asked. 'Another prisoner?'

'Yes,' said the King from the shadows. 'A prisoner of twenty-four years.'

The man in rags swallowed hard at the sight of his opponent. A thin layer of muscle covered his entire frame, as though a suit of armour had been placed beneath his skin. Bright blue eyes shone back at him, gleaming with the souls of those before him, and the prisoner shivered at the cold prospect of death.

The Priest clapped twice and the prisoner stepped onto the sand. The King paced the fringe of the pit with slow even steps, his eyes firmly on his opponent, who mirrored his movements shakily. The King listened to the quickening beat of his opponent's heart. When the attack came, it was wild and uncontrolled, and the King caught the prisoner's trailing arm and popped it free at the shoulder with a tweak. The prisoner fell against one of the marble columns and turned for another attempt, but was halted when he found his arm flopping limply by his side.

The Priest stopped the bout and entered the pit, motioning for the prisoner to stand still. He reattached his arm into its socket by the same method the King had used to dislodge it. 'You may use the weapons you see about you,' he told the prisoner, who looked around with renewed vigour.

The prisoner almost tripped as he took the steps from the pit and made for the mounted weapons without fully regaining his composure. He slammed hard against the wall and pulled a large broadsword from its display and threw its sheath to the ground. His approach was more cautious and deliberate as he stepped down onto the sand. The blade of the weapon glinted in the narrow beams of sunlight and the prisoner approached with improved confidence and launched his attack, swinging with all his might. The King let each swipe come within a fibre of him as he ducked and weaved with astonishing agility. When the prisoner began to tire and slow, he felt his knee give to an almighty blow and could do nothing but follow it to the ground. The broadsword dropped from his hands and he scrambled after it, but the King offered no race to retrieve it. Instead, he slowly backed up the steps from the pit and watched the prisoner rise from the ground with sparks of pain flaring up his weakened leg.

'Make it quick!' shouted the Priest.

The King glanced at the Priest before selecting a large and peculiar weapon made entirely from stone. It had a sword-like handle but a club-like extension which thickened towards the end before its four sides folded sharply into a shallow point. He swung it several times with such control as he approached that the prisoner felt the resignation of his execution coalesce into one final and desperate fury. The prisoner thought back to what the Priest had taught him and all fear and hesitation left him in that instant. The swinging broadsword became a frenzied shield before him with which he approached his royal opponent. He came within distance and the opposing challengers struck their final blows.

A shockwave passed through the prisoner and he felt his knees hit the sand. Everything turned black around him and a memory from long ago surfaced from the darkness. It was of a night long ago when he had had too much to drink and fell on the pavement outside a tavern. He could hear his friends call to him to get up and walk home, but all he wanted to do was close his eyes and lay there. Those same voices called to him now, but the soothing pull was impossible to resist and he went with it deeper and deeper. The King swung his weapon back and forth with cold disinterest before turning sharply and taking the head from his defeated opponent. It released a hissing fountain of red before the headless body slumped to the ground and chugged blood onto the sand like wine from a spilled decanter.

The Priest broke the silence by clapping three times and a team of maids entered the room. As they shovelled the blood-soiled sand into buckets and rolled the decapitated body onto a stretcher, the Priest descended the steps and took the King under his arm and led him from the arena.

'I have watched you grow from a baby, at the mercy of those around you, to the man you are today,' he began. 'I have watched you grow strong and powerful and fulfil the tests set before you. I have done my best to prepare you for what is to come in the days ahead. And I tell you now, as your brave father would have if he were here today, that I am proud of you.'

The King looked at him somewhat blankly. 'I will do as you say now.' He walked off towards his quarters, passing the arena without a glance, as several of his guards now lifted the stretcher upon their shoulders and carried his opponent's body from the room.

The Priest retired to his room atop the spiralling steps and sat for some time in quiet contemplation. He tapped on his keyboard and the screen of his computer started up. Through a series of codes so long and diverse that only a fluke of historical proportions could have arrived at it, he accessed his private system. He leaned forward and tapped a microphone before speaking. 'Persulaes?'

Static rattled in response before falling silent. 'Persulaes here.'

'I need you in the bunker, old friend.'

'It is time?'

'Yes. Bring our guest in without harm.'

– III –

The Message

Those in the wastelands who had not been swept up by the immediate whirlwind of excitement found the eerie silence that followed filled with the whispers of their darkest fears. Once the youthful ranks of their villages and communes had deserted them for the festivities along the wasteland perimeter, the vast open plain beyond seemed to hold a more ominous horizon. Most packed up what they could and travelled to their nearest fortified stronghold; those in the southern region opting for the sanctuary of Hexlon city. Thousands had now gathered outside its walls and were growing increasingly restless as the sun slowly set upon them. Huge pens reached out into the desert beyond, gathering the approaching crowd between their long and welcoming arms and bottlenecking at each of the city's three entrances. They passed through one by one, each waiting several seconds before their retinal identity had registered and admission to the city within either granted or denied.

Further out, in the soft untrodden dust beyond, Hexlon guards dug with pickaxes and shovels, locating the hatches to those bunkers and underground passages that zigzagged beneath this land. Once a bunker had been unearthed, a team of technicians manned the post and acquainted themselves with the dormant equipment. They formed an underground network of surveillance at the front line of Hexlon's defence, and their eyes and ears reached deep into the falling darkness above. But there was a bunker in its midst that lay unconnected to those around it and unknown to the Kingdom's defence system. Only the Priest and the trusted guard he had chosen for this task knew of its existence and the purpose it would serve this night.

The air conditioning system rattled above the hum of the equipment, and in the corner of the small and red-lit bunker was a seismograph that scribbled neatly on a page. An old and battle-scarred monster of a man balanced on a tiny stool and his deep-set eyes flitted among the screens all around him. His face had been horribly disfigured some years ago by a torture at the hands of those who wished to extract from him the secrets of Hexlon's forbidden Palace. This torture, which he endured with steadfast fidelity, and the years that he had guarded the restricted reaches of Mount Hexlon, was what had elevated him to this highly secretive and enlightened position. What was to come in the days ahead had been entrusted to his indisputable resolution, and this knowledge had brought his mind a sense of order. From this covert command post, Persulaes could monitor all other bunkers, issue directives as though they had come directly from the Palace, and even utilise the fortress's newly installed defence system.

The radar blipped for the umpteenth time that day and he pulled himself towards it and noted a small vehicle moving at pace from the lowlands in the direction of their city. Computers began to busy themselves all around the bunker and quickly verified that it was not one of their own and followed seconds later that the vehicle was not registered at all. Persulaes picked up the phone. 'The guest is approaching the outer marker.'

The Priest's reply was brisk. 'You have your instructions. A message shall be sent to your computer momentarily. Pass it along.'

Persulaes put the phone down without a word. He first issued the oncoming vehicle with a guard-pass and authorized it to proceed through the outer marker. This would clear the path before their guest and his approach would be disregarded by those in the bunkers around him. A message appeared on Persulaes' monitor moments later, which he dutifully forwarded to the oncoming cruiser's computer. When the message had sent, Persulaes leaned back on his stool with the unopened message blinking before him. What would it matter if he took a peek now? He glanced involuntarily around the empty bunker and pulled himself close to the screen. His thick eyebrows drew close as he ran his eyes along the message's unintelligible text. What he first assumed to be an encryption of some kind was then decided to be a strange form of language. But, despite the outlandish characters of which it consisted, there were two pieces of information which he could understand clearly; the coordinates B45977 – G55847 and the number 37842.

Persulaes pulled a map from a rack behind him and drew his fingers along from the top and side to the area stated in the message. It was right in the middle of a restricted area on a contaminated patch of land between the outer and inner markers. This area was to be avoided at all costs and guards gave it a wide berth when coming and going; its sanctity further enforced by grisly stories of gruesome deaths for those who had unsuspectingly wandered through it. Persulaes closed the map and perused the message on the screen once more, attempting to curl his tongue around the garbled text before deleting it and preparing for the subsequent steps of his duty.

As the ragged little cruiser passed through Hexlon's outer marker, its on-board computer warned of their potential threat and compiled lists of the weapons that they had now come within range of. An incoming message appeared on the screen seconds later and the stranger stomped on the brakes and slid his cruiser to a stop on the soft dust. He savoured the tranquillity of that moment as the motor fell silent and wiped the thick beads of sweat that hung from his forehead.

There it was before him, the gentle rise of Mount Hexlon way off in the distance, its base illuminated by the fortress installed in its lower reaches and the city at its feet. After reading the message, the stranger uploaded the coordinates to his vehicle's digital-layout and revved the weary cruiser for its final shunt.

There were no houses or encampments or buildings of any kind within Hexlon's outer marker, and the stranger felt much more relaxed with the blank and silent screen of the digital-layout staring up at him. His eyes become so dulled and acclimatised to the seemingly infinite desert that they immediately focussed upon something catching in his headlights up ahead. More appeared, scattered unevenly through the area he was entering into; signposts hanging crookedly on their posts, leaning in the direction of the most recent wind and each warning of what lay ahead through a varied depiction of danger and death.

A shudder passed through the stranger as he entered into this area and followed the coordinates towards a rocky area that rose from the flat plains around it. There were many cracks and crevices through the large mess of rocks, and he was led down a narrow inlet, just large enough for his cruiser to pass through. Total darkness enveloped the stranger and he could see a dull glimmer of light grow brighter up ahead as the distance from the inputted coordinates rallied down from twenty metres. When the counter reached one, he got out and found himself in a small opening, protected by the red rocks all around.

The stranger kicked about in the dust for some minutes, covering his mouth and nose as he did, and then fell to his hands and knees upon uncovering an old storm drain. He located a handle at each end of it and pulled the lid from its place, revealing a shiny metal plate beneath. In the centre of this plate was a dial with the numbers 1 to 9 along with a green and red button at each side. The stranger punched in a five digit code and hit the green button. There was a releasing of latches beneath and it opened slowly to reveal a cold and dank shaft with a ladder reaching into its darkness. He placed a foot upon the first rung of the ladder and felt a chill run its fingers up the backs of his legs and slowly engulf him in its icy grasp. The dull halo of evening light grew smaller with every step and soon the stranger found that he was no longer in a narrow shaft, but making his way down the wall of a large open space. As he stepped onto the ground, a series of lights above him began illuminating and revealed what appeared to be a long-forgotten subway station. The once-white walls had been eroded by the sulphurous desert that surrounded it and a thin layer of red dust clung to everything, all except for an awaiting carriage. The stranger walked along the edge of the platform and the doors of the carriage opened before him. There was an eeriness about it all that unsettled him.

Persulaes watched the stranger disappear from one screen and appear on another as he entered the carriage and took a seat within. The motor then started and the carriage began rolling forward into the dark tunnel ahead. Persulaes lifted the phone and held it thoughtfully for a moment before returning it to its place. Instead, he pulled open a drawer and from it lifted a framed photograph of a young girl in a school uniform. Underneath the picture was a bottle half-filled with a clear alcohol, which he set on his desk next to it. He poured a large measure of the liquid into a cup and emptied it with one sharp swig before reaching for the photograph and holding it in both hands. She would be twenty now... or thereabouts. Last he had heard she had passed her high school exams and was studying to become a defence analyst in Fortress city. All he had of her were snapshots of distant memories.

'I do this for a better future,' he whispered.

He lifted the bottle and drank what remained with five uneasy chugs and grimaced at its potency. With one final lingering gaze upon the photograph, he said farewell to the daughter who had grown up without him, before finally picking up the phone. 'Our guest is on the way. There were no complications.'

The Priest took a little longer to answer this time. 'You have served our noble cause well, Persulaes. Your reward shall be an incarnation in an enlightened world far from now, when only true peace has ever been known.'

'Thank you, sir.'

Once he had set the phone down, the Priest tapped at his keyboard and the screen before him lit up with the network of subterranean bunkers beyond the city walls. All the threads of their grand design had to be eradicated before the witch-hunt that would inevitably follow took off, and this purge began with the bunker and the underground station. The Priest looked out the window, high in the Palace's highest turret, as he executed the command to blow both of these places, and then bowed his head for a loyal servant.

His thoughts returned to the task at hand and the Priest began sifting through shots of the city's underground system on his computer. Each carriage he passed through was packed with people and charged with the excitement of the times, when suddenly he came across a lone figure sitting quite still in an empty carriage. His guest had already changed into the white overcoat left for him and affixed the security pass on his lapel as instructed.

The carriage then broke from its steady approach and began to ascend before levelling off and turning sharply, shuddering momentarily as it changed tracks. The darkness of the tunnel suddenly parted as a brightly lit underground station flashed by with a dense crowd of people waiting on the platform. Those there threw their hands in the air as the carriage zipped by without stopping. Several more stations whipped by in flashes of light until the carriage eventually began to slow and opened its doors to a crowd that filled almost instantly around the stranger. A disjointed medley of conversations erupted from them, which heightened gradually into cheers as they approached the end of the line. The doors of the carriage then opened and the exiting tide of passengers carried the stranger from the station and up the steps to the tumultuous commotion of the Gardens.

The fast-falling darkness of late evening had been pushed to the shadows, where the beams of the huge floodlights above could not reach. This famed expanse of green they called the Gardens, that stretched between the walls of the fortress around the base of Mount Hexlon and the city that lay beyond, had always been an attraction for outsiders to come and visit, and today had seen its largest crowd yet. Hexlonian families would often go there and congregate around its many barbecues, and friends would gather and divide themselves into teams and play games beneath the cannons of their Kingdom's mighty fortress. It was particularly renowned for artists and writers, who would come from all over to sit under the shade of a tree and feed from the inspiration that gathered there. But today, music boomed from everywhere as the festivities maintained their vivacity, and the stranger stumbled through the raucous crowd as he made his way to the walls of the fortress.

The changing face of the fortress had attracted the fascination of everyone and pulled people from every quarter of the small Kingdom and beyond to see the new level one artillery jutting from her positions up and down the mountain. A solid ring of journalists and reporters packed around the base of its wall, taking pictures and making notes so that this historic event could be properly documented. It was now almost fully operational, and there was even talk of a demonstration to test it all out when the last of the upgrades were finally in place.

Entrance to the fortress itself relied on a small and individual security pass rather than the logging of retinal identity; allowing the inner workings of Hexlon's compound to operate independently of the Company's omnipresent system. All of its employees had one, from cleaners and guards to senior advisers and Generals, and their rank and authorisation were contained in its metal strip. It would then be used as a keycard once inside the fortress, as its every door only opened with the appropriate authorisation being swiped through its reader. Guests were each given one with the nature and details of their visit logged alongside provisional access to the pertinent parts of the fortress. Though the crime of obtaining a security pass through unofficial means was as heinous and unthought-of to the Hexlonian people as entering into the forbidden reaches above, there were some reporters in the crowd daring enough to procure one unlawfully with a tempting offer of credit.

The steady stream of guards and civilians coming out through the gateway was matched at a much slower pace by the intermittent shuffling of those undergoing the rigours of entry. Four security booths, each no larger than a small shower, stood side by side, and the disorderly crowd were ushered through them one by one.

A burly guard swiped the stranger's security tag with a hand-held reader and pushed him along to the front of the queue. Signs asked that all electrical equipment be placed in the trays provided before stepping into the booths. The stranger shook his head when one of these trays was thrust into his chest and waited silently as the queue moved on. When the door to the booth before him opened, he stepped inside and stood with both arms held by his sides as the door closed behind him. There was first a flash that disorientated him momentarily and, as he recovered, a strange odour filled the booth. The smell faded just as quickly as it materialised and the front door of the booth opened to the compound within and the stranger stepped out to the final phase of the checkpoint.

'You have access to the Palace!' said the guard waiting there, more in awe than in conduct of his duties. 'Most of the information on your security pass is classified. May I ask, what is the nature of your visit?'

'I work for the Company and the nature of my job requires some discretion. Your fortress has recently been upgraded and I have been summoned by the Priest to instruct him on this personally.'

'The Priest?' said the guard airily. 'Instruct him… personally?'

The stranger nodded. 'That is correct.'

The guard looked to the peaks of the mountain and, upon lowering his eyes to the figure before him, his conduct regained some professionalism. 'It says you are to be escorted to the cablecar. I shall do this myself, if you wish, sir. Do you require anything before you go up?'

The stranger shook his head and motioned for him to lead the way.

The crowd inside was much thinner and their collective spirit more relaxed. People mingled on the grass that separated the paths leading through the red rocks to the lower levels of the fortress. The stranger's escort walked several paces ahead, his demeanour stiffened with determination and pride and he would have cleared the path before him with a voice equal to it had the nature of his duty not been so delicate. He led the guest off to the right and up a gentle hill that led away from the core of the commotion. The stranger looked towards the great mountain, presiding over all with its majesty and splendour, gleaming with the lights from its endless rows of reinforced windows, where the business of conducting a city went on. There was a constant and low hum that the stranger found oddly soothing, which was punctuated at intervals with the intermittent whir of the cannons close by, surveying the land beyond the city walls. His heart fluttered with joy upon beholding every detail of this mountainous structure.

The stranger continued along the summit of the hill in silence, until its downward slope revealed a growing sea of grey warehouses on the other side. Having never faltered from his purposeful stride, the guard before him then stopped and raised a hand to its midst, just as the cablecar was pulled from its tranquil surface. This, explained the guard as they continued down the hill, was the only link between the Palace and the world below.

They entered the maze-like corridors of corrugated metal, passing all kinds of workers submersed in their chores. The usual saturation of guards was much thinner today, the guard told the Palace guest. Duties elsewhere, he added with careful discretion. A few of those guards who had remained, however, were quick to detain them in this highly classified area, but the young guard who escorted the stranger dealt with them admirably and each was quickly dismissed.

They finally reached the cablecar stall, in the very centre of this warehouse suburbia, and the guard bowed slightly and informed the stranger that this was as far as he could take him. As he turned and walked away, the stranger found himself looking around somewhat fearfully in his new surroundings. He quickly climbed the ladder and sat like a mouse in the corner of the empty stall, his eyes drawn to the upper reaches of the mountain, now indiscernible against the black canvas of night.

The cablecar and surrounding area were almost as guarded as the enclosed gardens that surrounded the forbidden peaks, and there would usually have been two guards posted there, charged with overseeing the loading of provisions and ensuring that no one snuck aboard the cablecar. But today there were none and the stranger sat all alone with boxes of fresh fruit and vegetables stacked around him. His long journey had left him parched and he lifted some oranges and mangoes from one of the boxes and sated his thirst while he waited. Then the cablecar appeared, zigzagging its way down the mountainside and finally docked in the stall next to him. Its doors had to be forced open and it rocked about freely until the rope that held it tautened and started with a sudden jolt. He was on his way.

From the window of the rising cablecar, the stranger had a panoramic view of the vast inner compound and the specks of people moving to and fro like ants. The dense crowd beyond the fortress walls thinned gradually through the Gardens towards the forest that separated them from the city's residential area. The streets beyond, marked by the lights that lined either side, were perfectly regimented and the city of Hexlon deduced into manageable quarters of equal size, and looked something like a web in its design. More and more of its grand landscape was unfurled as the cablecar rose high into the sky, and the stranger could eventually see its edge marked by the outer wall. Two large fields of solar panels lay to the east and west of the city and collected all the energy necessary to maintain it. It was an awesome sight to behold, and the stranger placed his forehead against the glass and, for the first time, noticed the dull thud of a headache.

The cablecar moved close to the face of the mountain, where it turned and began being pulled up alongside it. It changed direction at several points as it made its way through the lower peaks and the expansive fortress they held, turning one final time before the long ascent to the top. It passed through clouds that enveloped the cablecar with its misty dew and eventually pulled through them to reveal the forbidden upper reaches. A faint light shimmered in the distance above, and the stranger watched with bated breath as the silhouette of tall trees revealed the spires of the Palace they hid.

A party of five guards stood by the edge of the precipice; each armed with an automatic rifle and sidearm and looked upon the approaching cablecar with an unusual excitement. More approached from different parts of the peaks, some led by snarling dogs on strained leads. It had been so long since the Hexlonian law had been violated that each of the guards were unsure on how to proceed. Then the Priest appeared and ordered each of them to stand down and return to their posts. He was wearing a white robe, held in form at the waist with a black belt. His face seemed as though a mix of emotions and his beard had been trimmed and his hair neatly brushed back. But what did he want with the stowaway? The guards began to disperse, seemingly disappointed at being robbed of some sport, and watched the strange encounter unfold as they walked away through stolen glances over their shoulders.

The cablecar docked and its doors were prised open. The stowaway emerged and held out his hand and the

Priest offered his in return, both bowing slightly as they shook. 'It is an honour to be here in the famed peaks of Hexlon,' announced the guest. The words had no sooner left his mouth when his head whipped to the side suddenly and a powerful sneeze snapped it forward. The guest wiped his nose with a bloodied rag and looked apologetically towards his host.

'Follow me to the Palace,' said the Priest. 'I have something that will cure your ailment.'

The Priest led his guest through a large and beautiful garden that lay like an oasis amongst the red peaks. Strange birds with large and colourful feathers wandered here and there and pecked at seeds strewn amidst the grass. Water could be heard flowing down the steep hill through several channels and collecting in a pool somewhere in the distance. Though black night had now fallen, the path was lit with burning torches that led to a wooded area just ahead. The gravel path on which they walked then became a trodden trail through its undergrowth, where deer and other livestock roamed. A distant glimmer of light appeared through the darkness of the small forest and illuminated a path beyond that tapered into a steep and narrow corridor, hedged by a single row of tall trees on either side. A strong wind blew as they walked along it and the men hastened onwards.

The Palace was a welcome sight to the guest, rising above the summit of the steep path, where it sprawled almost hidden in the darkness that surrounded it. No lights shone on it and only a pale glow flickered from some of its windows. It had been built with stones of varying sizes and a large oak door sat at the centre of it with some steps leading up to it. This door was opened by a guard as the two men approached.

A thick red rug with gold trim stretched along the narrow entrance and opened like a body of water in the large reception, up the stone staircase, and along the narrow corridors at either side. Candles flickered in the gentle draft, illuminating everything with their tender glow and there was nothing to suggest that the power enjoyed by the city below reached the heights of the Palace. Strange paintings of curious things gave colour to the grey interior and a large golden fountain in the centre of the reception bestowed much of the room's grandeur.

Two maids watched silently from behind the balcony of the upper floor with the demeanour of curious rats, as the Priest led this stranger into the secret heart of their world. It was the first time either had seen an outsider up there and they scurried off once the duo had passed to cool the burning coal of curiosity with gossip amongst their colleagues.

The guest followed the Priest along a narrow passageway to the left of the staircase, with doors leading off from it at intervals on either side. They stopped at the end of this corridor and the Priest pushed open a door to his right, revealing a small washroom. 'You may freshen up here,' he told his guest. 'Come on through once you are finished.'

The guest emerged some time later, washed and refreshed and draped in a white robe of the same design as that worn by the Priest. He pushed open the door at the end of this corridor and entered the small dining hall. In the corner was a large open fire on which burned huge logs; a luxury enjoyed by the few in this barren world. He found his host before it, enjoying the heat from its crackling flames. There was little else in this room. Three chairs around one end of a long and plain wooden table constituted all of its furnishings. From another door at the far end of the dining hall emerged a plump little woman in a patchwork dress, bringing with her the wafted rumours of delicious food being prepared. She had in her hands a bowl of steaming liquid and led their guest to the fireplace, where she wrung a cloth of the fragrant mix and handed it to him before returning to the kitchen again in silence.

'Place it over your face,' the Priest instructed. 'I had the same problem when I first came out here.'

His guest did as he was instructed and filled his lungs with the soothing vapour before speaking. 'He is ready?'

'He is. You will meet him soon.'

There was a moment of silence, through which the guest could be heard breathing more clearly beneath the fragrant cloth, before he resumed. 'It seems strange that with all that has been accomplished in the last century that our future should now rest in the hands of one man. These are exciting times, though such anticipation does not come without some doubt. There are those in our land who believe the King's seclusion from the world around him may have been a mistake, and this has somewhat perturbed the tranquil nature of our people. So it is with the greatest importance that I ask you now if he is ready? We must be sure.'

A second voice responded, youthful and with a tone that gave no hint of emotion. 'If you have come to fill my home with the doubt of your people then I suggest you go back to them without uttering another sound. This life chose me, and I have spent every day of it in dutiful preparation. Allay your senseless fears. I am ready, and have been for a long time.'

Their guest removed the cloth slowly from his face and rose to his feet. 'I mean no disrespect, valiant King.

Tales of your courage and resilience are repeated and embellished throughout our land. Whatever doubt has been raised surely comes from our own imperfection.' He then dropped to his knees and bowed his head before the famed King.

'Stand,' the King ordered softly. He was draped in the same white robe as the other two men. 'Address me as an equal for we have much to talk about this night.'

Their guest rose to his feet, warmed by the benevolence of the King, and reached out his hand. 'You are as handsome as your father,' he told him as they shook.

The King's eyes glimmered slightly upon this remark and he invited both men to sit with him. The door to the kitchen burst open as they seated themselves and the plump little woman in the patchwork dress reappeared with wooden plates and cutlery, which she set before each of them and returned to the kitchen.

'You spoke of my father,' said the King. 'Tell me of him.'

There was an enquiring glance towards the Priest, to which the guest received a gentle nod. 'He was a very brave and wise man,' he began. 'It had been foretold by our visionary father that it would be a King from the outside who would decide the future of mankind. Each and every one of his prophecies that came before had been fulfilled in one way or another, but there were some apprehensions about this one. As there were no Kings or Kingdoms in the unconquered land, we took it upon ourselves to create one. Through a careful study of candidates, we decided upon your father and gave him what he needed to create this Kingdom. Once his Kingdom had been established, we convinced ourselves that the time was at hand. As it turned out, we were premature in our decision. Your father was killed in the execution of the mission that now lies before you, and it was a time of great confusion and disillusionment for our people. We thought all was lost and the destiny of mankind consigned to another thousand years of aimless wandering. But in his wisdom, your father left us with a contingency by impregnating a healthy young stable girl before he departed on his mission. When you were born and found to be a boy, there were joyous celebrations from every inhabited square of our land and there was a solid renewal of faith. You became the focus of everything we had worked to achieve and were a symbol to all of what was to come. Where you were to be raised became the only uncertainty in our world. It was initially suggested that you live within the walls of our land and prepare for the mission there. But it was agreed thereafter that you should take the throne of the Kingdom your father established, and there, in the outside world, you would prepare for this day.' Their guest paused for a second and nodded towards the Priest. 'Our most esteemed spiritual leader took the place of your father and came with you to educate and raise you as he saw fit. Royalty is not a title that can be awarded, it must be passed from one generation to the next, and it is you, the first true King of Hexlon, who will fulfil the last prophecy of our people.'

The King remained silent for some time. 'I know nothing of my mother,' he said softly. 'Please tell me of her.'

Their guest shook his head. 'There is very little known about her. She died shortly after you were born. Her identity was never made public in the fear that it would adulterate the natural order to come.' He then added earnestly. 'It is known that she was a true beauty and that she died content with the knowledge that it would be her son who led our people into the age of enlightenment. Paegonaean blood runs through your veins.'

'I have never met this woman yet I feel the connection between us.'

Mrs Else, the plump little woman in the patchwork dress, made several trips from the kitchen while they spoke and loaded the table with the bowls and plates of a banquet. She was among the best at what she did and had perfected her trade cooking only for the Priest and the King. When she had finished laying the table, she bowed before the important gathering and exited the room. The men began to eat.

After the King had satisfied himself with his first plate of food, he set down his knife and fork and his guest responded by doing the same. 'I have lived alone up here all my life and there is much about the world I do not know. Books have been my window to it, yet I have never found its origin in any of them, only conflicting speculation. I suspect the people below are ignorant of anything beyond their own existence. Yet, you speak of prophecies and solid faith. It is my guess that the Paegonaeans know something... something that no one before them knew, something that has united your people.'

'You are also as wise as your father,' said their guest, and he began again with humility. 'Before our crusade had achieved final victory, our satellites received a message from deep space. We had been... contacted.'

'By another race?'

'The message travelled through both space and time. Those who had sent it claimed to be our descendants and spoke of Earth as the mother planet of a vast multiplanetary System. Only when the world had been united could this message be delivered, and it was entrusted to the harmony of the Paegonaean people. To do so beforehand would have only added fuel to the wars of man and hastened our self-destruction. There were, at last, instructions for us to follow; a divine path laid before us. We shall receive more information once your mission is complete and, when the time is right, we shall be joined by the first of these inter-dimensional travellers and the great span of time will become as one.'

'Then why, if time is so important, did the Paegonaeans not proceed with their conquest so near to completion eighty years ago? Why forsake what little land remained and delay this glorious event?'

'Harmony is of the utmost importance and is what elevates human nature to divinity. This is a process of evolution. Our people were not yet ready for this new way of life and had to be slowly introduced to its concept over time. An enemy beyond our walls was needed so that the darker aspects of human nature could be diverted upon it. Without this enemy, our people would have inevitably turned on each other and our new world would have become as fractured and imperfect as that which came before it. As the nature of our people became more accustomed to this new peaceful way, this supposed threat was lessened until a point when it was no longer needed.'

'And that point has been reached?'

'Our civilisation has reached its peak with the knowledge we have and it is time for us now to take the next step and begin the sacred journey bequeathed by our descendants. That is why I have come to you this night, on behalf of the Paegonaean people, and invite you to our land. You are to locate two others who were implicated in the prophecy, and the three of you are to travel to coordinates I am to give to you upon acceptance of this invitation, where you will be granted entry to our land. All will be explained there. Your accomplices have already been informed and await your arrival. Be advised that our defence grid will go back on at midnight, four nights from now. Do you accept this invitation?'

The King nodded. 'Of course. But who are these men I am to enlist on my journey? Are they noblemen or warriors? Have they been trained from birth as well as I?'

'All will become clear with time,' responded the Priest tactfully. 'Eat heartily and get on to your bed. You have learned much this night and will need your strength tomorrow.'

The King said nothing until he finished eating and then rose from his chair with a swift single movement. 'I wish to consult my father in prayer at his tomb in the city.'

'It is dark out there, but it will soon be light,' said the Priest. 'You can go with some guards at sunrise.'

'My heart cannot be advised,' he told him. 'I wish both of you a pleasant rest, as it will be late by the time I return.'

– IV –

Beyond the Palace

There was not a stir in the Palace but for the footsteps of those who patrolled her silent alleyways and corridors. There were twenty-two guards in total; elected from the ranks of the Hexlonian army to protect the shroud of secrecy that veiled the young King and his throne. The law forbidding those below from entering these protected reaches had been loyally upheld by the Hexlonian people, and only once had this stronghold ever been breached.

It was in the summer of the King's thirteenth year when a budding avant-garde magazine in Fortress city offered an incredible sum of credit for photographs of the secret Palace. The outcry from this blatant treachery was tempered by the curiosity it roused and there were many who set to work in the hope of securing this fortune. Defensive measures were tightened around the city and access from the outside restricted. Experts were called in to assess every possibility of infiltration and the people of Hexlon rested easy, convinced of their stature as one of the most secure establishments in all of the Free world.

On a cold Friday evening in late October, almost three months after the proposition had been put forth, someone somewhere inside Hexlon's fortress opened a seemingly innocuous message from the outside and perused its promotional pretence. The undetected virus it contained remained dormant in the system until triggered remotely later that night. It then spread to every extremity of Hexlon's defence network and began shutting down its various faculties. In the city below, the people noted the flickering lights of the fortress before huge sections went out one by one, until it was as though the mountain that watched over them was no longer there.

A small plane watched the lights go out as it entered into the restricted airspace unchallenged. As it flew overhead the mountainous peaks and the sanctum they cradled, a man jumped from the light aircraft and parachuted into the forbidden region with a camera in his hand. The Palace's private alarm system sounded as soon as he landed and its guards immediately began searching every inch of the grounds. They found this intruder some minutes later, lifeless, in a growing pool of dark red blood. His vacant eyes stared past them, with a fresh gaping wound from his groin to his shoulder exposing the mortal damage within. The young King sat a little distance off, the bloodied weapon sheathed before him, watching the commotion unfold with compassionless eyes. The magazine got its headline, and it was the Palace guards who took the credit for the kill. Never again had this restricted area been breached.

After the Priest and their guest had retired to their quarters, the King walked outside and moved through the blustery peaks with such stealth that not even the dogs sensed his passage. A solitary guard stood near the steps to the cablecar and looked out upon the dull glow of the city below. When he turned to make his way back across the stretch of garden, his eyes fell upon a shadow stealing through the darkness. 'Who goes there?' he called. When no response came, he dropped to one knee and trained a roving eye down the barrel of his raised weapon. 'Who goes there?'

A cloaked figure stepped out from the darkness and the guard dropped his weapon upon recognition of the King.

'Forgive me, your Highness. You understand, I could not see,' he stammered. 'Should I assemble a team to escort you?'

'Tell no one of this,' said the King in a passing whisper, and the guard dutifully nodded.

The cablecar's long descent was spent in a deep and thoughtful silence. As it began to weave through the jagged rocks of the lower reaches, the King's eyes found the huge spire of his father's Temple rise high above the landscape of the city. The old King had been among the first to show support for the Paegonaeans and put a voice to the unspoken hope for redemption by christening this Temple with a white flag of repentance. It was a controversial and unprecedented move that had brought both scorn and admiration in equal measure and heralded a new era of hope, with many more churches built in the name of forgiveness thereafter.

The night sky began to mizzle upon the city, but it did little to dampen the festivities that had not abated since the excitement broke. A lone figure passed through the crowd with eyes that would drop to the floor in an instant if ever they were to meet with a gleeful glance. A grave and uncomfortable sentiment fell upon the King in such sociable circumstances, which quickened his pace through the stifling throng. It was as though he was drowning amidst this sea of bodies and his mind was becoming frantic as he battled through them. His brusque passage grew wilder until he was almost running and, so haunted by dark thoughts of panic, he had not noticed that the crowd that engulfed him had suddenly fallen away and that he stood quite alone beneath the stare of huge floodlights above. There were shouts from those behind him to get off the pitch and the King looked down to find that he had strayed onto a marked perimeter, where a game of football was being played. He shuffled back to the sideline, where he stood for some minutes to watch the sport being played.

The fierce interplay tantalised the King and he licked his lips as he watched the defence of one team crush an attack from the opposition and quickly mount a counterattack. Such an exposition of training and skill had been strictly forbidden by the Priest, and the King was never to participate in any such frivolities. As he was about to leave, the ball rolled out of play by his feet and he picked it up and stroked the wet leather. An oncoming player accepted the ball from him without so much as a please or thank you, and the game again resumed.

The King continued on and entered into the thick fold of trees at the base of the Gardens that gently arched along its perimeter. This thin band of forest was a renowned spot for lovers and a congregating ground for the youth of Hexlon, as there were many areas off the beaten track that the watchful eye and keen ear of their protectors could not reach. Both were in abundance now and its depths buzzed with impish delight. The paths leading through it overflowed with people coming this way and that and chugged along like clogged arteries. Beyond the last of the trees ahead were twenty stone steps leading down into the city. The King perched on its edge for a moment and plotted a route from where he sat to the tall and colourful spire that dominated the skyline.

Choirs sang on street corners with retinal scanners beside them so that the tourists could make small donations. Vendors stood along the pavements of the streets and offered bowls of soup and stew to those passing by, for double the usual fee. The busy mesh of people offered adequate diversion for one not wanting to be harassed or questioned and the King pushed on, regarding nothing but the next step ahead of him. Every now and then, he would look up and note the steady rise of the spire until he was almost upon the Temple. A warm breath of air wafted from the entrance of a subway station at the end of the street and a drunken rabble emerged from it and made their way noisily along the opposite side of the street. When they had gone, the King noted how quiet the area was without them and entered onto the large square, at the centre of which, lay the Temple.

The Temple's magnificently coloured glass spire thickened from its pointed peak like a witch's hat and turned to stone at the brim and overhung the large circular building. Shops and cafes hemmed the square and simmered with the blunt excitement of the weary tourists that remained. Four neat and well-tended gardens lay at each corner around the Temple, separated by four narrow paths that were each lined with wooden benches. The entire square seemed empty now under the haunting spectre of the crowds that had gathered there earlier. A group of old men emerged from the Temple's large double doors and stood chatting under the roof's extended shelter, looking towards the mizzling sky before moving on reluctantly. The King stepped in from the rain and lifted the hood from his head.

There was a ragged hierarchy of thirty-three Temples in Hexlon, of which the King's Temple lay at the very apex, and they formed the underlying social fabric of the city. Speakers were invited up from the lower tiers of the smaller Temples, where the pulpits were open to all, and the careers of all speakers were dependent on their popularity. They were never constrained by strict house guidelines and their sermons flowed from their own personal philosophies, thoughts, feelings and viewpoints. In every foyer or surrounding veranda there would be posters informing its congregation of upcoming events and of various classes being organised in the community. The King's Temple had lost much of this chaste sentiment however, as it was given more and more to the cursory yet profitable attraction of the passing flow of tourists. Empty stalls lined the surrounding veranda and awaited local vendors to stock them with their goods at daybreak, having bribed one of those devout men whose honour it was to bestow these profitable positions. Money was to be made in such institutions, and the King's Temple was second only to the harvests when it came to bringing credit into the city.

A squat little woman hobbled alongside the King as he walked by and held a bag of watches and jewellery open before him. She did not speak, but nodded towards her merchandise with a smile of rotten yellow teeth and hissed contemptuously when the King dismissed her with a scornful glance. He pushed open the great double doors and entered.

Concentric halos of circular wooden pews emanated from a central altar of marble. As the sun rose and fell each day, this altar would be turned into a kaleidoscope of colour, as light streamed through the stained glass of the spire above. All was now illuminated by torches that burned along its curving wall and were tended by a hunched and elderly man in a brown robe, who smiled and bowed his head to those who passed him by. Though over five thousand people had walked through those double doors that day, only the most devout now remained, positioned sporadically in the pews with their heads bowed and hands interlocked, passing their private thoughts, whatever way they be inclined.

An immense silence filled the room and accentuated every noise with a trailing echo. A few heads rose from the pews as the King walked towards a small enclosed area at the far end of the Temple. He opened the door to this area and slipped inside silently. Three rows of pews stretched before a display of precious statues and symbolic artefacts, beneath which were a row of retinal scanners so donations could be made. At the centre of this display was a set of steps leading down into the crypt below and, once he had finished his silent prayer, the King arose and made his way towards it. The spiralling staircase wound down through fifty steep steps to a narrow corridor, lined with the remains of important Hexlonian men and women and, at the very end, lay the old King under a great tomb of marble. A frail and elderly woman knelt before it, gently rocking back and forth, deep in meditation. The King let her hear his footsteps as he knelt down beside her.

'He was a good man,' said the old woman after some time. 'Not only for what he did with this city. He was just as good as man can be. As great a King can be.' She looked over towards the young man beside her, who shifted slightly to avoid her gaze. 'You are most probably too young to remember him.'

'He died just before I was born,' the King replied softly. 'What can you tell me of him?'

The old woman turned towards the tomb again and looked upon it admiringly. 'He brought hope to the wastelands at a time when all seemed lost. No one can say for sure much more than that. He was a solitary being, and there are few alive today who ever saw him with their own eyes.' Her voice seemed to fade as her mind delved into thought and she began again refreshed. 'I had a dream... so vivid and clear. I dreamt that the good King had returned to us and told us not to be afraid, that things were only taking their natural course. He looked so youthful and strong.' She sighed deeply and turned again towards the young man beside her. 'I have not left his side since, hoping that he would return to me. But you seem thoughtful yourself, young man. Tell me your problems.'

'I have no problems, only questions,' the young King confided. 'I hoped that the King could direct me as he had you.'

'The dead do not give answers,' she replied. 'It is the silence they offer... therein lies all the answers.' The old woman dropped her head and returned to her meditation.

The King reached out and placed a hand on the tomb and closed his eyes. He thought of his father and to all those who had done their part, the sacrifices that had been made, and to all who looked to him now to finish their grand scheme. A sense of duty welled within him and he rose slowly to his feet with his spirit invigorated with this honour. 'Take heart from my words, wise old woman. Something beautiful lies ahead for all mankind and there is no reason to be fearful. Go and be with your family and loved ones, for they are more important than anything and need you now more than ever.'

He then returned to the Palace, burdened heavily with thought, and slept soundly in his bed until morning.

The sun began to rise over the Kingdom and its light streamed through the windows of the Palace and crept slowly along its floors and walls. The King stirred from his slumber and opened his eyes to the important day ahead. It was unusually cold in his chamber that morning, but the King carried on regardless with his routine of stretches, which he then followed with a quick shower. The water was cold and remained so throughout and he walked back to his chamber shivering slightly. He took a little longer selecting his clothes on this special morning and ran his eyes along the row of ceremonial garbs in his wardrobe. In the end, he selected a neat pair of trousers and a plain white t-shirt, over which he pulled his favourite long coat that he had made himself from the hides of twelve desert dogs. There was no strict fashion in the world below and it seemed that one could wear what one wanted. He looked at himself in the mirror and, once satisfied that he looked just like one of them, gathered some belongings into a backpack along with whatever else he may have needed on his journey.

There was an unusual silence throughout the Palace and the King called out for his two Doberman Pinschers. When they did not arrive, he called out again, perplexed as to where they could be. They would be the last in a long line of pets that the King had been given through the years. The first was a rabbit upon his fifth birthday and the Priest told him to nurture and feed the small animal.

This the young King did until twenty-seven days later, when the Priest ordered him to kill it, suggesting that he snap its neck cleanly. He then received a small kitten, which he called Ginger, who lasted fifty-seven days before meeting a similar fate. Since then, the growing King had had a varying range of animals, and from this cruel conditioning learnt the consequences of attachment. Cerberus and Famine had served him loyally since they were given to him three years ago and followed him everywhere; be it jogging through the jagged peaks of the mountain or guarding his tent when on one of his few expeditions outside the Palace.

The King ate breakfast and supper alone each day at a small table overlooking some peaks and was served personally by Mrs Else. When she did not appear, the King went in search of her and found the small adjoining kitchen empty with all its surfaces scrubbed and sterilised. This was most disconcerting. His stomach rumbled until he found some fruit and a small bowl of olives in a cupboard. He brought all to his solemn little table, where he ate his meal hungrily and, once he had finished, the empty silence of the Palace resumed.

With one final glance around his chamber, the King said farewell and slung his backpack over his shoulder. The corridor outside was empty and the usual assortment of guards and maids that wandered through the courtyard it overlooked were nowhere to be seen. He now suspected that the entire Palace had been cleared out. Would the Priest still be there? he wondered.

Every step of the spiralling stone stairs echoed through the winding passageway and he pushed open the door to the Priest's diminutive living space to find that it too had been vacated. His bedclothes lay wrapped in a neat bundle upon the frame of his wooden bed and his computer was gone. The King stepped into the room and his browsing eyes caught sight of a folded piece of paper on the bundle of bedclothes. The paper itself held no message, but inside was a small disk, no bigger than his little finger, and a smile broke across the King's face with the realisation of what it was. Though it existed only as a fanciful possibility in the world below, its people referred to it mythically as the Shadow-disk; a program that allowed its user to override the Company's security code and alter all that it protected; from the military under their control to the personal accounts of every registered citizen. In the wrong hands, it could bring down everything that had been so diligently constructed and return their world to chaos. The King's eyes flickered with an unfamiliar sentiment, which he then shook from his head before putting the disk into his backpack.

There was a sudden patter of feet in the distance and the King shot upright as they drew near. He held tight against the wall as the footsteps made their way up the spiralling staircase and awaited for the intruder to present himself. But it was the plump little figure of Mrs Else who hurriedly entered the room and jumped several inches off the ground when the King spoke behind her. The lunchboxes she carried flew into the air and fell all around her. She dropped to her knees to gather them. Once she had handed them over, Mrs Else looked at the King with a mix of maternal pride and sorrow. She pressed herself against him and whispered in the midst of their embrace to be careful.

With nothing left to do or say it was time for his journey to begin, and he drew a long breath at the prospect of his mission.

The Priest's private study lay beneath the courtyard, at the very heart of the Palace, and was its most highly secured area. Retinal and palm scans that recognised only the Priest and the King were to be followed by a thirteen digit code that changed every three days. There were several loud clunks as the bolts released their grip and the heavy metal door slowly opened. The King walked through the aisles of literature towards an elevator at the back of the room. He stepped inside and turned around as a red blanket-like beam appeared above his head and moved slowly down over his body. Once it had finished its scan, the elevator began moving down into the very heart of Mount Hexlon.

It arrived with a thud that echoed through the dark cavern and stirred the bats that clung to its roof. The large empty hollow was suddenly filled with an unearthly fluttering of wings above his head. Lights flickered on and illuminated the secret lair, still some distance above the fortress below. Red rock lay all around and its roof was supported by huge metal columns. A narrow metal bridge stretched from the elevator to the main platform that stood surrounded by a moat of darkness.

There was an assortment of vehicles on this platform, and it was there that the King learned about mechanics, maintenance and on-board defence systems. The Priest would spend hours quizzing him on every nut and bolt and together they constructed and stripped everything from small attack buggies to the more sustainable armoured trucks. Shortly after receiving confirmation that the Paegonaeans' defence grid had gone down, the Priest had summoned the boy and told him to wash, polish and thoroughly check Elena. Elena was a small assault cruiser the King had built under the guidance of his tutor and had used on his trips outside the Palace. He whipped the cover from her now and ran the tips of his fingers along her aluminium frame. She had come to represent freedom to the King, and now she sat poised to take him further than he had ever travelled before.

Meters jumped to life as he started her up and blew the cobwebs from her motor with a few stiff jabs on the accelerator. A widening stream of sunlight hit the back of the cave as its great doors began to open and a drawbridge, held by two metal chains, began to lower upon the chasm between. The King checked everything one final time as Elena's motor simmered in anticipation. With the drawbridge only halfway down and propped before him at a forty degree angle, the King took off with a spin of the wheels, up the makeshift ramp and through the air and into the outside world.

Elena's back wheels met the ground some distance down and her frame snapped forward as they did, asking everything of her powerful suspension as she took the rough terrain in her stride. She jumped about wildly as the King descended the fierce mountainside and warnings rang out as she weaved through the jagged rocks. The fortress did not extend this far back from the front of mount Hexlon, nor were there any houses or buildings of any kind; its ground too steep and uneven to build upon. When the sheer gradient of the mountain began to moderate, the King pushed forward on her thrusters and they ignited with a powerful and simultaneous whoop. His arms stiffened to fight the mounting g-force and his face contorted in the battle, as Elena tore through countless wire fences and continued down the mountainside with all the characteristics of an avalanche.

Two and a half hours passed by, dodging the oncoming medley of vehicles on their way to join in the festivities, and the King felt uneasy that he should be the only one heading in the other direction. A wave of relief washed over him when the Company's great Trade-convoy appeared on the digital-layout some distance ahead. It kept going and going, like a gigantic mechanical caterpillar that almost reached the entire length of the digital-layout's screen. From a list of options on its menu, the King selected to contact it, and sent a message that he wished to hitch a ride with them to the edge of the wastelands. Within a few minutes, he received a message back from them, telling him to disarm his defence system and pull in behind while they scanned his vehicle. The King shifted his course and soon found the huge tracks left by the wheels of this motorized monster and followed them until he was right behind it. Elena's on-board computer began to hum as they scanned her system to ensure against attack. Once satisfied that the vehicle or its occupant deemed no threat, another message appeared on Elena's system stating that it would cost one hundred credits and that bay 3766 was now opening. He pulled out from behind the monstrous vehicle and sped up alongside her, counting down the bays to 3766, and he found its door already opened and trailing along the ground on small wheels.

Once inside the empty storage container, the ramp the King had just driven up was pulled shut behind him and sealed the bay in darkness. There was an unmistakeable smell of oranges as the King climbed out of his cruiser and immediately noted the glow of a fluorescent light hanging above a small exit. The King opened it and stepped out into the daylight and walked along a metal gangway that trembled slightly as the colossal vehicle trundled along. At the end of this gangway was a door that led through into the belly of this beast.

Ribs of steel stretched overhead from front to back and there was not a being in sight. Forklifts lay abandoned and empty crates were strewn everywhere. The King wandered through the desolate hull with a nonchalant stride and eventually arrived at a small seating area. On the table lay some cards and poker chips from an abandoned game. A television in the corner fuzzed between stations. The King threw a searching glance all around before producing a small computer from his backpack, into which he inserted the Shadow-disk.

In the Company's fledgling years, the importance of a universal security code capable of protecting their system became clear. They therefore founded the Academy; a school where they trained young scholars in the field and it soon became the seat of all power. It was a man known only as the Professor who had developed the current security code, and it was he who had been chosen to assist the King on his mission. His artificially intelligent security code inaugurated every attempt made against it into its makeup, thus strengthening it and enabling it to evolve with the best of those around. Never had this security system been breached in its twelve years, until now.

The computer screen opened on the Hexlon homepage and, with the help of the Shadow-disk, the King scrolled through the forbidden reaches of cyberspace. He would need an identity and an account with some credit, and this task took only a few minutes. In a carefully monitored wing of the Company's Academy, a new account was created with every new registration and was subsequently deleted upon death, but with the Shadow-disk in his possession, the King was free to be anyone he wanted. He took the name of his favourite author and filled out the rest as he wished, finally adding his own retinal identity before saving it to the system. With a few more keystrokes, he had been invited to the Academy on official business. There, he would make contact with the Professor, and together they would continue on their quest. Before he closed his computer however, that same strange sentiment that had tickled him upon first beholding the Shadow-disk resurfaced. He brought up the accounts of those large industries, owned mostly by the Company or their friends, and looked upon the millions they had assiduously accumulated through the years, now interchangeable digits at his mercy. But such a mortal sentiment quickly shrivelled when placed in the shadow of the mission he had been honoured with, and he closed his computer and looked around for something in the way of entertainment.

He ran the length of the empty hull several times and exercised for some hours before settling down to a meal of seasoned chicken. By now he suspected that they must have been close to the border and he climbed a nearby ladder and opened a heavy hatch to the outside. A strong wind blew against him as he climbed up and looked out upon the surrounding landscape.

The sun had just set and night was creeping close. Patches of unassisted green broke from the orange soil here and there and, in the distance, was a large old oak tree that had somehow survived the blitz and seemed now to sigh from beneath its orange foliage. The King returned to his cruiser in bay 3766 and, after sending a message to the Trade-convoy's control, the door began to open and Elena backed out into the howling wind. Once upon the firm orange dust, the King sat for some time as the last of its gigantic wheels rolled by and finally unveiled the jagged silhouette of the mountain range against what remained of the evening sky. A trickle of adrenalin coursed through his veins as he set off towards them.

The military installation that stretched along the face of these mountains had been built long ago as a last stand against the Paegonaeans, with those who had survived the war so far huddling behind its line. Whatever little armour and weaponry that remained in the weakened resistant state was put into its construction and the area was to be known henceforth as Tyra. Those who controlled the missiles at her disposal however, were never given the chance to let them rattle upon the final advance of their enemy. Instead, they watched with consternation as the land before them was gradually blitzed by the incoming sweep of the Paegonaeans' defence grid, stopping miraculously by their very feet before retreating back to its position just beyond their wall. Everything beyond had been left unscathed, and the installation then became a hotly contested commodity in the power-struggle that followed the war's unexpected conclusion. Once their defence network was in place throughout Fortress city, the Company consolidated their authority with its acquisition, and there they watched over everything. As the King approached, more and more of the base came into view, and he could just about make out the missile launching sites, high in the peaks of the mountains.

The sandy grit of the wastelands soon gave way to the tarmacked roads of the central suburbia of their little world, and huge floodlit signs assorted the oncoming mess of traffic into lanes. One by one, the queues moved forward as the border patrol inspected those passing through. The King had come through there before, but never had he seen so many guards about it nor waited so long in one of its queues. When he approached the barrier, a youthful guard held up his hand for him to stop and wind down his window.

'Where are you going?' he asked, handing the King a hand-held retinal scanner.

'The Academy,' replied the King, pressing it against his eyes like a pair of binoculars. 'I am expected there.'

The guard looked at the computer screen beside him and nodded slightly. But there was a hesitation in his movements and he took several steps back and observed Elena with lingering appeal. 'You a bounty hunter, Mr Sagan?'

'No,' replied the King, seemingly amused by this accusation. 'Only a fool would travel through the wastelands without some protection.'

The hesitant guard did not change his stance while he delivered the Company's rules of conduct and was somewhat distracted by the customised cruiser as he spoke. 'You will be sent the full conditions of Fortress city by message once inside. Any breach of these and you will be before the justice court. Any other weapons to declare?'

The King shook his head.

Horns began to honk from the long queue behind and hastened the distracted guard to a decision. Again he looked to the screen before him and then shook his head of his instinctual suspicions. The barrier was raised from before the King and he was waved through into the grassy hub of their little world.

– V –

The Suburbs

Beyond the bubble of light that surrounded the checkpoint there lay a deep and impenetrable darkness, falling about the countryside like a blanket and merging the humble lights of the mountainfolk to the infinite cosmos of stars and galaxies in the sky above. Elena's headlights illuminated the narrow valley road and strayed occasionally into the rising slope of the green fields on either side as the King meandered through the corridor they made. The dreary landscape was reflected in the silence of the digital-layout until it gave a short sharp bleep to notify some inns and hostels clustered along the path up ahead. Their lights eventually appeared through the darkness like the breaking hue of dawn and grew brighter until he was upon the first of them.

In its brightly lit forecourt, there was a group of twenty youths sat around their vehicles, interacting with obvious excitement. Some flirted brashly while others held onto lovers and listened to the jocularity of the group with subdued participation. In their midst was an attractive young girl with long golden hair and the King found his eyes drawn upon her as he passed. Once the bright lights of the forecourt died away and darkness resumed around him, the excitement that he had felt upon beholding this young girl soured into something akin to loneliness. The King had often wondered what his life would have been like had chance willed otherwise and he just like any other boy, free to enjoy an unshackled life. Knowledge, he thought, was a tyrant that made slaves of all who possessed it. In an enlightened world, all would serve the truth with complete obedience and there would be no place for subversion. This was to be the burden for our young King; a slave amongst the free.

A thin sliver of moon looked down upon the thoughtful King and offered only the faintest silver shimmer to the world around him now that the oppressive mountains on either side had withdrawn a little. Some way in the distance, a small spark rose high into the darkness and caught the King's somnolent attention. It began to fade as its trajectory waned when suddenly it exploded brightly in an eruption of sparkling colours. How jaded must these people be, he thought, that they greet news of indeterminate change with fireworks. Many more were to follow along this route, unwittingly serenading the intrepid King as he set forth on his surreptitious mission.

Once the mountains had withdrawn completely and the surrounding landscape flattened, voices began to surface through the static of the radio and the King searched for any morsel of information or news that may have been of use to him and stopped upon hearing the name of his Kingdom.

'... The people of Hexlon have reacted vehemently against a proposal, put forth by some lower members of the Company, to send in a team to find out why they have lost contact with their Palace, claiming it a violation of their most sacred law. This proposal has also been condemned by senior members of the Company, who have always been keen to maintain their profitable relationship with the city. Only a few have ever seen the uncharted region atop mount Hexlon or the Palace it holds, by order of the late King and creator of the city. Not only is it protected by this law, but it is also heavily fortified and patrolled by an elite selection of guards. Next to nothing is known about it or those who live there. Many Hexlonians and circles beyond believe that it is now home to the King's rumoured son, a claim criticised by others as fanciful. But with communication going down after the Paegonaeans' defence grid, the coincidence is sparking off fresh debate in a possible link between the two. Many are now asking, after the Company's rash decision to upgrade Hexlon to a level one installation, could they turn those new guns upon our city? We have our resident defence expert, Martin Klimp, in the studio with us tonight. Martin?'

'Well,' began a ponderous male voice. 'While it is, in theory, possible...'

A dull grey unease settled about the King's mind as he turned off the radio. It was all a game and its rules were being divulged as it went along. Time was its currency, and these latest revelations had just inflated its value. It would not be long before they were after him, whoever *they* would be; sniffing at the track he inevitably left behind.

He pushed hard upon the accelerator and counted down the distance to the city on each of the road-signs he passed. But Elena would soon be running low on fuel cells and a full recharge out there would mean that she would need no more until she was leaving the city with the Professor safely onboard. The balance of this decision was tipped at the thought of some food and the King consulted the digital-layout for a mutual solution. It flashed with various possibilities, and the nearest was a Burgerbar just ahead, nestling amongst the warehouses of the industrial estate that it served.

A message appeared on the digital-layout that he was now entering into the jurisdiction of Cobra Security. Almost immediately, there appeared one of their vans by the side of the road; its two occupants stuffing huge burgers into their mouths and washing them down with cold drinks. Neither paid any notice as the passing cruiser slowed and turned in to the industrial estate.

As the King looked around its seemingly deserted lanes, a sense of familiarity dawned on him. He had been there before. It was at the end of his first excursion beyond the Palace grounds, he remembered, just after his sixteenth birthday. The sudden memory of the delicious meat sandwich and the thin strips of fried potato made his mouth water and his stomach began to rumble. Cobra Security signs were on every building and fence as the King wound through the alleyways of the dull concrete maze. At last, upon turning one final corner, he was greeted by a large neon Burgerbar sign with the famed fast-food restaurant beneath.

Seven charging ports lined the top of its forecourt and, on a small placard, were the words *Top up while you fill up*. Three vehicles were already charging there: a suburban land cruiser with brown muddy treads, a family vehicle slightly tinged with red dust, and a recreational vehicle with the luggage of five young males piled high in the back. Elena took her space between them and shuddered as the port attached itself to her. The King then got out and stretched himself, breathing in the freshness of the air as he walked towards the entrance of the restaurant.

Those inside did not stir as he entered and the King slid quietly into a booth looking out onto the forecourt. Hot oil sizzled from the kitchen and filled the large room with the aroma of food cooking in it. At a table in the centre of the restaurant sat the group of young males, conducting themselves noisily at the expense of everyone else's tranquillity. Near them was a young farmer's wife, feeding a child in a highchair while two others played quietly by her feet. In the far corner sat a young couple looking deep into each others' eyes with gently touching hands. A middle-aged waitress with heavy makeup perched on a stool by the counter and was watching a news report on a television in the corner of the room. There was a shout from the kitchen that made her jump to her feet and she made her way towards the seated King.

'I apologise for the noise,' she said as she arrived, in a tone that suggested her mind was elsewhere. 'Welcome to Burgerbar. What would you like this evening?' She set a retinal scanner before him and arranged his settings with the robotic movements of a deeply ingrained routine.

'Do you still sell the Monsterburger?'

Her eyes gained focus upon the King and she smiled with a slow stretching of her mouth. 'It must have been a while since you were here, sweetheart. We haven't sold the Monsterburger in years. We do, however, sell the Megaburger. It's more or less the same. You want the meal... that's with fries and a drink? And you are at port three, refuelling at 1.56 credits per cell. Would you like it topped up?'

Prices, it seemed, were constantly rising while the credit of the Company's monetary system devalued steadily. He remembered that on his first excursion, the Priest had spent just over thirty credits and all of their entourage had eaten and all of their vehicles had been fully charged. Not that this mattered to the King now. Once his order had been inputted, he placed his eye upon the scanner and the transaction was made. The waitress tore off a receipt and handed it to him before walking to the kitchen with his order. The King closed his tired eyes for a few seconds and reopened them as a wave of light rolled across the forecourt. Another vehicle entered and pulled in next to the King's cruiser. It was a standard Ford, armoured dune-buggy, and from the fresh red dust on its treads, it had just come in from the wastelands.

Its door opened and a worn leather boot stepped out onto the ground, followed by a short and chubby little man of about sixty. A lengthy yawn and stretch revealed a holster on his belt and small sidearm, and his dusty clothing was of a man fresh from duty. He took great interest in Elena and inspected her thoroughly, even lying on the ground to look underneath. It reminded him of something one would see at a show; the best of all parts put together with precision and knowledge, although this one had certainly not been contained to the showroom. There were scars on its frame that intrigued him, as did the buttons and controls on its dashboard. He seemed to depart from it with some reluctance and stopped twice to gaze at it from over his shoulder as he made his way towards the double doors of the Burgerbar.

His entry was announced by the wail of an alarm and the waitress emerged from the kitchen, stiffened by a sudden jolt of panic. Her eyes flickered with recognition upon beholding the familiar figure and her stricken demeanour relaxed. The youths fell silent momentarily and even the lovers broke from their gaze to glance in his direction. He stood there for some time, smug in his own self-importance, slowly surveying the room before taking a seat at a table next to the King. His eyes darted between the cruiser parked in the forecourt and the silent young man next to him. 'That's a sweet cruiser you've put together there, boy,' he said finally. 'You do that yourself?'

'A friend did,' answered the King, in a tone that politely asked for no further questions.

The wastelander lifted a menu and skimmed his eyes down its listings before closing it again and throwing it in front of him. 'You coming in from the wastelands?'

This time the King turned to face him and answered more curtly. 'Yes.'

The wastelander nodded to himself, either oblivious of his imposition or seeming not to care, and then turned towards the King again. 'You heard anything lately?'

'Nothing.'

At this he laughed heartily. 'It's hard to hear nothing these days. What we lack in fact we make up for with rumours. Anything from the Company?' he prompted, before continuing himself. 'It seems they may have been premature in their upgrading of Hexlon. Apparently, the Company are divided themselves over the issue of taking action against them. Hexlon makes a lot of money for a lot of people within the Company, and they'll be careful not to offend them. Seems that they can't make up their mind and some of the younger members of their board are taking the initiative. Word is that a team have already entered the city. Something is happening under our very noses and the authorities have no idea what it is. That's why a few old colleagues and I are operating a kind of roving patrol about this area. Maybe we'll see something that those young bucks at the checkpoints have missed.' He then extended his hand towards the King. 'Jones is the name.'

The waitress appeared from the kitchen with the King's meal and broke the ensuing silence between the two men by leaving all before him and asking if there was anything else he required.

'Just a peaceful few minutes to enjoy it.'

As the waitress pulled away with the empty tray, the old wastelander took her arm and asked if there had been any news in the past ten minutes.

'Nothing yet,' she answered. 'But the Company seem to be at war with themselves, and there is definitely something going on at Hexlon.'

'You be a good girl and tell me the minute there is anything.'

The King ate his meal with such haste that he had almost finished by the time the waitress had returned from the kitchen and sat down again upon her stool. As he got up to leave, the waitress rose from the chair with an excited outburst that rendered all in the restaurant at her attention. 'This is it!' she exclaimed, running towards the television and turning it up loud for all to hear.

A female newscaster listened carefully through her earpiece before looking at the camera and clearing her throat. 'We have just received confirmation that a team have entered Hexlon's Palace and have found it deserted. Reports are somewhat sketchy at this time, but it is claimed that there is evidence to suggest that a young male, perhaps the alleged son of the King, has lived there until recently. The whereabouts of servants and other workers remain unknown at this time. Sources within the breakaway branch of the Company who authorised this action say that they are to issue a statement shortly, and it is expected that they will offer bounties on each of these workers, including the Priest, who is also missing. Photographs of each of them can be found on the Company's website. It is believed however, that information leading to the whereabouts of the young King, if he does indeed exist, might come close to one hundred million credits... a record by any standard. It is thought that he is between twenty to thirty years of age and is taller than six foot with a large athletic build. It is added - and this has been stressed by all three of our sources - that he is to be approached with extreme caution.' The screen then cut to an artist's sketch of the old King in his youth and explained that his son may look something along these lines. Though the portrait lacked the King's fine features and the sharpness of his face, the link between father and son could easily have been bridged with a little imagination. The newscaster reappeared. 'At a time of many questions, it seems that the first pieces of the jigsaw only add to the confusion. More on this as it develops.'

'The whole thing stinks!' shouted Jones, slamming both fists down hard on the table. 'It's obvious now. Hexlon and the Paegonaeans have been plotting together since the reign of the King. They have been waiting for this day, and now it's here all we have is an artist's rendition of what his son might look like. It is probably he who will deliver the final blow upon us while our troops twiddle their thumbs on the front line.' He turned towards his table in exasperation and placed his head in his hands. 'What could all this mean?'

There was a silence as those in the restaurant took in what they had just learned and eventually the slow murmur of conversation began to rise. Jones remained with his head in his hands as the King slipped out behind him.

Four cameras swept the length of the restaurant's forecourt at overlapping intervals. The King stopped before entering into their field of vision and observed the overall pattern of their sweep. Blind spots were opening up here and there for brief seconds only, but he found that one in particular opened up near his vehicle that gave him ample opportunity to deal with the wastelander should he continue to harass him. He would need to be clinical and precise, but first he would need patience. When the time came, the King stepped onto the forecourt, just as the doors behind him opened and the voice of the wastelander called out to him. The King continued as though he had not heard his shout and again Jones called out to him. His pace then quickened and the King listened to his footsteps draw near. With his right hand, the King pulled a concealed blade from the buckle of his coat and with his left pressed a button on a small remote control. Elena's motor began to whir and her headlights shone brightly in the eyes of both men. With the press of another button, a storage compartment at the front of her yawned open; large enough for the lifeless body of one short little wastelander. Just as they stepped into the blind spot, Jones reached out to take his shoulder and the King prepared to turn for the covert and fatal finale. As he did, the doors of the restaurant again opened and the undisturbed silence was shattered by the rambunctious youths who made their way out behind them. The King returned his blade to the buckle of his coat.

'You'd be more than welcome to join us,' said the wastelander. 'Nothing like a little purpose to give life meaning. Let me make a call and my men could meet us here.'

'I have some business to attend to,' replied the King. 'However, I wish you well without me.'

'Before you go,' interjected the wastelander quickly. 'Could I have a look at some identification? Maybe even get a retinal scan. Wouldn't be doing my job otherwise.'

The window had passed and the opportunity had gone. There would be a screen somewhere in the offices of Cobra Security featuring both of them now and, if anything untoward was to happen, his mission would be over before it even started. 'Come with me, Jones,' said the King. 'I have something to show you.'

Jones frowned at the young man's change in approach towards him and his curiosity was piqued. The youngster opened up his cruiser and from it pulled a computer which he sat upon its roof. The screen illuminated and both huddled before its glow.

'It is the Shadow-disk,' the King told him, demonstrating its might with a few taps on the keyboard. 'I am taking it to the Academy in Fortress city.'

The eyes of the old wastelander widened and he looked towards the young man with wide incredulous eyes. 'It *is* you. You're the son of the King.'

'The King you speak of is dead and I am his successor. You want answers, my friend? I can tell you now that

I am on a mission of the utmost importance. The Paegonaeans' defence grid went down to allow an emissary to visit my Palace and it will stay down until I have delivered the Shadow-disk to the Academy. I will need someone to escort me there, and in return for your help, I will tell you everything that I know along the way.'

The old man licked his lips at this proposition and his imagination flourished with the secrets such a position could hold. But sentiments of enlightenment were quickly replaced by thoughts of more primitive riches and he moved his hand towards the weapon he had concealed in his belt. His eyes narrowed upon the King as he spoke. 'What is to stop me turning you in and collecting my reward?'

'Then you remain ignorant. However, if it is earthly delights that you hunger for, I am sure we can come to some arrangement,' he said, holding open the door to his cruiser.

Jones's eyes glazed with the balance of this decision. 'You have seen beyond our wall?' he asked.

'We do not have much time. But I promise that I will answer your every question truthfully and to the best of my ability along the way.'

Jones spent a moment longer in self-deliberation and then nodded at his own decision. He climbed into the back of the King's cruiser and made himself comfortable in the cramped compartment just behind the cockpit. His first questions concerned the cruiser and the functions of its many switches and levers. Many more followed the roar of its motor as the King took off out of the forecourt, out of the industrial estate, and onto the highway in the direction of Fortress city. They passed through small villages with remote clusters of farmlands in the distance, and Jones's questions grew in their scale; each answer leading on to another question. His relentless barrage only faltered when the King began to slow and turned off the highway down a small country lane.

'Linch island?' cried the old man. 'What business could you have there? It is as uncivilised as the furthest reaches of the wastelands! Even if we make it through the Black forest, they'll tear us to shreds and eat our flesh!'

'Have no fear, my friend. The island is a Hexlon colony. We will be welcome there.'

The old man sat back in his cramped quarter and looked around uneasily. His only fear in life was the occult and superstition that centred around these woods. When the Black forest appeared on the digital-layout further along the path, he leaned forward and asked the King had he not heard the stories. A wooden sign hung by the side of the small path, just before the dark forest, with a warning for all those who entered written in an archaic language of the old world.

LA MORT EST PRÉSENTE.

The King sensed his passenger's anguish and reassured him as they entered into the fold of trees. 'Those stories are put about to frighten people from coming through here. There is no truth in any of them.'

'People nailed upside down to trees. Human organs strewn amidst its undergrowth. I heard that a group of youngsters were picking mushrooms in here some years ago and saw a strange figure standing seven feet tall with a mist of red all about him. They say that he was in the middle of some twisted ritual with a small gathering of people around him.'

The forest watched through many eyes and strange noises filled the air. The wastelander's heart could be heard thumping in his chest and his great fearful eyes darted all around. The cruiser's palpable silence was then broken by a sharp bleep from the digital-layout and Jones withered behind the King. 'We're dead.'

'It is nothing but a fallen tree. I should be able to lift it from our path.'

The wastelander's voice now trembled. 'You're getting out... here? Can't you blast it?'

'That could start a forest fire.'

'Would it be a bad thing?' said the wastelander, looking all about him with great unease. 'This forest gives off a strange energy.'

The obstructing tree appeared before them in Elena's headlights and the King slowed down and got out. There was an eerie silence in the cold air outside, as though someone or something had just shushed the spectators that surrounded them and all now watched with bated breath. An owl hooted as the King lifted one end of the fallen log and shifted it from the path with small side-steps, pines crunching beneath his feet like snow. The old wastelander climbed into the cockpit and poised himself for takeoff should any sign of danger or loud noise demand it.

Once the path had been cleared, they continued through the dark heart of the forest and out the other side, where the trees began to subside into shrubbery. A large body of water, one of many within the walls of the Free world, opened up before them and the path turned sharply to the left along its edge. The King slowed to a halt as he turned the corner and looked out at the lights in the distance. 'There it is,' he said. 'Linch island.'

The silver moonlight reflected off the restful water and there was not a sound in the air above the gentle hum of Elena's idling motor. Memories of that day, when he first beheld this view, returned to the King now as he looked out upon the water. He had just turned sixteen and had never before been beyond the boundaries of his secluded Palace. Never before had he seen or touched the things that lay about him and the world was opening to him like a blossoming flower. This first expedition, the Priest had told him, would make him become a man. Though the sixteen year old King was unsure how this transition would come about, he did what he was told and set forth upon his journey with youthful zeal and an appetite to learn all that he could about the people of this world and their societies.

It began with a long journey in a helicopter, from the familiar setting of the young King's Palace to the top of a snow-covered mountain in a land he did not yet know. He was given no map, no food or warm clothes and told to descend to its base, where he would meet with the Priest in three days. What had once been tedious lessons during long afternoons at the Palace were now practical steps for survival. The young and inexperienced King did what he could to protect himself from the fierce and howling winds by day and sheltered from the dangers brought on by the darkness of night. On the morning of his second day, the young King descended into forest and saw things that had existed only in the pages of his books before that day. He stumbled upon a village that night and took a position high in a tree outside its perimeter to watch the customs of these mountainfolk. A tall fire burned near a totem pole in the centre of their village and the people came out from their huts and sang and danced around it with seeming cordiality. As the festivity reached its climax, a shackled young woman was led from one of the wooden cabins and stripped of her clothes before the baying crowd. She was then put upon a cross and hoisted above the fire and the flames began to lick her feet. A low chanting broke out amongst the crowd, pierced by the shrill screams of the woman, which seemed to continue long after she had been totally engulfed.

Inexperienced as the young King was, ethics and morality were not lost upon him, and he watched their barbaric display with revulsion. However, he also felt that personal judgement was inadequate to condemn the custom of an entire tribe, no matter how outlandish it may seem to an outsider. The young King understood that the world beyond his was diverse and lacked the unifying confirmation of any one deity or system. It was human nature to create such religions and their traditions would continue to flourish until the day of universal enlightenment. Only then could they be judged and all would inevitably pale in the glaring light of truth. With all this in mind, the young King pondered the fate of these villagers and decided that, unenlightened as he was, it was not his place to cast judgement upon another. This was what makes a man, thought the King, an individual sense of justice, armed with opinions and beliefs about humanity.

He arrived at the campsite early on the third morning and found the Priest and his guards still sleeping. After some breakfast, they packed up their belongings and brought the young King to the spot, where, eight years later, he now found himself again. The Priest took him

DAVID BLAIR

under his arm that day as they walked along the water's edge, explaining that the island in the distance lay independent from the rest of the Free world and that these waters and forest kept its secret. His mission, therefore, was to cycle around this land and map everything from its buildings, road network and terrain, as accurately as possible, adding that he should include anything else of interest or strange goings-on. After some final advice from the Priest and a round of 'good lucks' from his guards, the young King set off on his bicycle, submersed in the contentment of his freedom.

Back then, the island was connected to the mainland by an old and rusted bridge that stretched across the calm water below. In the middle of this bridge, parked askew, was a big and bulky armoured vehicle that presumably served as a roadblock to obstruct heavy vehicles from entering into the territory beyond. A narrow path continued on from the bridge with rows of trenches dug on either side, zigzagging their way back to a puny cylindrical stone tower. There were no signs of a defence system that the adolescent King could see, which meant that these islanders were perhaps as primitive as those he had encountered upon the mountain. All was deserted but for a hidden figure at the apex of the tower, watching the young cyclist approach and turn up the hill towards the village beyond.

Now… eight years later… the old building had been appropriately renovated and served more properly as the village's primary watch-post. A small garrison had been built around its base, where thirty guards were now stationed to protect their new-found wealth. A robust automatic weapon had since been installed at the top of the watchtower and jumped to life as the oncoming cruiser crossed the new bridge that had replaced the old and rusted one. To the left of this now-modernised building and behind some trees, in what had once been an old potato field, stood four great heat-lamps, shining down on rows of blooming marijuana, and the air was thick with the smell of it.

'Let's just turn and get out of here,' said Jones pleadingly.

'We do that and they'll kill us for sure.'

The automated weapon followed them as they crossed the bridge and turned up the hill to the right. Another gun of equal proportions waited to relieve its comrade as they descended the other side and another followed them all the way into the village. How different it all looked now, thought the King. It could almost have been a quarter in Hexlon city.

The arrival of this strange vehicle awoke the dormant weaponry around the village square and aroused the interest of those in the surrounding houses and taverns. A group of youths, who were seated on some steps leading up to a laundrette, took it upon themselves to greet the new arrivals and quickly gathered around Elena. One of them tapped on her window with the back of his hand. 'You gentlemen lost?'

Her armoured door opened and the King stepped out. He had always felt uneasy around those of the same age as himself and he looked at each of them now in silence. They laughed at something he did not understand.

'Nice coat,' sniggered one of them, raising his hand to sample its texture. But before his fingers made contact, the King had taken his hand and dismissed his advance with a forceful push. Those around him stiffened suddenly and their mood became violent in an instant. The first to step forward was swiftly dispatched with a punch to the face and those thereafter each received a debilitating blow of some kind that left them weakened or unconscious by the feet of the King. As the crowd thinned around him, there was a loud whirring of machinery and the clunk of heavy ammunition being loaded. A loud robotic voice spoke. 'Put your hands in the air and face the scanners. You have ten seconds to comply.'

Those who could backed away from him. 'Better do what you are told, stranger.'

The silence of the standoff was broken by the residents of Linch spilling from the surrounding buildings and gathering all around. There were gasps and whispers, and the Mayor himself pushed his way through and stood in astonishment upon beholding the scene before him. 'You!' he cried.

Someone somewhere deactivated the defence system and there was a unified gulp as the situation was made clear. Slowly, the people dropped to their knees and bowed their heads in apology. The youths looked around, first bewildered and then panicked. 'We didn't know!' one of them explained. 'How were we to know?'

'I see you have not lost your particular brand of hospitality,' said the King.

'We apologise with all the treasures we have to offer, your Highness,' said the Mayor; a stout little man dressed in fine attire. 'It has been a long time. When you said you would return one day, we simply... Please, you must be famished.' He then turned and announced to the crowd that a banquet was to be prepared in honour of their royal guest, but the King interjected that all he wished for was some rest.

'You wish to rest!' the Mayor called out theatrically. 'Then you shall rest in our finest lodgings!'

Jones had watched all from the safety of Elena's berth, but had now opened the door and ventured outside, confident in his position as the royal escort. He cleared his throat to speak when the King began before him.

'As a token of my personal appreciation and my Kingdom's gratitude for your bountiful harvests, I bring a gift that should give your men some sport.'

Hungry eyes turned to the old wastelander as his mind slowly adjusted to the new horror of his situation. His sidearm was removed from its holster by someone behind him and held towards his back. A crowd enveloped around him and subdued the old wastelander's weakening attempts at freedom. Jones's last bursts of energy were directed at the King for having duped him and his protests died into the calm and silent night as he was carried off.

The crowd parted with a wave of the Mayor's hand and formed a corridor up the steps to the village hall. He led the way with a determined stride through a brew of excited whispers and the King followed with obvious unease at this attention. Up the steps they walked and into the luxurious reception of the village hall, where the Mayor again began to rattle. 'We need a room prepared at once for his Royal Highness! Our best room at once!'

A lazy eye opened from behind the front desk and the figure there stretched himself out and yawned. 'All the rooms are the same, Artie,' he said sleepily, before the glint of recognition in his hazy eyes turned to a furore of panic. 'Ahh, right away, sir.' He turned and pulled some keys from the rack behind him with a shaking hand. 'Room 10 has just been cleaned.'

They walked up the stairs to the first floor and down a narrow corridor, where they entered a room overlooking the village square. The Mayor remained at the doorway while the King looked out the window at the dissipating crowd below.

'It is surely no coincidence that you should return to us on the same week the Paegonaeans' defence grid has gone down. These are exciting times. And I assure you that your stay here tonight shall be guarded by the same secrecy that has defined our allegiance to your royal throne.' He faltered at the door for a moment longer and then added. 'Perhaps some relaxation is what his Highness needs after a day of strife we mere mortals could only imagine.' He pulled a clay pipe from his pocket and set it on a table alongside a small box of matches. 'Perhaps you would like to sample some of our most recent harvest?'

The Mayor shut the door after him and the King began checking the room with meticulous scrutiny. Everything was neatly in place. He first pulled at the bedcovers and arranged the pillows as though a sleeping body lay beneath them. An armchair sat in the centre of the room and he moved it to a darkened corner and brought the table beside it. He lifted the clay pipe and savoured the scent of its content. Its distinct aroma took the King back to those nights outside the Palace when the Priest was fast asleep in his tent and his guards would pass around a pipe similar to the one he now held. The match flared in the darkness and he held it to the end of the pipe as he puffed life from the smouldering weed. Upon the first draw, he closed his eyes and let his mind drift back to that day when he first encountered these strange islanders.

– VI –

That First Encounter

It was the heat that he remembered first when he recalled that day, eight years ago, setting off up the hill on his bicycle, into the secret island of Linch. In the peaks of Mount Hexlon, the young King knew only high winds, rain and snow, and this stagnant warmth was something new to him. The sights and sounds of this strange new world seemed to sing the praise of his liberation and, at the same time, warn him that all was not as it seemed. He knew that this would be a test of some kind, and it seemed unlikely that the Priest would be satisfied with the completion of a simple map. And so, it was with an open heart and eyes and ears alert to danger that he continued on into this exotic land.

At the top of the hill, the path forked in two with a crooked little signpost pointing in each direction. The path that continued straight ahead and down the other side was marked *Village* while the one that pointed further up the hill to his right was marked *Heller's point*. At that junction, the King settled for some minutes while he drunk from his water-bottle and regained his composure in the rising heat. A soft and persuasive breeze blew towards Heller's Point that filled the sails of the young King as he continued further up the mountainous path.

Crows rustled and flew off from the branches of the trees that lined the narrow road and there was a thin smell of smoke in the morning air. Eventually, the rising slope began to recede and, once he had reached the flat of its summit, the young King got off his bike and climbed a tall tree with a pair of binoculars in his hand. Much of the land below, he noted, was farmland, though it rose into a peak along the middle and formed a spine that ran the length of the island, hiding much of the other side from view. The path on which he now stood fell sharply through some forest ahead and dipped and weaved its way through the island and up the imposing mountain that rose from its far end. That was where he presumed to find Heller's point, and there he would be able to finish his map more comprehensively.

He pulled some paper from his backpack to begin work on the map when he noticed some faint plumes of smoke rising from an encampment below. Through his binoculars, he counted thirty camouflaged tents with some military vehicles parked around them. He added these to his initial rendition of the island along with estimations of the force they contained. As he carefully etched the contour of the land, his attention turned inexplicably towards the village way off in the distance to his left, where he focussed his binoculars upon a curious gathering of men.

The leader of the group was on his hands and knees, drawing with his finger in the soft dirt with five men gathered attentively around him. Behind each of these men was a further group of twelve, to whom the message of their leader was relayed along with individual instructions. Then, suddenly, the group dispersed and headed in each their own direction. Two men climbed into a small truck nearby and started up the road from the village. The young King jumped from the branch of the tree and took off on his bicycle until he was speeding his way downhill through the small forest and emerged on the other side moments later.

If he was to understand his situation more fully, he would need a closer investigation, and he looked around for a suitable spot to do so. A wooden gate appeared in the long stone wall to his left and he pulled hard on the brakes and slid to a halt. He opened the gate wide and threw his bike on the ground beside it, and then hid amongst some bushes on the opposite side of the road.

The appearance of the truck through the corridor of trees gave the young King his first taste of fear and he shrunk deeper into the bushes as it approached. He could see the eyes of its two occupants fixed upon the open gate and it slowed and stopped just before it. The words *Fortress City Waste* were emblazoned along the side of it, though the young King could see that this vehicle had been modified with armour-plating and reinforced wheels. Both its driver and passenger jumped out and looked all around with keen eyes before venturing into the field to continue their search. Not a word passed between them as they guardedly advanced, yet they heard nothing as the door of their idling truck was opened and the young King crept inside.

He hoped to find a radio to listen in on their communications or perhaps even a weapon should he need one, but there was nothing to be found in the pristine cab but a crumpled ball of paper on the floor. The young King's eyes widened as he flattened it out upon the dashboard and his blood ran cold. It was a picture of him.

As unanswerable questions bounced about his head, he noticed that the gentle rattle of the vehicle's motor was not confined to the acoustics of the cab, and he looked to the curtained area behind. When he drew back the partition, he found that the vehicle's waste disposal unit had been removed and replaced by a large and complex machine with an array of flashing lights and buttons. A voice then startled him from any further investigation of this machine, and he slipped from the truck in silence and returned to his place in the bushes.

The truck started off down the road and reappeared moments later doubling back, only slowing this time to allow its occupants a quick glance around before disappearing back up through the forest. Once the noise of the motor dipped beneath the soft breeze, the King climbed out from his hiding place and looked around. Though the path ahead swung back and forth through farmhouses and farmlands along the shore, a direct route through the fields would give him a much-needed head-start to ascend to Heller's point and stay one step ahead of these islanders.

It was a bumpy ride through the fields and the young King had to cross a wide and fast-flowing river at the bottom, where he lost his bike to its torrent. His clothes dried quickly in the morning sun as he raced up the side of the mountain on foot, jumping over stone walls and fences without breaking his stride and sprinting the lengths between them at full speed.

It was close to midday when he finally reached the summit, decked invitingly with wooden benches and marked by a sign as Heller's point. The young King caught his breath upon its very edge and hydrated his parched system with the last of his water. Having regained the faculties of his former self, he sat down upon the cliff and produced the unfinished map from his backpack. He added the winding roads leading up through the mountain and all that had earlier been hidden from his view. There was, however, much that still lay beyond the reach of his binoculars. As he added what remained of the buildings and houses within his view and speculated on those indistinct clusters beyond, a faint hum of a motor began to rise through the silence, like the buzz of a mosquito drawing near.

An older model of cruiser, something akin to Elena, stripped of all luxury and technology, arrived at Heller's point moments later to find the area deserted. The driver took advantage of the desolation by throwing the rear end of the vehicle around several times, submersing itself in a cloud of roused dust. The young King could hear laughter from within the vehicle as it stopped and a back door flung open. An old and serious figure emerged from it. His stride towards the edge of the cliff was very stiff and, once there, he gave the order that the equipment be set up beside him. He stood looking out over the land below with his hands held behind his back, as his two young accomplices dutifully obeyed his command. They carried from the cruiser the components of a long-range surveillance post and slotted together the constituent parts. Once everything was in place, the old leader took a radio in his hand and lifted it to his mouth and spoke. 'Eagle eye, in position. Nothing yet, but will contact you as soon as we have visual.'

Back and forth their equipment swept many times, but there was no sign of the boy anywhere. The heat and motion sensors that had been positioned at points all over the island revealed no solitary wanderers anywhere. It was as though he had become a ghost. While they chatted amongst themselves, the young King quietly eavesdropped on the threads of their conversation, but heard nothing as to why they were searching for him. It then began to mizzle lightly and the two youngsters soon grew impatient with their repetitive obligation. The conversation between them digressed into mirth and, after one final perusal, the youngest gave up and returned to their vehicle.

The two that remained continued their search back and forth across the landscape below when the remaining youth picked his head up and turned somewhat quizzically towards his elder. 'Did you hear something?'

The youth then got up to search for their colleague and the old man cursed the idle nature of his subordinates as he continued with their operation alone. Footsteps then drew near from behind him and he asked if everything was okay. The silence that ensued turned the air to a crispy chill and slowly the old man took his eye from the telescope and turned to face the young man they were searching for.

'It seems that all this is in my honour,' he said.

The old man seemed to relax a little after his initial shock and allowed himself a more leisurely look upon their prey. 'So, you have stumbled upon our plot. It is of no importance, you will be dead within an hour.'

'You speak with such confidence,' said the young King, genuinely impressed. 'May I impose upon this confidence with some questions?'

The old man nodded that he could.

'Who are you people and what do you want with me?'

'We bought you, fair and square, like the others. We are the People's army and we buy prisoners to use in training.'

'The People's army? Who do you serve?'

'We serve the people of the Free world. That is all you will get from me, you worthless piece of dirt!'

'Beware your words!' warned the King sharply. 'I am no worthless piece of dirt! But tell me, who is your enemy?'

The old man sniggered and looked away, his former reticence toughening into a stubborn refusal to speak. A condition easily cured. The young King grabbed his wrist and snapped it with a sharp pirouette. There was a scream that reached an inaudible crescendo and the old man dropped to the ground and nursed his shattered wrist with delicate fingers.

'The Company!' he repeated. 'The Company!'

This *Company*, the young King had heard of. The Priest had spoke of them before, neither as friend nor foe but as the keepers of the Free world. They were a greedy and oppressive government and their role was vital in maintaining and controlling its people until the day he set forth on his mission. An uprising of any kind, therefore, would surely jeopardise everything that came after. It was then that it all became clear. 'This army you speak of is no match for the Company,' said the King. 'They surely outnumber your force many times and possess technology superior to anything I have seen here today. Unless, of course, you possessed an electromagnetic device of some kind with the capability of taking down their defence system, thereby bringing them down to your level for a dogfight. And I presume that was what I saw in the back of the armoured truck you sent searching for me this morning.'

'You will never leave here alive,' said the old man, his voice dripping with venom.

It was without tribute or ceremony that the old man was dispatched and his body joined those of his young colleagues in the trunk of their cruiser. The young King then picked up their radio, and in a cold and hoarse voice, similar to that of the old man, announced. 'Eagle-eye unit, nothing yet.'

There was a moment of static before a voice shouted back that he must be there somewhere and the transmission went dead.

With the surveillance equipment of the Eagle-eye team, the young King now finished his map in detail, including everything that had before lay beyond his range of vision and all information pertinent to his attack. The primary target was a building in the village that stood out from those around it. He suspected it to be a communal village hall of some kind and was the hub of all this excitement, pumping constant streams of guards in and out through its front doors.

The secondary target was a compound and charging station that he found huddling beneath a camouflaged sheet amongst a cluster of farmhouses, packed tightly with military vehicles above an underground storage of charged ions. If he was to cripple this army, he would also have to take out this site.

But it was the unstructured patrol of the roving units below that the King feared most. He watched them come this way and that with no pattern in their search and their number was increasing steadily as more and more of the rebellious islanders were drafted in the hunt. After some time spent watching them, the young King lifted the radio and spoke in the same voice as before. 'This is Eagle eye, we have just seen the boy by the old mill and he has gone into the trees to the north. From watching his movements, we suspect that he has somehow acquired one of our radios and is evading our patrols by listening to our broadcasts.'

'What! Someone let this son of a bitch steal one of our radios!' There was a crackling of static. 'All periphery teams to Mc Merson's lane by the old mill. He's in the forest. Converge from all angles and watch where you are firing. Get the dogs over there as well… and maintain radio silence for thirty minutes. Go!'

The young King pressed the button on his radio. 'Make that an hour. We think he may also be armed.'

The roving patrols were redirected and many of the stationary checkpoints packed up and vanished; everyone now hungry to claim the scalp of this scallywag. This army had underestimated their young purchase greatly and this had proved to be an invaluable advantage for the King. Only a few patrols remained between Heller's point and the recharging compound, and the enthusiasm in their duties suffered greatly as they waited expectantly for the crackle of gunfire to rip through the air as their comrades entered the final phase of the hunt.

A cruiser descended the mountain with the face of its driver hidden beneath the peak of a cap and then entered onto the narrow network of paths that zigzagged back and forth between the farmhouses along the spine of the island. There were many dead-ends and twists and turns that would have exposed someone unfamiliar to them, but the young King drove with such confidence that those he passed along the way suspected nothing. By the time the compound came into view, he saw a truck leave with the last of the heavily armed personnel onboard to join the widening search around the mill and surrounding forest.

Having abandoned the cruiser and now approaching on foot, the young King stalked the compound's perimeter in search of a weakness in the four metre high fence that surrounded it. Mechanics and technicians wandered from one vehicle to the next and only a handful of guards had remained by the front gate. A control room was situated at the very back of the protected compound and the young King stole from shadow to shadow towards it.

As he entered the control room, his silence was betrayed by the creaking hinges of the door. The guard inside turned immediately and made for his holster upon sight of the youngster. But the King burst forth like a flash and broke his neck with an audacious kick; the lifeless body of the guard slumping to the floor without uttering a sound.

The young King observed the control panel and familiarised himself with its features. Down in the secret cave in the heart of mount Hexlon, the recharging of their vehicles worked on a similar system, and his lessons had taught him all there was to know about them. After overriding its security features, he began reversing the flow of charge from each of the vehicles back underground; a procedure that turned the volatile storage beneath into a ticking time-bomb. A series of warning lights began to blink. So well had the young King been schooled in this procedure that he was able to calibrate the flow and calculate the moment of instability to within a few minutes. There began a slight rumbling beneath the ground as he undressed the guard and walked out of the control room in his uniform.

The plan, at that point, was to take one of the heavier trucks from the compound and deliver it through the front doors of the primary target, and from there he would rely on his training to do the rest. But upon entering into the field of vehicles, he found there before him the armoured waste disposal truck that had pursued him earlier that morning. The young King quickly pulled it from its port before the last of its power had been drained and checked to make sure that the electromagnetic device had not been removed since. He exited the compound with a friendly wave to the guards at the gate and took off up the road towards the village.

The top floor of the village hall was the command post for the People's army, and there they watched the clock tick by nervously. Thirty-seven minutes had passed since their surveillance team had spotted the target and they had been waiting in silence since. No one dared give voice to them, but there were worries in the air that they had been duped and this boy an agent of the enemy. They had tried to find out what they could about him and found only that he did not exist. Suddenly, the lights went out and their equipment whirred to a halt, and the dull red glow of the emergency lighting rose from the darkness.

'Everything is down, sir,' shouted a guard. 'We have basic functions only.'

'This boy must be near.' The controller then lifted his radio and spoke. 'Outer periphery teams check in.'

The young King pressed the button on his radio and held it close to his mouth. 'You were burned in your deal. I will be making my way to the main building, where I have watched your men come and go all day. Once inside, I am going to take you out.' And with that, he dropped the radio to the ground, just as a siren began to wail. There were loud clunking noises as the building went into lockdown around him and the echo of marching feet resounded from every floor. He had already been in the village hall for several minutes and had used this time to study its layout. A soft female voice began to repeat through the speaker system that all guards were to go to the armoury, adding periodically that all non-military personnel should assemble in the main hall, and that this was not a drill.

Three guards ran past the young King and he started off behind them. They turned corner after corner with more guards joining their group as they all made their way towards the armoury. There, a woman was handing out rifles and other pieces of equipment to the lengthening queue of soldiers. The young King received a backpack and a rifle and followed the rushing crowd on their way to the briefing room. He dropped on one knee before entering and fiddled with his shoelaces, watching carefully for the last of the soldiers to pass by. Once all had been bundled in, the young King took the butt of his rifle to the door's keypad, locking the room down automatically.

He then turned and walked back along the corridor with a sense of calmness about him. Two uniformed guards stood with their backs to him, feeding the oncoming crowd of civilians and high ranking officials into the main assembly hall. To his right was a door marked *STAGE* and, once through it, the young King followed a narrow corridor of dark steps up to an area overlooking the bewildered crowd below.

He pulled on a pair of night-vision goggles and, with the flick of some switches, submersed the large secured hall below in darkness. Confusion turned to panic in an instant and many scrambled for the windows and doors, all now locked up with metal shutters. Two gunshots rang out, followed by many more and screams ripped through the darkness. Twice the barrage lulled as the King reloaded and continued his reign of terror. The room then fell silent and light was restored. The bloodied corpses of their leaders lay lifeless and slumped in their seats. There was not an armed guard left amongst them and a chorus of horror resounded. A strange voice then spoke and silenced its terrified audience.

'Now hear this!' began the young King from his elevated position. 'You brought this war upon yourselves and your army has been defeated. I am the King of Hexlon, and today I claim this land under my growing Kingdom. Remember the price you have paid here always. I promise wealth to you all from this day forth. Reject me and feel the full wrath of the Hexlonian army and be erased from the pages of history. Now, kneel before me and accept me as your King.'

Slowly, the crowd obeyed and fear rippled through them as their new monarch jumped down from the stage. Everyone was now whimpering on their hands and knees, too afraid to look up as he made his way through them. A sudden and deafening boom shook the ground as the recharging compound went up and every window in the village shattered. Cries of grief, fright and anguish broke from the crowd and the King glanced back upon his cowering subjects before making his way towards the exit.

The explosion was heard by the Priest and his guards and they watched as a great plume of smoke mushroomed above the island. There was a few minutes of silence followed by sporadic eruptions of gunfire, which was followed some time later by a loud crashing noise on the bridge ahead. The large truck positioned there had just been forced into the water, and a smaller, heavily armoured truck, badly damaged from the impact, hurried on towards them. The Palace guards took defensive positions and the Priest walked some steps ahead of them and told the men to lower their weapons. The armoured truck slammed to a halt just before them and the young King got out and placed the barrel of his rifle under the chin of the Priest.

'I have kept my last bullet for you! You send me into such a place with no word of warning? I should take your life in recompense!'

A smile broke across the Priest's face. 'You left here this morning calling me sir and now hold me to ransom with this gun.' He pushed away the rifle and looked at the boy earnestly. 'I am filled with joy to see that you have returned. You are truly the one, and some day soon you will set forth on a mission that will change the course of humanity forever.' His voice then adopted a lighter tone. 'Now come, my boy, you must be starving. I will treat you to a hamburger.'

The people of Linch awoke that next morning to find the King's personal guards patrolling their streets and the sound of huge trucks arriving with all manner of weaponry. Within a month, their island had been transformed into a highly fortified stronghold and they grew rich from the crop they were instructed to grow there. A Temple was built and enlightenment flowed. They had just become the first secret colony of Hexlon.

– VII –

Fortress City

The King crossed the bridge from Linch island early the following morning and his cruiser reappeared on the digital-layout once through the Black forest and returned to civilised territory. Along the empty stretch of highway rolled the headlights of a single van marked Cobra, and the bleary eyes of its driver turned instinctively towards the light emerging from the fabled woods ahead. The van should have passed long before Elena reached the junction of the highway, but had slowed to coincide with her arrival. They passed with a slow meeting of the eyes and the van then took off with a burst of acceleration on its way towards Fortress city. It was an omen that the King did not wish to pursue.

Upon searching for an alternative route on the digital-layout, the direct path of the highway became a jagged course of country lanes that rose high into the mountains, adding two hours to a journey that had barely been one. The King set off up the highway for the short distance it took for the detour to begin and was soon rising high along winding lanes into a forgotten world above.

No official jurisdiction had claim to these highlands, and those who lived there protected what they owned themselves. Though there was never any effort to civilise these mountainfolk, the Company's media portrayed them as despicable thieves and the ills of their society were blamed upon them and their kin in similar regions elsewhere. When the theft rate began to rise inexplicably one year, the people of the registered territories cried out for protection against these unregistered villains. The Company responded by decreeing that all merchandise of value be tagged, enabling them to track that which had been stolen. Then one day, a story broke of three children who had gone missing while playing in the family garden and terrified parents everywhere cried out that their children be tagged also. Within a year of this outcry, tagging had become mandatory, and every newborn since had received the small microchip in the palm of his or her right hand as part of their registration. The whereabouts of every individual could now be monitored constantly rather than following the dots of each of their transactions. A new crime of ingratitude was introduced more quietly later that same year to control the vocal minority who spoke out against such policies, and the punishment was always de-citizenship and expulsion. But even those cast out from Fortress city, who spoke of liberty and justice for all, did not dare to take up residence amongst these vilified mountainfolk, so damning was the Company's portrayal of them.

Barking dogs on long chains rushed to the fences on either side of the King as he passed through the first of these villages. Every house had a large wooden shed that lay packed to the rafters with bails of hay and old farming equipment, while decaying wrecks lay scattered here and there in the surrounding fields like the unburied dead of a battle long ago. A few residents had already risen and warily eyed the passage of this stranger through their community. The King looked around at their desolate world and wondered how these people passed their time when not working and to where their thoughts escaped. He continued along the mountainous track, through many more little clusters of houses and large sheds; each village much the same as the one before with the exception that more of those who lived there had now risen and were setting about their daily chores.

The promise from the slumbering sun was becoming evident as all was now touched with the faintest glow. It would be rising just ahead, thought the King, and he consulted the digital-layout for a suitable place to enjoy the daily spectacle while he ate some breakfast. A small public area appeared on the far side of the mountain, just before the steep descent into the city, and he pushed his foot upon the cruiser's accelerator for fear that the show may have started before he reached it.

Trees appeared up ahead at the site the digital-layout had led him to and hugged around the small and secluded park. It was no surprise to find it empty at this hour and the King got out and walked towards the railing that stretched from one end to the other and took in the sight before him with a contented smile.

Fortress city: the Company's factory of consumerism and home to two million citizens. It was perfectly pentagonal in shape, with five carriageways running from its tips to the Academy at its very heart, dividing the city into five equal boroughs. The Academy itself was set within a pentagonal wall and beyond each of its faces was a garden of individual beauty, each separated by one of five wooded areas. As the King swept his eye across the dormant city, the deep red of the horizon softened and darkness cowered in the city's dying shadows.

He ate a breakfast of flavoured oats and juice while he watched the sun rise and bring morning to the city, listening to its sounds slowly rise from the slumberous silence. Once he had finished his meal, the King took a walk along the trees to stretch his legs and there he noticed a spider web glistening amongst some branches. He reached out a hand and strummed one of its lines and watched as the pearls of dew rearranged themselves upon its intricate design. The little spider retreated to the corner of his web as it shook with the violence of an earthquake. Its work was undone in an instant, as the line the King played with snapped and the web fluttered free amidst this storm. Only when the fury had subsided and the darkened sky gave way again to sunlight did the humble creature venture forth on his masterful repair.

The path down the mountainside was a track of hairpins and straights that no driver in search of excitement could resist. Perilous drops cradled every corner and the uneven surface of the road would have cast a lesser driver to his death at such speeds. Elena slid around its last corner with precise geometry and the King slowed her down upon reaching the flat of its base. He was now in the suburbs of Fortress city and cameras and sensors were popping up everywhere on the digital-layout, none more so than in the heavily fortified village that lay ahead.

The leafy and civilised suburban village of Foxborough was one of several sprawling landscapes of wealth and decadence that had grown through the years to become the Heaven of the Company's world. Only those who had lived in accordance with their rules and played their game correctly could afford the exorbitant fees of these houses. They consisted mainly of the

Company's elite and those who had amassed fortunes through the various industries that kept their wheel of consumerism turning. Though the King longed to see the wondrous palaces contained within this village, it was an unnecessary risk. There was a large security base nearby owned by the Techtorian guards, whose duty it was to patrol the streets of Fortress city and guard the elite in its suburbs. A stranger such as himself would most likely attract attention in such an exclusive area and his schedule could not suffer any form of detainment. That meant he could only admire from a distance as he passed by and continued on towards the city.

One by one, the narrow country lanes began to converge on one another and developed into a thickening highway, which would eventually rise and become one of the carriageways through the city. A message appeared on Elena's on-board display and the King opened it to find that the Techtorian guards had just registered his arrival and that he was cleared with access to the Academy. He then fell amidst the camouflage of daily commuters along the extensive carriageway as the city unveiled itself.

On either side of him lay what the citizens of Fortress city referred to as the Outside; a vast forest beyond their outer wall, where those without jobs were forced to live. Employment in Fortress city had been maintained steadily at ninety percent of its citizens for some years now, meaning that there was ten percent that could not afford to live within the city's residential zone. This ten percent jumped to fifteen two years ago because of the recession, and they were now preparing to move that up to twenty. Mounds of food and tankers of pure alcohol were delivered to various locations out there each day, and these they used more than anything as currency in their own primitive system. But with more people being forced out there due to the rising rate of unemployment, the citizens were pressurising the Company to act. A solution was proposed in that several of their factories were to be relocated to this area, allowing the growing numbers there to earn a subsistent level of credit. The fact that this proposal was met with little or no resistance should demonstrate the power of the Company's propaganda, and how far the will of their citizens had been subdued.

Shabby houses built from wood occupied the branches of old and sturdy trees with lines of drying clothes hung back and forth between them. Children ran free with wild delight as their parents cowered in the shadows with crushed and inebriated spirits. There were patches of open garden, where the King could view the feral population more clearly and saw a gathering of them before a religious leader and a large mob dispense justice on two young boys.

Up ahead, the King could see the rising wall that separated the Outside from the residential zone beyond. The carriageway passed overhead and, once beyond this wall, the forested and uncivilised landscape was replaced by rows of stringently regimented streets that stretched out like the waves of a vast ocean on either side. Each house was identical in every dimension to that next to it, and only a little smaller than those in the row just ahead of it. An occasional taller building, a depository or factory, would rise above them and blend into the surface of its surroundings. Vehicles weaved through the lanes of the carriageway, as some joined from the slip roads and others peeled off, distributing themselves about the city.

Huge billboards stood at intervals along the route, advertising more expensive products as they went along. After some time on the long and monotonous route, the King could just about make out the other carriageways to his left and right, narrowing in upon the Company's private sector and connect with the bridges over the moat that had once protected this highly secured area. His on-board computer registered some scanning as he crossed the bridge into this new-age metropolis.

Buildings now rose around him at their own discretion and the footpaths on either side were packed with citizens dressed in fine attire. The workers of this world lived in the residential sector outside while here the elite maintained their establishment. Decision-makers gathered in the offices of high buildings, and there, the future course of the city was deliberated. These people had long been corrupted by power and this had blinded them to the glorious concept of evolutionary progress for all. Many technological advances that would have paved the way for a more efficient society had been suppressed during their tenure due to the implications it would have had on public spending. For example, the technology for a simple and economical sonar detection system had already been developed and its implementation would have eradicated all vehicle collisions on the city's carriageways and streets. However, this would have meant the loss of revenue generated from the lucrative insurance industry, as well as hospital fees and repair bills, and so, it was suppressed and ultimately forgotten. To move on in any way was to threaten their deeply imbedded institution, and not even the lives of those people they would save each year could persuade them to overcome their greed. In any form of monetary system, life will eventually have its price, and like the worth of their credit, this too, will devalue with time.

The Company logo was everywhere, as though fearful the people may forget who it was in charge of their city. Up ahead were those towers that the King had seen surround the gardens of the Academy. It was now eight o clock and students were pouring from them and they flooded the streets of this exclusive hub. Only the wealthiest could afford to educate their children there, with those rare geniuses who arise now and then offered scholarships. Their number poured over the footpaths on either side and spilled onto the road and their swarm proved too dense for Elena to pass through. The King slowly directed her into a residential car park and he got out and said farewell to her, just in case. He slung his backpack over his shoulder and joined the marching throng of students.

The five blissful gardens that surrounded the Academy were in stark contrast to those outside the city. It was only by special invitation that one from beyond could come and enjoy such a privilege. In the centre of this particular garden was a small lake and the garden itself was hedged by woods on either side from which people emerged and disappeared into on their morning strolls. Some lounged around the lake while others jogged its perimeter or fed the tamed animals. At the far end of the garden ran one face of the pentagonal wall, approximately twelve metres in height, at the centre of which, was one of the Academy's five entrances. A large crowd gathered around it and the King walked along the forest's edge to observe its procedure.

There was a gentle hum in the air from the Academy's transmitters, which sounded something like the subliminal symphony of an orchestra to those with ears attuned to it.

An elderly man walked by and stuffed a newspaper into a bin before strolling off into the woods. The King watched him disappear from the corner of his eye before retrieving the crumpled copy of *Academy Weekly*. As he flattened it out with a few rubs of his forearm, he saw that news of Hexlon had made the front page and, upon venturing further, almost every other page thereon. It seemed that the rebellious students of the Academy were putting pressure on the upper members of the Company to take action against Hexlon by showing support for the breakaway group that had already exposed the vacated Palace. Hexlon could no longer be trusted, they said. Should outside forces take it, Fortress city would fall. A demonstration had been organised outside its walls in the wastelands tonight and every night that followed until the Company were installed in its turrets. The King returned the newspaper to the bin and looked around the garden. This was the very debate heating conversations all across the Free world right now.

However, the final year students of the Academy had more pressing issues at hand on this particular morning. They could be identified easily amongst the crowd, tapping at their keyboards and comparing screens with those beside them. Today was the deadline to submit the piece of code they had chosen as their personal project and, upon which, their future careers would depend. The complex and seemingly infinite code that protected the Company's system was segmented into different fields of education and students were trained in everything from repairing downed feeds and administrative work to the more critical applications of enforcement and protection.

The King's eyes turned again upon the crowd gathered around the Academy's entrance and watched as they filtered through. The guards were from Techtor, most likely highly ranked, though their black uniforms gave no distinction. As each student passed, a scan was taken of a small metal tag that each wore upon their lapel and their identification verified thereafter with a retinal scan. Those few visitors who wished to pass through without one of these tags endured a more rigorous search. They were taken to one side and their equipment and belongings tested to ensure against attack or theft. The King's mighty heart fell at this imposition. The Shadow-disk would undoubtedly be detected upon inspection of his computer and, even if he could procure one of those metal tags, using it there to reconfigure his account would surely set off the sensitive equipment that protected this area.

He looked at the face of the surrounding wall and sized it up. Many of the branches offered by the trees next to it could easily be scaled and then one final bound would take him over it. But with this he risked being seen and he did not know what lay at the other side. Then an idea struck him. What he needed was a student with a metal tag to carry the Shadow-disk to the Professor for him, leaving him free to walk in through the gate empty-handed.

The King's hawk-like eyes scanned the garden for a likely candidate. Under a nearby tree sat a young girl all alone, working at her computer with an air of dissatisfaction. Every now and then she would look at her watch and this seemed to deepen her frustration. She was pretty, in a way, with thick-rimmed glasses and wisps of curly dark hair that fell loosely about her shoulders. She did not look up however as the King approached and dropped to his knees before her.

'Yes?' she asked frostily, as his presence persisted, the incessant tapping of her keyboard undisrupted.

'I can help you,' said the stranger.

The tapping stopped and she beheld him with a mix of uncertainty and annoyance. 'I don't have time for this. My codes have waited until now to start falling apart. I'm sorry, but no…' Her concentration was again called upon by the discovery of yet more flaws in her work and she shook her head woefully.

'I can help you, if you let me see.'

She drew a long sigh and studied this stranger with a little more attention than she had done before. 'Do I know you?'

The King shook his head. 'But I can help you with your system nonetheless.'

There was something about this stranger, something about his eyes that captivated her and she found herself staring without a word. She shook herself free from this daze and her cheeks reddened slightly. 'You're not a student,' she said, dipping her eyes coyly. 'Do you work for the Company?'

The King nodded.

'And you know about security codes?'

Again the King nodded. Taking her new-found sociability and blossoming attraction as an invitation to venture further in his pursuit, the King sat down beside her and took her computer on his lap. As he began to type, the young girl slipped off her glasses and pushed a few straying strands of hair behind her ear. She straightened herself up and stole a glance at this dashing young man before joining his eyes on the screen before them. Having already slipped the Shadow-disk into her computer, its files were now downloading and replacing the girl's paltry system, and the King watched as the percentage of this procedure slowly rose to completion.

'You will be careful, won't you?' she said. 'I know it's not perfect, but I have spent a lot of time on it.'

When it had fully downloaded, the King checked through its main alleyways and corridors to ensure all was present in their new location and handed the computer back to the young girl. She accepted it with a bashful smile and began her assessment of his upgrade. There was a moment of incomprehension in which she just stared blankly at that before her, after which her eyes began to sweep back and forth in receipt of the endless rows of data. As they did, her mouth opened gradually and her eyes began to blink more rapidly. She struggled to make sense of it all and contented herself with some simple calculations. The fundamentals, along with those bits and pieces within her grasp, all seemed to be withstanding and in place. Never before had she seen such complexity. The intensity of her perusal eventually gave way to gratitude and she turned towards her mysterious benefactor to thank him. But he was no longer beside her. She rose to her feet and searched the surrounding crowd, but could see him nowhere. As she sat back down again upon the grass, the young woman lifted her computer to check that she had not just fallen asleep and the whole encounter just some wishful dream.

The King walked into the adjoining forest in search of a place of seclusion and followed its winding path until he entered into the shallow depths of the neighbouring garden. With one final glance around him, the King pulled his own computer from his backpack and broke it in two like a cookie, depositing each half in separate bins along with the now-shattered Shadow-disk. Once purged of all incriminating evidence, he walked out into the splendour of this new garden and admired its beauty as he made his way towards the entrance.

The procedure there was the same as before; each passing student was allowed through with a swipe of their security pass and verification upon a retinal scanner. The King waited in the jumbled queue until he was taken aside and the few remaining contents of his backpack emptied onto a metal tray. After a retinal scan, the guard told him that he was early and that there had been some problems this morning with a double-booking. He then turned towards the King and stepped from the path before him and waved for him to go on. Getting in had been easy; a simple amendment on the security list... the Professor's private schedule, however, had remained unaltered. He would have to make contact with the Professor himself.

The surrounding pentagonal wall was two metres thick and the tunnel through this particular entrance decorated with the random graffiti of those who passed through it every day. Beyond this tunnel was a large triangular ledge, one of the surrounding five, that jutted some way over the chasm below that separated each point of entry from the raised island on which the Academy sat. Five monorail tracks converged upon the island from the tip of each of these triangular ledges, and their carriages shuttled back and forth all day long, twenty metres above the floor of this chasm.

Once a carriage docked, and those inside herded off along another route, the awaiting crowd shuffled forward with tiny steps towards the tip of the triangular ledge. It was not until the current of the crowd had drawn him into its very depths that the King was struck by a sudden sense of drowning and he grappled desperately at those around him as he tried to free himself from their swift engulfment. The throes of his panic were quickly relieved as the carriage arrived at the tip of the ledge and those waiting there poured into it. Cold morning air fell about him once more as the sweep of the tide brought him to the very brink of the platform, where he stopped with a measure of horror in his eyes. Those inside the carriage had been squeezed in one by one, like bullets into the chamber of a gun, and now stood pressed tightly against one another.

'One more,' shouted a guard with a great booming voice.

Those in the crowd seemed to step back from around the King and a shudder ran the length of his spine once alone upon that tip. Solitude was bearable in the peaks of Mount Hexlon, but in the midst of this crowd it carried a troublesome weight. With all eyes upon the clandestine King, he eventually stepped forward and pushed into the soft mass of bodies within. The doors closed behind him and the carriage took off with the helpless King held tightly inside.

Someone sneezed and another coughed, breaking the silence of the carriage and consenting the slow mumbles of conversation to rise. There was a dull stench of body odour in the trapped air that fused with the mix of synthetic fragrances and the King felt nauseated by it. As the black pit of panic opened beneath him once more, he pulled helplessly at the carriage's doors. He could hear the whispered thoughts of his fellow commuters grow louder as his impending attack began to lack discretion. The sense of drowning returned to the King more forcefully than before.

A sudden gust of fresh air filled the carriage and a collective gasp arose. The doors now hung crooked with a large gap between them and the mechanics on which they operated lay sparking. The King looked like a wild animal as he stood at this opening, and the palpable silence erupted into screams of horror as he then leapt from the carriage. The pitch of their squeals and shouts reached the guards at the other end, who listened closely as the lop-sided carriage approached.

'Someone fell out!' was their chorus.

A stream of guards ran down a metal staircase to the base of the chasm as the elusive King crawled up its underside and emerged amidst the camouflage of the resulting chaos. A solid barrier of guards was forming along the edge of the chasm, as the crowd they held back struggled to get a view of this excitement. The King bowed his head and hurried on lest someone from the arriving carriage should recognise him and all this attention turn upon him.

The Academy itself was a prestigious building that merged the traditional and the modern schools of architecture that were popular at that time. There were fifty lecture theatres contained within its walls along with two hundred small classrooms and offices. The King had learned from the Academy's official site that the Professor taught his final year students in lecture theatre one and that he had a class with them first thing this morning. He hoped that he would find the room without further trouble.

Students and teachers alike poured down the grand steps leading up to the Academy, as the news from outside made its way through the corridors and classrooms of the sprawling building. The King took the steps two at a time until he reached its huge doors and found himself at the head of a long and decadent hallway. The floor was decked with precious marble and its two walls panelled in rare oak. Masterful paintings and various artefacts lined each side between the doors that led off to the other parts of the Academy. He pushed through a serenade of students, forcing flyers of all kinds into his hands and proclaiming the news according to them. A sign hanging from the ornate roofing pointed towards a set of double doors to his right and was marked *Lecture theatres: 1 - 10*. The corridor beyond was much quieter, with only the last of the stragglers running to see the commotion for themselves, and the King quickly located the room.

It was with some relief that he found its door unlocked and the silence it held put his settling nerves at ease. Widening rows of seats rose from the front in a semicircle around the teaching area, with a total capacity for two hundred students. The King took the first row upon entering and followed it along to the very end, where he could overlook the entire room. Shortly after he had taken his seat, the first of the students began to trickle in and arranged themselves as near to the front as they could manage. By the time the doors were locked and the lesson about to begin, the rising tide of students reached three quarters of the way up, with the King all alone in its uppermost corner.

The teaching area was enclosed within some sort of reinforced glass that separated those behind it from the class before them. There was a small door at the side of this area, which the King could only presume was locked and would open only at the touch of a button somewhere within the protected area. Another door, lying open, lay at the back of the cosseted zone with several technicians entering and exiting from a passageway behind as they arranged for the presentation of the class. Above this open door was a huge blackboard that stretched from one end of the wall to the other and had drawn upon it the endless threads of code that formed the very basis of the overall security system. There was no sign of the Professor as of yet.

The crowd settled down, plugging their computers into their stations and checking over their systems one final time before they were uploaded and graded. Those scoring in the top marking bracket; having highlighted and improved a piece of this code, would have their work inaugurated into the overall system, thus reinforcing it with another generation of protection. They would, of course, be paid for their contribution with a profitable future guaranteed for them somewhere in the upper echelons of the Company's world.

The clock ticked past nine as the level of noise began to rise and a few paper aeroplanes took to the sky. At four minutes past, the last of the technicians exited the area and the King's eyes narrowed upon the figure that entered. He was a small and insignificant-looking man with a protruding belly that had come with middle age. His head was perfectly spherical and was crowned with an orange tuft of hair. The features of his face added nothing to his unremarkable demeanour and it was only his stiff sense of dress that had distinguished him from the others. The King put his age at forty-two.

A cup of tea was brought to him and he sipped at it unhurriedly as he leafed through the pages stacked in front of him. The private conversations of the classroom began to stir and he looked out reprovingly over the rim of his glasses. He tapped a small microphone attached to the collar of his shirt and the large speakers along each side of the room boomed its magnified equivalent. 'Quiet, please,' he said.

There was a shaky confidence to his voice, thought the King. He had most likely come from a humble background and had been educated amongst the children of wealthy and powerful parents. His rise to the top would not have been easy; his confidence both fortified and damaged by the experience. The Professor continued to consult the notes before him in silence before leaving them down and clearing his throat. His eyes swept along the sea of faces at the other side of the divide and snagged momentarily on a lonely figure in the very corner of the room.

'Our civilisation,' he began, 'depends upon these codes, and, in learning their various strands, you have been elevated above the common man by knowledge. Once you have uploaded your coursework at the end of this class, it will be your duty to take with you what you have learned and use it in the virtue and maintenance of our system. Many of you will take positions within the Company. A few will continue their research here and take various jobs in and around the Academy, while others will find themselves relegated into the lower reaches of our society in search of employment. No matter where you find yourselves or whatever position you take, you must always remember that you are forevermore disciples of the code, and bound by oath never to use what you have learned for personal gain. You students are the soldiers of our world.'

The crowd seemed uninterested; they had heard this rap before.

The Professor then stepped upon a small, electronically-controlled podium and his tone lightened substantially in his further address as he rose alongside the face of the blackboard. 'Though I am still waiting for someone to crack my code, I hope you all have challenged it with everything that you have. Perfection is an evolutionary state and complacency its downfall. The code will always need those who protect and nourish it with constant revision.' He then turned towards the board to begin his lesson.

The minutes ticked by as the monotonous voice of the Professor prattled on, repeating numbers and letters in an endless cycle while the lecture theatre was alive with the taps of fingers on keyboards. As the end drew near, the tapping began to wane and the Professor's voice became less strident. The electronic podium descended to its starting position and, once there, the Professor stepped off and clapped his hands together as though about to receive a promised gift. 'It is time,' he announced. 'Please upload your coursework to the front and I wish you all the very best in your prospective careers.'

There was one final flurry of keyboard tapping as their coursework was uploaded and most began packing up their belongings while others indulged in conversation. The Professor watched the usual stream of data roll down the screen of his computer when something peculiar caught his attention. A frown crumpled the features of his face together and he fumbled on the desk beside him for the small microphone he had just taken off. 'Row B, seat seventeen,' he stammered, before repeating it again more clearly. 'Please come here for a moment.'

The Professor pulled a chair under him while he waited and returned to his computer for a more assiduous inspection. The volume of data this particular piece contained was immense and its components seemed immaculate. There were parts of it that even he would require some help in understanding. He looked up and saw a young girl emerge from the thinning crowd with a huge smile beaming across her face. Still delving the depths of this new system, he unlocked the door between them and returned to his computer. 'It's amazing,' he said, turning to face what he expected to be one of his female students.

'Consider it a gift,' said the King, turning to the girl and asking quietly that he be allowed a few minutes with the Professor.

The Professor rose from his chair and backed away slightly. 'Who are you?'

'What you have in your possession should interest your superiors,' said the King, as he walked some steps into the protected booth. 'All I ask in return is that you listen to what I have to say before presenting it to them.'

The Professor sighed at this helpless decision. While it undoubtedly seemed an advantageous exchange at this point, he suspected there would be much more to what he had to say than what was implied in the innocent plea for his ear. He looked this stranger up and down with a scrutinizing eye. This young man was no ordinary person and this tale he brought would be of equal rarity. Whatever he wanted, he could at least give him some time to explain himself in compensation for the trouble he had gone through in coming here. 'My private chambers are through here,' he said pertly, and held the door open for the King to enter through.

The passageway beyond was carpeted in crimson and the walls painted a dull yellow. There were portraits of high ranking officials and a series of display cabinets, holding various treasures and keepsakes, though its overall impression did not reach the decadent heights other sections of the Academy were keen to boast. The Professor walked several paces ahead and turned his head twice towards the stranger with a quizzical frown upon his face and hurried on towards his room.

Columns of paper and files lay stacked on the floor and anywhere else there was room for them. Books lay scattered with equal abandon, though there was not a dish or crumpled shirt to be found anywhere amongst the academic muddle. Little coloured memorandums were stuck everywhere and on them were everything from the names of students he needed to see or inspired ideas that he hoped would revolutionise whatever it was he was working on.

'You've been expecting me?' asked the King, as he sat down at the desk.

There was no response, but he heard the clink of a bottle behind him, followed by the pouring of a large measure of whiskey. The Professor's hands were shaking when he appeared before him and he sat down on his chair at the far side of the desk. 'There *was* someone here,' he began somewhat hesitantly. 'May I ask who you are?'

'I am the King of Hexlon; son of the city's creator and saviour…'

That was enough for the Professor, who raised a hand that he need go no further. 'Then it's true,' he said finally. 'A few weeks ago… a man I had never seen before knocked at the door to my chamber and sat down where you are sitting now. When I asked him who he was or how he had passed through my security, he simply dismissed my questions and told me that I would be contacted by a King sometime in the future and that I was to go with him on a mission of the utmost importance. While it did seem strange at the time, I reasoned afterwards that some students had found a glitch in the system and hoped this colourful ploy would gain them some attention. Such things have been known to happen. As time passed, I became a little suspicious when I heard nothing more of it, but I expected that they would come to me when they were ready. Then, when the Paegonaeans' defence grid went down... I feared that perhaps it was all connected.' He leaned forward on his chair and placed his forearms along the desk between them. 'What is it we must do?'

'I know little myself at this point,' replied the King. 'There is another person who we must find and the three of us are to travel to the Paegonaeans' wall. I have been given coordinates where we shall be granted access to the world beyond. Our mission awaits us there.'

These words weighed heavily upon the Professor and he struggled to cope with the sudden derailment of the comfortable world in which he lived. 'It is not possible,' he said. 'I have classes after lunch and several appointments after that...'

The King leaned close to the Professor. 'Listen to me carefully and do not doubt a word that I say. We have been chosen by powers beyond our own volition and I suggest that you take a few minutes to realign your objectives. All that matters now is that we leave this place unhindered, find the last member of our team and reach the coordinates I have in my possession before the defence grid goes back on-line. Are you with me?'

The Professor swivelled around in his chair to look out the window at a solitary tree that sat amidst a small enclosed garden outside. His first reaction was to have security come and arrest this man and take what he had given him to his superiors. If it was what he assumed, it would guarantee the Company and their system another fifteen years of security at least. They would pay whatever it took for such an asset and this would elevate him into the guarded cloister of the elite. He would then be matched with the daughter of some rich old man and their descendants would live like royalty in the luxury and comfort of this world. But none of that was real anymore; this young man had shown truth to lie elsewhere, within a larger scheme of things. Should he stay in the luxury and comfort of his invented world or step out into the void?

The matter settled itself in his mind like clouds being swept from a clear blue sky and he nodded yes towards the King, he was with him.

The Professor downloaded the Shadow-disk onto his personal computer, gathered together some clothes and necessities and said goodbye to his old life with a heavy heart. Photographs that had once brought him happiness now brought only grief. Awards that once held such pride for him now seemed empty and foolish. When he finished packing and took one final glance around him, the Professor found the King looking rather uneasy and asked him if everything was okay.

The King's face strained towards him, tinged slightly with shades of grey and he spoke in a slightly altered voice. 'Is there any way out of here that does not involve crowds?'

They entered into the secured corridor and hurried along it to a set of stairs that reached deep into the bowels of the Academy. It was on this downward journey that the true depth of the Company's protection system was unveiled. Endless floors of research facilities and laboratories whizzed by as they hurriedly descended the steps. Those they met along the way greeted the Professor with surprised cordiality and then stopped and turned after the rushing duo with an inquisitive stare.

The King reached the bottom of the staircase long before the Professor and entered onto a dark pentagonal garage. He looked around while he waited for his new accomplice and saw a tunnel leading through each of its walls and there were cars parked randomly throughout. 'Where to now?' he asked, as the Professor finally arrived behind him.

He turned when there was no response to find the Professor buckled in two with his hands on his knees and he begged for a moment to regain his composure. Slowly, the colour returned to his cheeks and the wheezing howls of his breathing grew less desperate. 'Where is it you want to go?' he asked, at the first chance he could.

'My vehicle is parked beside some towers marked H.'

The Professor shook his head. 'No... We can take one of these vehicles. The five tunnels leading from here exit upon its corresponding carriageway. Where is it you want to get to beyond the city?'

There was a moment of silence as the King thought of Elena and then looked around for her replacement. 'There is a train station in an area known on the digital-layout as Sachem, with lines that reach out to the old mountains. We must get there before midnight.'

'No problem,' announced the Professor. 'I will have you there in time for dinner.'

– VIII –

To the Jungles of B-75

The train station appeared on the digital-layout as a dark grey rectangle with a surrounding area of lighter grey to represent its car park. The broken lines of three railway tracks ran from the west side of the station and continued off beyond the screen, in the opposite direction of the city. There was little else of interest; the station being neighboured on all sides by endless rows of fields and the two roads that cut through them from the north and south. The King scrolled through the list of options offered by the digital-layout's menu. He reserved two tickets for the midnight train to Arramay, at the very tip of their world's grassy shores, explaining to the Professor how he had used the Shadow-disk to create a new account from nothing. The Professor sighed, feeling slightly cheated by the irreverent blow this dealt him. His lifelong achievements were redundant in the new world that he had just ventured into and, as well as that, he was now involved in treason. He checked his watch... his next class had just begun.

The station appeared before them like a huge warehouse, put together with strips of corrugated metal, and was somewhat of a blight amidst the natural beauty that surrounded it. Techtorian guards walked around in groups of two or three and their equipment was positioned all around the station. Some were stopping people at random and searching their luggage while one group checked the treads of vehicles in the car park. Above all this commotion was the ranting of an old beggar, standing by the entrance of the station. He proclaimed in full voice that the end was drawing near and begged those within earshot to get as far away from the city as they could. By the time the King and the Professor had parked and were making their way in his direction, a few guards had had enough of this vagabond and were leading him away from the station doors despite his wilful resistance. His protest suddenly quietened as his eyes fell upon the figure that had haunted his dreams and he was filled with a surge of terror. 'It is him!' he shouted, as the King made his way up the path. 'I have seen that face before! He is a devil and brings with him Hell!'

More guards were called to restrain the old man's riotous disruption and he threw them off him with extraordinary strength. Neither the King nor the Professor looked at him as he shouted and they only glanced in his direction once he was finally subdued. Despite his loud accusations, the old beggar had effectively cleared the way before them with his performance and both men entered the station without being harassed or pursued.

They first passed through a small office, where both were asked to submit retinal scans and received their tickets upon verification. The doors before them then opened and they walked onto the platforms beyond. There were no trains in the station and the muted bustle of those who waited there was held beneath the squawking of the birds that had taken residence along the rafters of its roof. A few unconcerned-looking guards with dogs wandered amidst the medley of commuters.

The King nodded for the Professor to follow him, and walked to the far end of the platform to escape the main body of the crowd. He took a seat near the large open face, through which the trains came and went, and fell into a reverie as he looked out at the mountainous world beyond. Why he had been paired with this odd little man, he did not know, but he felt weaker with him by his side. Upon such melancholy reflections, he was reminded of the unspeakable blackness that had consumed him at the Academy and, for the first time in his life, the King felt the ivory pillars of his confidence challenged. An evening meal of chicken soup restored him somewhat and he felt somehow safer as night began to fall. The crowd alongside the platform thickened steadily as they waited for the arrival of the train from Arramay.

The moon formed a crescent of reflected light and the King sat watching it when his eyes suddenly shifted towards a small speck of light in the distance. Some of the dogs in the station began to bark as it grew nearer and the awaiting crowd shuffled in anticipation.

The Mag-Lev-10000 pulled in silently; each carriage hovering an inch or so above the magnetic charge of the railway line on which they sped. This technology was one of the few fragments of the Paegonaeans' system that had been successfully replicated before their wall was erected and their technology and culture hidden forevermore. Train journeys were now much smoother and faster and the pollution of the old system long forgotten. It gently lowered itself upon the track once it had stopped and opened its doors, flooding the platform with currents of exiting passengers. Those gathered outside waited till the train had emptied before boarding.

Two elderly ladies poured tea from a flask and the King squeezed by them to an unoccupied seat next to the window. They did not seem to mind this interruption and continued their conversation unaffected while they sipped their tea. Using his rolled-up jacket as a pillow, the troubled King rested his head and let go of the dark thoughts that had constrained his mind that day.

The Professor, however, would not fall asleep so readily. He had found the entire row behind these old ladies empty and had positioned himself behind the King with his short legs outstretched. It had been a most unusual and trying day and, as the reward of sleep drew near, a large gentleman with several hefty pieces of luggage pushed in beside him. With his body now wedged against the frame of the carriage, the Professor's eyes turned dolefully to the last of the crowd on the platform as they waited to board.

The doors closed and the last of those to enter took their seats. With a barely perceptible hum, the train rose slightly and held firm above the track. It moved off slowly into the moonlit countryside.

Sleep had now been pushed from the Professor's reach and his mind turned helplessly towards the commotion that now surrounded him. The alarm would have been raised when he did not show up for his second class and they would have traced his steps through the security archives of the Academy. They would know the vehicle he had taken and would inevitably follow its trail to the station. Could they be waiting for him now at Arramay? His eyes eventually closed and he found himself wading out into the murky depths of a haunted sleep.

A slight shudder awoke the Professor some time later and he looked out the window to find the morning sun rising upon the endless fields of yellow corn that whizzed by. Powerful bursts of excitement and fear fused within him to form something that he was quite unable to express, like bitterness and sweetness upon a dulled and unaccustomed tongue. The large man beside him, along with many others, had departed from their carriage during the night and those who remained slept soundly. The King had not moved an inch since he fell asleep and, only now, as though sensing the Professor's attention, did he begin to stir and stretch himself.

'We are near,' he announced, joining the Professor in the row behind.

'We are at Arramay already?'

'We are not going all the way,' the King explained. 'Our destination lies at the summit of a mountain up ahead.'

The Professor did not like the sound of that. Shortly after, the train began to slow and the King and the Professor gathered their belongings and prepared to disembark.

They stepped from the train onto a long wooden platform that had been left in a state of untended decay and its boards laboured and squeaked beneath their feet. A small wooden sign lay crooked on its post with the name *B - 75* engraved on it. So vast and unimportant was this land that the Company just worked out a quadrant system and assigned each area its points. The Company owned almost all of the cornfields and farmlands out there and employed the locals, from whom they had bought the land, to tend their produce. It was then sent back on the trains that ran along these lines to feed the hungry mouths of their city. At the end of the platform was a small ruin of a building, perhaps once a station, with a wall reduced to a pile of rubble at one side.

The train moved off silently and the platform trembled slightly. Only when it had passed from before them were they fully submersed in the immense desolation of their surroundings. Never before had the Professor stood at the centre of such a wide open space and, for a moment, he felt as though he could drown in it. The King, however, jumped from the platform, much rejuvenated by this new environment, and began to plot a route through the tributaries of the forested mountain that stood before them. When the Professor joined him at the base of the platform, the King pointed towards some trees just ahead. 'We can follow this path to the top,' he said, tracing a parting through the forest with his finger and stopping at a small clearing at the edge of the summit. 'You see the ridge?'

The Professor sighed and searched with little endeavour. 'Yes,' he said wearily.

'We will make it there for nightfall and set up camp. We can approach the village by the light of tomorrow's rising sun.'

What importance this village held for them, the Professor did not know, only that there was something up there that they would need for the next leg of their journey. The King walked ahead and entered the fold of trees with quick long strides that left his unconditioned accomplice lagging further and further behind.

Never had the Professor seen such a place. This was a world extinct of man, where more natural laws prevailed. Everything flourished equally knowing nothing of greed and mistrust. Grass grew long and withered, replaced by the endless flow of newer generations and flowers blossomed with arbitrary beauty. Huge silky cobwebs hung between trees, as the cousins of the timid spiders under mankind's rule had grown strong and dominant out there.

The sun now perched overhead and drained the Professor with its merciless heat. Each step grew heavier along the steepening forest path and everything was slowing as he struggled onwards. The incline then veered left and narrowed along the face of a cliff. He eventually caught up with the King, who was now bathing in a stream and enjoying the cool and refreshing course of the mountainous water. With his body now depleted of energy and shaking uncontrollably, the Professor sat down upon the edge of the path and cast his eyes upon the impressive view below. His head was beating with the thuds of a headache and his tired limbs could go no further. All of his features had taken a life of their own; puffing and panting their own exhaustion. He lifted a water bottle to his mouth and then fell back lifelessly upon the ground.

The King emerged from the stream and produced a small glass bottle from his backpack. 'Drink it,' he told the Professor.

The cork shot out with a pop and the Professor sniffed at its content. He recoiled at its odour and asked stiffly. 'What is it?'

'Nutrients,' replied the King in his usual flat tone. He then prepared himself for the remaining trek ahead and started off once more, leaving the Professor with his private elixir.

Again the Professor sniffed at it before throwing the thick green liquid down his throat. After trusting that it had settled in his stomach, he rose to his feet and set off behind the King.

Things seemed more interesting and vibrant around the Professor since drinking the King's potion and he eventually began to enjoy the mountainous trek. A new way of thinking was beginning to emerge from the old and things just seemed to make sense. There was a harmony with that around him which fed his every muscle and he maintained a steady pace in pursuit of the King. Excitement coursed through his veins now that the secrets of the world lay just ahead. He had risen above the clouds of fear to the glorious sunshine of enlightenment and would hold this feeling always in a vault within his heart.

With the sun already set and night fast approaching, the King sat upon a rock and watched as the fatigued figure of the Professor grew near. It seemed that his potion did not last forever.

'Tell me we're there,' he just about managed to say, before falling at the King's feet.

The King pulled him upon his shoulders like the prize of a hunt and carried him through the final stretch of forest.

The very sight of the ridge made the Professor weep for joy and he asked that the King set him down so that he may rest upon its surface. Many of the large rocks that poked from the ground had strange markings and words scrawled upon them and there were animal bones strewn all around. In the centre of this clearing was a small scorched area surrounded by stones, and the King told the Professor to gather some wood for a fire. The King followed him into the forest and wandered off into its depths.

The Professor did not have to stray too deep into the woods to gather his collection of firewood, which he then piled neatly beside the scorched ground. Strange noises lurked around the forest's edge and his eyes darted fearfully between them. Then came an unmistakeable rustle from the forest just ahead and the Professor crept towards it with a pounding heart. 'Hello?' he repeated nervously.

A hand then seized him by the shoulder. The Professor fainted and fell to the ground like a wisp of smoke.

His eyes groaned open some time after and flickered in the brightness before him. A great fire now roared and cooked the meat of two large rabbits, skinned, gutted and skewered above it. The King stood before it, gazing into the flames with ancient fascination. Only the crackling of the fire broke their shared silence. When the rabbits were done, the King set the first of them upon a large leaf and handed it to the Professor. He did the same with the second and both ate hungrily.

'You don't talk much,' remarked the Professor, juggling the hot meat in his mouth as he spoke.

The King considered this observation. 'I speak when I have something to say. People talk too much.'

'You don't believe in conversation?' the Professor retorted quickly. 'Talking for the sake of getting to know someone or to discuss an opinion?'

The King's tone was lighter when he spoke. 'I was raised in the Palace upon Mount Hexlon by a man who those around me called the Priest. He told me that I was special and that I was preparing for a very important mission. I obeyed his every word and he taught me everything I know. Upon turning sixteen, I took the first of several journeys beyond the confines of my home to perform various tasks. About a year ago, the Priest told me that the time for my mission was near and I never left the Palace again until two days ago.'

The Professor scratched his head. Questions about the Paegonaeans and the King's secret world would wait. 'This man, the Priest, taught you all you know of the world. But it is a very grand and diverse little patch of land on which we live. Would you not now like to add another perspective to that which he gave you? You may ask me anything... about my experiences... or my opinion upon some moral subject.'

There was indeed something that had been lurking in the narrow consciousness of the young warrior King. 'Why do you think you were chosen for this mission?'

It was a question that he had asked himself many times since setting off with the King, but it failed to serve his purpose. The Professor shook his head. 'You see, that is still about the mission.'

The King looked at him blankly.

'Something personal perhaps, for the sake of getting to know each other?' asked the Professor, hunting again for a glimpse of that personality buried deep beneath his armoured exterior.

'What can you tell me of Mack Tennerson?'

He gave up. 'I know nothing more than any citizen. He was banished from Fortress city many years ago. Is he the man we are looking for?'

The King nodded. 'What was his crime?'

'He stole something of importance from a museum, I do not remember what. All of the newspapers reported on it and there was a huge uproar at the time. What he did after that I do not know.'

'A thief?' said the King with sudden interest.

'That's right, a common thief.'

The King lay back and looked up to the stars in the night sky. 'A king, a wise man and a thief,' he said, and then repeated in a melodious tone. '*A king, a wise man and a thief, to decide the fate of mankind.*' It was a story he had heard long ago from his childhood. But how did the rest of it go?

They finished their meal, and the Professor commented that it was the best he ever had. Rabbits forced to survive in their natural habitat, explained the King, would always taste better than those raised in captivity on the Company's farms. The fire burned low in the calm night as they talked.

The Universe shone much brighter out there in that wilderness and settled the eyes of the weary travellers upon a tall and sprawling tree. The King climbed up into its branches and lowered a helping hand to his accomplice.

'I don't like heights,' said the Professor in a shouted whisper.

'You'll prefer them to what crawls around down there at night.'

The Professor cast a timorous glance all around and then accepted the King's offered hand. Tiredness had fallen upon both of them like the blanket of night that now shrouded their surroundings. There was little conversation between them as they settled themselves for sleep. Nestled there, in the arms of this ancient forest, the Professor felt a glimmer within him of life's deep essence.

Morning was proclaimed all through the forest by those that inhabited its branches and undergrowth. The Professor awoke and called out to the King and received nothing but silence in return. He sat upright to find that the persistent aches which he awoke to each morning were not there to greet him today. The cool night air had refreshed and revitalised him and he was eager to begin again on their journey. He should have slept in a tree a long time ago, he thought.

The King stood naked at the edge of the cliff, already bathed and with a selection of fresh fruit and berries by his feet. When his body had dried in the soft morning breeze, he pulled on his clothes and carried all that he had gathered back to the thick trunk of the tree. As the Professor watched him from high up in its branches, he noticed a small star-like scar positioned between his shoulder and neck. He did not make a noise as he observed it and almost fell from the tree in alarm when the King spoke.

'You have noticed my scar.'

The Professor was taken aback, but composed himself enough to ask what had happened.

'I was hit by an arrow,' replied the King, studying it for himself. 'My life had been spent avoiding them, and so, I grew curious as to how one should taste.'

They ate breakfast and pulled their packs upon their shoulders and walked some way down the path they had travelled the night before. An overgrown and barely noticeable path led off to the left and snaked its way up through what remained of the dense mountainous jungle. The King took the lead and battled through the relentless foliage with the Professor following close behind. Eventually, they crossed a small stream near the summit and ventured into a more lightly wooded area.

Something metal lay on the ground ahead and the King approached it cautiously. He looked back at the Professor for him to observe, and demonstrated its principle by pressing upon its central plate with the tip of a stick. The contraption's jaws snapped shut with a mighty crunch and the Professor jumped back with fright.

'Be careful,' the King warned him.

More traps snapped shut as the King hastened on and, though their jaws had been closed, the Professor allowed a wide berth for each of them. The ground slowly levelled until they had passed the mountain's summit and were beginning to make their way down its far side. It was with nimble feet that the King approached a large boulder and he huddled behind it until the Professor caught up with him. Their destination lay just beyond.

Thirty-three huts of varying shapes and sizes formed the heart of this village along with a stream that meandered through its midst. The ground was thick with heavy mud, and the animal pelts and fleeces that its people wore as clothing were stained with it. Pigs ran about freely, in an uneasy alliance alongside the villagers, with one squealing for all its worth as an old man chased after it. Huge pots boiled and the squalid inhabitants gathered around them, as more ingredients were brought from the forest and fields beyond. The Professor marvelled at the primitive scene before him.

The King pulled him back and spoke softly. 'They will kill us unless we can present ourselves first. You must follow me carefully.'

With that warning only, the King slid over the boulder with the agile and fluid movements of a lizard and crawled down the loose banking on the other side. His stealthy descent was interrupted by a small avalanche of dirt that was followed seconds later by the more rapid and uncontrolled descent of the Professor. No sooner had he reached the bottom and gotten to his feet when a horn sounded and there arose a scattered roar from the village. Within seconds, the first of the villagers arrived, some brandishing primitive weapons, and the Professor instinctively raised his hands. The King rose to his feet beside him and did the same. They remained under close guard until a small man wearing a robe made from the brown pelt of a cow arrived before them. He stared upon the intruders before shaking his head and ordering his men to drop their weapons. 'Has he been gone so long, our own secret King?'

One by one, the people dropped to their knees and bowed their heads. Those just arriving did the same and all knelt before the two men in absolute silence. The village elder, dressed in the brown pelt robe, was the first to rise and waited until the last of his people were on their feet before he addressed their King. 'We would be honoured if you and your friend would join us for a banquet. We did not have the opportunity to show our gratitude when you last visited us. There is not a soul in this village that is not owed to you.'

The crowd watched with bated breath and a wave of joy swept through them as the King accepted their offer. He was taken immediately under the arm of the village elder and led through the parting crowd.

'We have had fourteen new additions to our little family here, including a grandson of my own,' he began. He then proceeded to lavish praise upon every building they passed and every invention that had revolutionised their society since the King had last been there.

'Is the package I left still here?' asked the King.

'Of course,' he cried out with supreme delight. 'It was cared for as you requested, but first you must eat and replenish your strength.'

The crowd followed behind as they made their way to their village's banquet hall, some way further down the mountainside. Six huge erect stones of similar proportions held up a roof made from wooden beams and mud, and the empty rows of seating beneath quickly filled. Barbecues were set sizzling and mugs of brown ale were passed around. Song after song broke out and the merriment of each table was momentarily quietened by the arrival of huge platters of meat. The village elder rose to his feet and cheered their King three times. Eruptions of laughter pierced the merry air of song and banter and the villagers swayed back and forth clinking mugs. As the King ate quietly with his head bowed, those around him settled upon the Professor to answer their many questions. The Professor quickly found his feet in their topics and told them of the complex workings of Fortress city, the role of the Company, and of his involvement in all of it. His stories were muffled as he ravenously chewed and washed all down with ale. Before another question could be asked, the Professor reached out and lifted an exceptionally large drumstick and opened his mouth to take a bite.

'I wouldn't eat that,' warned the King, reaching across to stop him. 'They call it sacred meat. The flesh of their enemies.'

The Professor looked at him blankly for a moment as these words settled into comprehension. His eyes darted fearfully around the banquet hall and the bone he held dropped from his grip. 'They're cannibals,' he muttered.

The King wiped his mouth after eating his fill and stood up from his seat of honour. A silence fell across the banquet hall and slowly they all rose to their feet. He bowed his head in appreciation of their hospitality and walked from the hall with the Professor and village elder following directly behind. The banquet hall then emptied and the crowd that spilled from it swarmed around the important duo and their leader. They walked further down the mountain to a cluster of tall trees, within which, lay a wooden construction. Some men rushed ahead of them and waited for the command from the village elder. Upon his nod, its four sides dropped to the ground.

And there she sat, on the very spot he had landed her after his heated escape two and a half years ago. She had belonged to the rogue security firm he had just taken out; a group who had threatened the liberty of these mountainfolk and the supremacy of the Company.

'Exactly as you left it, your Highness. Cared for upon your instruction as though divine will. My people and I wish you every success on your next mission and thank you once again for saving us.'

The Professor was swallowed up by the excited crowd and he battled his way through to the King. When the helicopter started and its blades began to turn, he called out in desperation, lest he be forgotten in this place. By the time he was pushed free from the tightly packed crowd, the rotors had become a constant halo and the King sat flicking switches and reacquainting himself with the controls. The Professor was bundled aboard and the door closed after him. He peeped out the window as they lifted into the air and felt a whirlwind of relief and disgust swirl within him. Such places had not existed until now.

The helicopter hovered above the cheering crowd for some time before the front of it dipped slightly and slowly began to move off. The forest below stretched all the way down the mountain and continued right out to the channel of water that separated this land from the reddened shores of the wastelands.

– IX –

Mack Tennerson

A huge bear-like figure, draped from head to toe in camouflage, raced along a narrow track through the forest on horseback. The steed was a sturdy and impressive animal, black in colour, though draped in the same jungle camouflage as its rider. Across the saddle lay a lifeless stag with the arrow-tip that had killed it still deeply embedded in its skull. Though hunting was prohibited in these parts by the Forest Alliance, stags and the other woodland creatures did not pay taxes. The Forest Alliance had grown from a neighbourhood-watch-scheme to become a security agency in their own right, unaffiliated with the Company. This meant that they could charge unofficially for special privileges, and Mack Tennerson was amongst the best protected under their watch.

The narrow forest path opened out into a widening corridor of trees and the fresh scent of pine fused with the salty air from the sea beyond. At the end of this corridor was a gateway with a twelve foot wall on either side that arched around Mack's six acre estate. Automated weaponry, positioned at intervals along both arms of this wall, scanned the area as he approached, and a fortified gate sealed the entrance once his horse had passed through it.

The estate was now a faded and overgrown memory of what it once was. The building itself was one of the oldest in all of the Free world and had served as an exclusive hotel for two hundred and fifty years before the war. It had then been requisitioned by the resistance during the war's final years and used as their headquarters. In the aftermath of the war, the Company then claimed possessionship and put it on the market at a price that had yet to be acquired by any of its citizens. Its one hundred and twenty rooms and remote location were ideal for Mack's enterprising ambition, and the thief, renowned throughout the Free world, stumped up much of the asking price. This secluded and prestigious old building was then to become known as *The Academy for Young Men* under Mack Tennerson's ownership.

They came from all over and from every tier of the Free world's societies. Boys as young as five or six were taught how to lie, cheat and steal, how to fight and defend themselves using a variety of deadly weapons. Mack produced lethal assassins and silent thieves and built an army that served only profit. He grew rich with the bounties of those his boys had killed and from the items they procured in his name. All was well and business was good until the Company began cracking down on his operations and claiming more stake upon these lands. Since then his army had disbanded and Mack lived out there all alone, semi-retired, dealing in anything that would bring his name a few more credits.

Three paths stretched out from the inner perimeter of his home to the large outer wall, separating its semi-circular garden into four equal segments. There were photographs and paintings inside the old building that testified to the beauty this area once held and its sad demise since the war. Had it not been for the horses and cattle that roamed about freely, these gardens would have grown untended to form an impenetrable barricade of wildlife.

Mack galloped swiftly along the middle of these paths, as his security system went through the usual provisions to verify that it was their programmer who now approached. Upon reaching some gravelled ground, just before the inner wall, he dismounted from his horse and took off its apparel and the stag they had carried from the forest. With a full-blooded slap on its rump, the animal was sent back to the others. As the horse galloped off, something caught Mack's attention; a sound hovering just above the silence of his isolated retreat. He pulled a small handheld computer from the pocket of his overcoat and checked the air traffic schedule of the Forest Alliance. Nothing out of the ordinary had been permitted to enter, though the sound grew ever closer. Whoever they were, they would not make it past the Alliance's defence system, he thought. However, Mack was a cautious man, and entrusted no one more than himself for his own personal safety.

His private armoury and bunker lay at the bottom of a winding set of steps within his home and could only be accessed through a well-rehearsed sequence of timed inputs. Ten inches of reinforced steel would stand between him and the end of the world when it came, and he had enough provisions in there to last him several years. All he would need to survive the apocalypse and re-establish himself in the aftermath was stored in these cupboards; canned goods, fresh water, radios, gas masks, gold sovereigns and many other items. Weapons ranging from bows, knives and small pistols to supreme automatic weaponry were mounted in displays all around. At the far end of the bunker, below a selection of antique swords, was a large brown duffle bag with something hefty inside. Mack made straight for this item and took a few minutes to browse the remainder of his collection.

He carried all back up the winding steps and to one of the old hotel's lower roofs, where he would often come and pass the unfilled hours shooting birds. The sound of the oncoming helicopter deepened steadily and he tried to work out its distance. Where were the Forest Alliance, he wondered, should they not have already dealt with this problem? His mind cast back to the strange visit he had received just three weeks ago and he prepared himself for action.

The helicopter finally appeared just above the canopy of the forest and glinted in the evening sun. There could be no doubt that it was coming for him. He unzipped the duffle bag, lifted its bulky content upon his shoulder and fixed his eye upon the digital sight. The target came within range and the screen flashed red to denote that it had locked on its heat signature. His breathing steadied and he pulled on the trigger. The device fired with an overpowering whoosh and Mack tumbled backwards, scrabbling at the roof tiles as he fell.

A soft and indecipherable word escaped the King's lips at the sight of the oncoming missile. He undid his harness with one hand and pulled hard right on the steering stick with the other. The helicopter veered sharply and the King threw the Professor from the condemned vehicle with only his backpack beneath him for protection. Everything then erupted and the King felt the warmth of the explosion reach out after him as he freefalled into the forest below. The first of the branches brushed him jaggedly but then struck more solidly as he made his way through them like an unfortunate human pinball.

He did not feel the pain just yet, but could hear himself groaning as he surfaced into consciousness. His eyes struggled open to a blurry world and his entire body began to ache. Upon an initial inspection of his injuries, the King found everything still connected with no serious damage to his internal organs. His nose, however, had been broken and his entire body blackened by the branches of the forest that had beat him like the feet of an angry mob. There was a rustling from above, and the King strained his eyes up just as the Professor dropped to the ground before him, followed moments later by his backpack. There was no brace for impact as he landed and each part of his body hit the ground with equal luck. He lay there as though dead, and the King worried that the mission had just been lost.

Every movement sent jolts of pain coursing through his limbs and the King winced with the combined effort of sitting upright. He brought his hands to his face and gently massaged the bridge of his nose. The break was rectified with a short and concise readjustment, watering his eyes with tears of silent pain. He then looked towards the unresponsive figure before him. The Professor had not been so lucky.

His right arm lay twisted with its bone broken. The King gently rolled him over to begin his examination. There were teeth missing from his bloodied mouth and his nose had been broken in similar fashion to his own. A few fingers had been broken on his right hand as well. There was little way of knowing what damage had been done internally while he lay unconscious. Both legs seemed fine, though his left foot had also been injured.

The King proceeded to knead gently from his shoulder and corrected the bone with an audible crack. At that, the Professor awoke like a vampire from a coffin and released a squeal that made the entire forest tremble. He lay back down again into a seemingly comfortable slumber and the King splinted his arm with a thick branch and tied all together with some reeds. He tended the rest of his injuries in order and then slapped his face till he awoke.

'What's happening?' the Professor asked feebly.

'We were hit by a missile. You are hurt, but it is not serious. We must assume that Mack Tennerson has mistaken us for an enemy. Therefore, we must act accordingly. He will be making his way towards the wreckage site to search for survivors and will have with him heat and motion sensors. We must avoid detection.' He then added more thoughtfully. 'We passed a small river some way back. We can hide there for the moment.'

He helped the Professor onto his one good foot and walked alongside him slowly as they made their way to the river. The Professor winced in pain with every step as he heaved himself along. This nightmare, it seemed, would cost him his limbs one by one.

The river the King spoke of was wider and more wild than it had seemed from the air, but it served their purpose just the same. The blackened face of the Professor turned to dismay as he watched the King lower himself into it and wave for him to follow. They held onto the muddy embankment with only their heads above the cold and fast-flowing water, where they remained for twenty minutes until the King pulled himself from the river's current. 'Give me a few minutes,' he told the Professor, 'then move to the crash site and await my return. Do what you can to heat yourself.'

Upon delivering those words of advice, the King stripped off and smeared handfuls of mud on his chest and body until there was not an inch of flesh showing. The Professor's computer had remained intact within its protective case and illuminated the creature-like face of the muddied King as he began typing. To use the Shadow-disk to shut down Mack's defences may have forced him into fleeing by air or by sea and they would then be unable to follow him. What they needed was to lure him into a false sense of security. The King typed his command and then closed over the computer before gathering some things and setting off into the forest.

The burned-out shell of the helicopter still smouldered and pieces of wreckage lay scattered all around. With some rummaging through it all, the King located the fuel tanks and found that they each contained half of their unexploded capacity, such was their design. He siphoned the fuel into some containers and disappeared again into the forest, moving from treetop to treetop and stealthily approaching the perimeter of Mack's estate.

Mack sat at his command post, with the screens all around him covering every inch of his land. There had been no bodies in the wreckage and this had troubled him. To escape unscathed from such a blast would require the instinct of a true survivor. Nevertheless, should they be fool enough to persist after this warning, the full wrath of his defence system awaited. There was a sudden glint from one of the heat sensors and Mack pulled himself close to the screen. Something was rapidly snaking its way through his garden from the edge of the outer perimeter, leaving a thin trail as it moved towards the...

'No way!' said Mack softly, a fraction of a second before his fuel dump erupted.

Many of his screens now buzzed black and white, having been knocked offline with the blast and all of his heat sensors in that area had been rendered useless. This attack had blinded him and crippled much of his defence system, reliant as it was upon these eyes and ears.

'If that's the way you want to play,' said Mack, lifting an automatic weapon and walking out upon a small balcony overlooking the front of his home. The fuel dump burned brightly with black fumes falling like a mist upon his garden.

'You wanna play games?' he shouted, opening fire in the direction of his fuel dump. There was a joyful glee on his face as his weapon rattled and he threw it to the ground in anger once its ammunition had exhausted. Mack returned to the control room and his eyes were wild as they searched through the screens that remained intact. He was eventually rewarded with a glimpse of someone climbing through a window downstairs. 'Gotcha now,' he said with a huge bright smile.

He pulled a sidearm from its holster and prepared for some close quarter combat. As he turned to make his way down the stairs and confront this intruder, he was blinded by a flash of white and he found himself tumbling backwards. He fell upon the ground and the pistol dropped from his hand. His eyes glanced towards it and then to the mud-covered figure before him. He dismissed the pistol with a grunt and smacked his fist on the ground. 'How did you move so quickly?' was his first question. His voice was a deep and resonant growl that had kept his students in line through the years and there was a powerful disappointment in his eyes as he waited for the King to respond.

'A slight adjustment in the relay of your cameras. I was in the building before you saw me.'

Mack smirked. 'I'm getting too old for all of this. Did the Company send you? I see they have been making moves all over this territory and are now beginning to take out key targets before they claim it for themselves. A good strategy, I must admit.'

'The *Company*?' the King repeated in a perplexed tone of voice. 'I come with a proposition. Were you not contacted?'

'Contacted?' said Mack, his face now frowning under the pressure of the upcoming confession. 'There was a man who came out here... maybe three weeks ago now. Bypassed all my security and just knocked at the front door. He warned me that there would be someone coming for me in the weeks ahead.' He shrugged his shoulders and concluded. 'I thought he was from the Company. I killed him. Buried him out in the forest.'

'Had you listened to him you would have known to expect me!' replied the angered King. 'You may have jeopardised the mission.' He then took a deep breath and the hardened glare in his eyes softened. 'We have little time to spare. Come with me and I will explain all on the way.'

There were doubts and suspicions on both sides as they talked, but the prospect of money soon seduced Mack's greedy mind. 'How significant is this reward you speak of?'

'Very,' replied the King, misinterpreting their values.

The crash site still smouldered and the King scanned the wreckage for any sign of the Professor. Mack had talked for most of the way and digressed inexplicably into unconnected fields of conversation without finishing what came before. It was as though his mind had been uncorked after years of patient silence and now spewed excitedly with the fragments of his thoughts like a geyser. He had just started a speech on the necessity of hygiene when the badly-injured Professor jumped out from the bushes behind him with a heavy branch raised above his head. Mack turned and dispatched him instinctively and the Professor fell to the ground once more.

'Who was that?' he shouted.

'That was the other member of our group.' The King then waved his hand over the smouldering wreckage. 'And that was our transport.'

'No sweat,' said Mack. 'I have transport at the harbour. It's not far, but we will have to wait until morning.'

The walk back through the forest and through the gardens of his estate was a path of enlightenment for Mack, and he listened eagerly as the King laid all before him. They carried between them an improvised stretcher, upon which lay the bruised and broken body of the Professor, still out cold. Though details of this mission ended at the Paegonaeans' wall, Mack could only wonder what lay in store for them beyond. He would come out of retirement to fight alongside the King of Hexlon. What a formidable force they would form, with their intelligent little friend to aid them, wielding his expertise of defence systems like a weapon and making all levels of security crumble before them. This would be a tale that would be remembered forevermore.

All that remained of Mack's academy was the red and black emblem that hung above the gateway of the inner compound wall. Within lay a collection of antique and revolutionary vehicles and weaponry that had been arranged along the front of the old building, as though for viewing pleasure. There was something ghostly about the building itself, as though lowly bemoaning its former existence from some remote afterlife. Windows had been broken and never replaced, haunting its corridors with a sharp and whistling draft. Mack had localised his living space to a few rooms in the centre of the large building and had left everything else for the ivied tentacles of nature to slowly reclaim. The King wondered what the academy would have been like at the height of its years. How it would have felt to be trained alongside other boys the same age and the camaraderie this would inspire. But now all had passed, the King asked why Mack chose to remain way out there, all alone.

'I like to be reminded of those days,' he answered in his formidable growl. Should this man ever find himself in a directive seat of power, the evolutionary path for mankind would be set along rigid lines. Young boys and girls would be regimented into soldiers and everyone would be charged with protecting themselves. There would be no security companies or governments, just schools like his that taught its students how to fight and become practised in the wily arts. Complacency and dependency were the crimes that restrained this evolution, thought Mack, and perpetuated the dull stupor found in abundance along the endless rows of housing in Fortress city.

The Professor began to stir as they carried him up the steps and along the narrow reception. At the end of the entrance hall, towards the back of the building, was a kitchen and seating area, where Mack would prepare and eat his meals all alone. On an island in the centre of the room lay the stag which had been killed earlier that evening with a selection of knives poised next to it. The Professor then began to rouse from his blackout, murmuring something about his arm before finally opening his eyes.

Mack lit a fire before radioing through to the Forest Alliance to give an explanation for the explosion. After tending the Professor's injuries more carefully, the King wandered out through the back doors of the kitchen onto some decking and sat down upon a lounger. He peered out into the darkness beyond with tired eyes and listened to the hypnotic lapping of the sea upon the shore. Inside, the Professor was rising unsteadily, holding his battered arm and dabbing the ground with his injured foot to see how much pressure it would take. Where was this place that he now found himself and what new nightmare awaited him there? He hobbled across the kitchen to the heat of the roaring fire and stood shivering before it. On the fireplace was a photograph of a young boy with a stern expression and a scar that ran the length of his face. He could have been no older than sixteen, though his eyes were hardened and tinged with sadness; already experienced in the atrocities of man.

'That's Tony,' said Mack, as he re-entered the room. Nostalgia seemed to gather around him as he took the photo-frame in both hands and looked upon the youthful visage. 'Tony's my boy,' he started. 'Left a woman pregnant during a brief stint in the wastelands and got Tony ten years later. His mother couldn't deal with him any longer and didn't know what else to do, so I put him to work. He was one of my best… a chip off the old block, you might say. He earned over one hundred thousand credits in bounties and fifty more in stolen items. Not to mention taking out targets such as Mayor Tomlinson in '58 and Colonel Rourke two years later. He scrapes a living out in the wastelands now. Haven't seen him in years.'

'Colonel Rourke?' spat the Professor incredulously. 'He died in an accident on one of the carriageways. There were witnesses. And Mayor Tomlinson… he stepped down from office and retired. He is living somewhere in the hills to the east of the city.'

Mack looked at the poor fool before him. 'You ever see him with your own eyes?'

The Professor shook his head glumly.

'Rourke was a visionary, and he was popular. He understood what the Company were doing and that was why they had to get rid of him.'

'The Company?'

Mack nodded. 'I bet you believe that the reins of the Free world were just handed over to them without any bloodshed or resistance, as though it was their birthright, and all they care about is looking after their citizens.' At this, he scoffed. 'The Company are very good at what they do, taking out anyone who poses a threat while slowly turning their citizens into slaves. They're buying up everything before they do away with their monetary system. With no money and them controlling everything, the future does not look too bright for the people.'

'But I work at their Academy... I would know if this was what they were doing.'

'Their world is all misdirection and confusion, like a sleight of hand. The closer you follow the magician's hand the more he guides you from his trickery. You watch their television and listen to their radio; they control what you think and do. More and more people fill their factories and buy their products. All they know is working and buying, working and buying, working and buying. But, some day soon, it will all come crashing down, and the people will find themselves with nothing while those at the top have everything. It happened before.' He then shook his head as though in admiration. 'They did pay well though... when they needed me.'

The Professor sat stunned as what he had just learned razed the settlements of his mind and replaced them with this new reality. His head became dizzy as the old connections broke and struggled back to sense again with this new understanding of the world. Any liberation of this kind was never easy, but it is man's duty to never settle upon what was once, but what is now.

The patio lights turned on and the King startled from his somnolent respite. Night had been thrust out to sea in an instant and he rose from the lounger to survey the newly illuminated area. Two thin barriers of loosely gathered rocks stretched out into the sea some distance to his left and right and curved together to create a small private harbour. The patio continued down several steps onto the beach and narrowed into a jetty that reached out between these arms with several small boats tethered to it. What a perfect place, thought the King.

The tearing noise of flesh being ripped from the stag in the kitchen and the subsequent hacking of its limbs was followed by the more delicate sounds of its preparation. Both the King and the Professor now sat in the tranquil ambience of the patio, savouring the smell of roasting meat as it wafted from the kitchen. Mack then arranged three chairs around a table further down by the shore, which he loaded with pots and plates, and invited his new friends to come and join him. The very sight of the thinly carved slices of tender meat made their mouths water and there was enough vegetables and breads to ensure that none of them would leave unsatisfied. Memories of the village from earlier that day came back to the Professor as he pushed the meat about his plate. He placed a sliver in his mouth and was immediately cured of all apprehension and joined the other two in this tasty meal.

'I have some grog, if you boys fancy it,' said Mack whilst they ate. 'Something to toast this illustrious union.'

'Grog?' said the King inquisitively.

Mack excused himself from the table and walked up the steps to the kitchen. They could hear him rattle about inside and he reappeared moments later with a small wooden barrel, which he carried down the steps and set on the sand next to the table. A pipe was inserted into it and Mack sucked on it until it began spewing a thick translucent liquid. He filled a large tankard for each of them and they drank to the mission.

They returned their tankards to the table after a long and refreshing draught and took a moment before resuming with their meal. The King felt the heavy liquid find the pit of his stomach and his head grew dizzy with the fumes. Empty tankards were quickly refilled as they struggled on with the feast before them. Mack regaled them with endless tales while they ate, embellished, of course, to serve his own reputation favourably. Once their bellies had been filled, they sat back on their chairs contentedly and finished the last of the grog. It was about then that the world began to spin and the King stood up as though a tornado was slowly forming around him. He excused himself from the table and wandered off along the beach on his own.

The King's bare feet sunk into the soft sand and were submerged intermittently by the roll of the sea. There was something about the tide that made him feel secure, as though the entire universe was in perfect order and out there waiting to be understood. He looked up towards the moon with blurry eyes and wondered what this world would look like from its cratered surface. A wave rolled over his feet as he stood there looking up and he fell upon his rear on the sandy shore. He sat there laughing to himself for a moment before rising unsteadily to his feet. What was this grog that robbed a man of his balance and rendered him as giddy as a child?

The King continued along the shoreline until he reached the great arm of jagged rocks that reached around Mack's bay. He clambered onto it and jumped from one rock to the next until he stood at its very tip. There, he let his feet hang limply in the surrounding water as he again looked up to the night sky.

When he tried to stand up, the King's foot slipped on a wet rock and he tumbled helplessly into the cold water with a splash. The shock to his system immediately sobered him and he reached out for the surface and kicked with his powerful legs. But something seemed to pull at him from below and he fought hard to escape its grasp. Exhaustion slowed his flailings until he hovered motionless in the depths like a foetus in the womb. There was a faint noise in the distance before it all fell silent. An indistinct figure appeared before him and brought light to this dark place. It offered him a hand and the King reached out to take it.

– X –

To the Great Wall

A soft ambrosial breeze roused the King from his deep slumber. His entire body was stiff and every muscle ached as he struggled from beneath the thin white sheets that covered him and then browsed his unfamiliar surroundings. But for the soft bed that he sat on, the room was empty, and its four walls, ceiling and floor were all of the same bright white complexion. On the wall opposite was a window with white silk curtains gently rustling. Through the window shone a light so bright that the King had to shield his eyes from it and his head rang out in echoes of pain. It was then that he noticed he was naked. He looked around for his clothes, but found nothing. There was a strange purgatorial feeling about this place and his mind tried desperately to conjure something that would help explain his whereabouts. He tried to shout for someone to come and help him, but his voice failed to make any discernible noise and his throat and chest felt raw. A sickness fell upon him and he lay back on the bed and stared helplessly at the ceiling. Something about a helicopter came to mind. With supreme effort, he pulled himself to his feet and lurched unsteadily towards the door.

Beyond the door was a long windowless corridor that seemed to sway back and forth before him. The rocking motion of this corridor unbalanced him as he struggled up the middle, with an endless series of doors leading off from it on both sides. His head became dizzy and his weakened limbs ached vociferously. He stopped and steadied himself against the frame of one of these doors and then opened it to inspect what lay on the other side. It was exactly like the room he had just woken up in, with the same bright light shining through. He closed the door again and hastened on towards the elusive black door at the end of the corridor. A strange sensation grew inside him as he approached and reached out his hand to push it open. There was a mumbling on the other side; two voices perhaps, joined in muted conversation.

The voices quietened as the King's eyes struggled against the harsh brightness and there was a smell of fried fish in the air. Two shadowy figures appeared from the glare and grew to recognition as his eyes acclimatised to the morning sun. Both Mack and the Professor stared at him silently with curious expressions on each of their faces. A refreshing breeze rolled in from the sea and through the kitchen, reminding the King that he was naked.

Mack got up and gave a slight bow. 'I have your clothes right here, your Highness. Breakfast has been prepared.' His voice was a little jagged, wavering with unease. He got up and exited the room and the King sat down at the table.

The Professor resumed half-heartedly with his breakfast, stealing intermittent glances at the obviously disorientated King. 'How do you feel this morning?' he asked finally.

'Confused,' the King answered in a crackling voice. He coughed. 'What happened last night?'

Mack reappeared with a bundle of neatly folded clothes and the two men looked at each other when this question was put to them.

'You gave us a fright,' began Mack, setting the clothes down beside him. 'We were walking along the jetty when we heard you fall into the sea. I dived in after you and brought you to the surface. I feared that it was too late, but the Professor here gave you mouth to mouth and pumped on your chest till you coughed up the water that had filled your lungs. We then carried you to your room and watched over you until a few hours ago.'

'There have been so many close calls in my life that I believe it to be truly charmed. I am indebted to you both for saving me.' He drew a deep breath and placed his head in his hands. 'I have such a headache and everything around me seems to be spinning.'

'That would be the grog,' answered Mack. 'It does that on the morning after.'

A breakfast of fried fish and coffee restored enough of the King to contemplate the important day ahead. 'The defence grid goes back on-line at midnight tonight,' he announced pertly. 'Where is this harbour you spoke of yesterday?'

'About an hour up the coast.'

The King shook his head. 'We will use one the boats out back.' This harbour was an unnecessary imposition.

Mack nodded. 'Those are good vessels, but not fit for a King. I have a boat at the harbour that will cross the channel in a fraction of the time. We shall be at the wall before sunset. Besides, Customs would likely board us if we did not register our journey with them first. Miserable scum that they are.'

The very mention of the channel filled the King with dread. 'Very well,' he conceded.

They took ten minutes to themselves before setting off for the harbour and each went in their own direction. The King walked to the end of the jetty and looked out thoughtfully upon the water. He had always felt the unseen presence of some protective force and there were times when he believed that he had witnessed its interventions. An enemy's gun would jam at an inopportune moment or an escape would appear from nowhere when trapped amidst the wreckage of a crumbling building. These interventions had bestowed a sense of invulnerability upon the King. But, what if his colleagues had remained on the patio last night and did not hear him splash into the sea? What if they had been just a minute or two later? Had something whispered in their ears to walk along the jetty and be vigilant? Or had they just been lucky?

The Professor approached and stood next to him, both now looking out to the sea in silence as the fresh breeze blew against them. 'How do you feel?' he asked.

The King nodded. 'Better.'

'That's good. We will need you fully restored if we are to keep from harm. There is not much further to go now,' he said, nodding out over the body of water that remained. 'Put last night behind you and move on as before.'

His words had a profound effect on the King, who then placed a hand on his shoulder. Whether it was he who had breathed life into him or some unseen force that had acted through him, he now owed everything to this little man. The Professor would need him to be strong and clear-minded, and that is what he resolved to do.

They walked back along the jetty together, the Professor now hobbling upon a crutch, as Mack appeared through the kitchen of the large hotel and made his way down the steps towards them. He had changed into short-sleeved combat gear and shorts and wore large sunglasses that almost covered the entire upper half of his face. In his hand, hanging heavily by his side, was a duffle bag that fell to the ground with a heavy thump. His eyes were filled with expectant praise as the King lowered to his hunkers and began rummaging through it. Rifles, handguns and military equipment; the best of his large collection summarised within this sack. The King shook his head and zipped the bag up again. 'We will not need any of this on our journey. Do as I say when I say and no harm will befall us.'

There was a trodden pathway along the back wall of Mack's estate with the shore lapping to and fro on their right. This wall then turned sharply to the left and arched along the front to form the outer perimeter of his estate, separating Mack's land from the forest beyond.

The sun was now rising high above them and the King suggested a break before continuing any further. He pulled out a map and had Mack explain every detail of the harbour and what sort of security awaited there. The Professor wandered down to the shore as they did and scooped some water into his hands and splashed it on his face. With the other two still deeply engrossed in their discussion, he boiled a kettle of water and brought both a cup of tea before they set off once more.

Traffic out upon the great body of water, the largest within the walls of the Free world, grew heavier as they continued on and there was a deep clamour of commotion that grew louder with every step. Mack led them some way into the forest to their left and they climbed a steep hill as the trees around them grew smaller. At the peak of this hill, they looked out over the harbour below.

Many years ago, this harbour had been a quiet and simple little cove, where local fishermen drew their catch upon the shore each evening and loaded carts to be drawn by horse to a nearby market. Then came the war and the obliteration of the land beyond the channel, whereupon it became an important port for trading. In the nineteenth year after the war, one year before the proposal that saw their jurisdiction extended to the wastelands, the Company purchased the site, and the little harbour became a fortified cove. Business of all kinds had passed through there since; chiefly the export of wood to the wastelands, with a constant stream of trucks belonging to the Company passing through each week. They now controlled the marijuana and fresh food trade and were forcing their way into whatever else there was. What little they did not control was divided up amongst the few surviving, smaller and privately-owned trucking firms who had yet to be put out of business with their recession.

Huge cannon-like weapons watched over the harbour from each of its four corners and perused its alleyways or skimmed along the traffic out at sea. Each had the capability of sinking a boat ten kilometres from the shore and requiring only seconds to readjust itself and take out a single target amidst a crowd of one hundred. It was these that would pursue them should anything go wrong down there and the King was doubtful whether they could survive their combined effort. Armoured boats lay at anchor in the bay while others went about their business. There was somewhere between seventy-five and one hundred guards patrolling this area with cameras on every corner. A large boat made its way into the port and security seemed to gravitate towards it.

'How long will it take us to reach the lockup?' the King asked Mack.

He shrugged his shoulders. 'Fifteen to twenty minutes.'

The King looked out upon the tightly secured area below. 'We must now assume that the Company are looking for the Professor. Should any of those cameras catch sight of him, his whereabouts would be reported immediately. Is there any way of getting to the lockup without passing any of these cameras?'

Mack shook his head. He didn't think so.

'What if we were to leave him somewhere by the shore and come and collect him once we have the boat in our possession?'

'That could be risky,' said Mack. 'Customs look out for that kind of thing... vile motherless swine. I once dabbled in a little smuggling before the Company started cracking down on it. Now, everything has to come in through the port and taxes paid in full. Their radar would pick us up travelling across the shore and stopping, then heading out to the wastelands. We would have their boats coming at us from all sides.'

'What if I wear a hat and sunglasses?' asked the Professor.

The King thought for a moment and then shook his head. 'We will use the Shadow-disk.' He sat down on a rock and could be heard mumbling to himself as he deliberated its most effective use. 'To bring down their cameras or block the feed to the Company may force the harbour into some kind of shutdown. What I propose therefore is that we corrupt the Company's system temporarily. The feed from the harbour will still go through, but the Company's facial recognition system will have lost the database of those it is looking for. Those at the harbour would be none-the-wiser.'

Mack's jaw nearly hit the floor. 'You can do that?'

'I can do anything,' the King answered, without so much as a hint of humour. He pulled the computer from his backpack and, with a few keystrokes, claimed that it was done. To verify that it had worked, he entered the address of the Company's homepage and was redirected to a blank screen, claiming that the site was temporarily unavailable. Both men shook their heads in amazement.

'Let's move,' said the King, closing the lid of the computer. 'We have no idea how long this will hold out.'

A wire fence ran along the perimeter of the harbour with a highly guarded checkpoint at each of the three roads leading into it. All three were clogged with slow moving trucks, stopping and starting periodically as retinal scans were taken from the drivers. A steady flow of people walking in and out moved without restriction; the sensitive equipment ensuring that none were armed or wanted by the Company. The King held his breath as they passed under the gaze of the first of the cameras.

The narrow influx of people that shuffled through the harbour gates then dispersed through the maze of buildings and warehouses beyond. No alarm sounded as the three men proceeded further into the harbour, nor did any of its guards rush to detain them. The huge cannon above continued scanning the sea beyond. 'So far, so good,' Mack mumbled, taking the lead with an energetic stride.

Security guards passed them by and, upon recognising Mack, most tipped their hats and bid him good-day. He was a regular at the port, whether it was business or pleasure that had brought him there. There were few in these jungles who did not know his name, and almost all thought him to be one of the richest men beyond the suburbs of Fortress city. Should the Company ever declare war on this land for whatever reason, in a bid to claim it for themselves, it would be him many would look to in the hope of forming some level of resistance.

The storage facility was privately owned and lay separate from the harbour in a small contained area next to the sea. A portacabin sat upon stilts with a huge winch dangling overhead to transport the boats from the lockups at the top of the compound into the water. Mack made his way towards the small office and a guard came out to greet him and waved him inside with a smile.

Both the King and the Professor stayed some distance behind and watched this affable exchange out of sight. Once both had disappeared inside the portacabin and its door closed behind them, the King and the Professor set off into the compound. The King could only hope that Mack was doing his job in distracting the guard, or, should the guard spot them on his screens, have the good sense to take him out before he alerted anyone else. But no such action was necessary and they reached the sanctity of the lockups without being spotted and hid from view up one of the narrow alleys between them. They could hear the two men laugh out loud as the office door opened and listened to Mack's heavy footsteps as he approached.

There were five blunt notes from the lockup's keypad as he entered the pass-code, with one final higher chord when it was accepted. The door opened and Mack whipped off the tarpaulin that covered his motorboat and flapped the dust from it outside, where it caught in the wind like a kite. This gave his accomplices the cover they needed to emerge from their concealed position and enter the lockup unseen. Mack followed once they were safely stowed inside and closed the door after them. The King, being a lover of fine machinery, admired the customised BT1000 with his keen eye for detail and nodded approvingly as he rounded her. 'This will do nicely.'

Mack seemed pleased and looked proudly upon his vessel.

The winch was summoned at the touch of a button and both the King and the Professor climbed aboard and lay flat on the floor. From the pinnacle of the lockup's pointed roof slid the metal shutters that formed both of its sides to allow for the winch to be lowered through.

'What about heat sensors?' asked the King from his concealed position.

'The guard saw me come in alone and should not think to check them.'

That would not do. 'Go and distract him until we are safely in the water,' he ordered. 'There can be no incidents now.'

Mack exited the lockup once the boat was being hoisted into the air and called out to the guard, shouting about the possibility of rain out there today. The guard did not respond as he guided the motorboat through the compound and left it suspended above the water so that he could check the weather reports scattered about his desk. 'Perfect day for sailing,' he shouted back. With that, the boat was lowered the remaining distance into the water and Mack climbed aboard. He released the boat from the winch's grip and gave a signal to the guard that he was ready to take off. The motor erupted with a mighty roar before simmering down to a hum.

'Do not exceed the speed limit for the harbour,' ordered the King, still hidden.

'That would be a sure way to arouse suspicion,' smirked Mack.

Once clear of the harbour mouth and her patrols, the stowaways crawled out from their positions and stood up against the roaring rush of wind. The harbour shrunk into the distance amidst the surrounding coastline until it too began to disappear beyond the watery horizon. With the watchful eye of the Company left far behind, the King took out his computer and restored their system with a simple click. It reappeared on the screen in all its former glory and seemed to exude the relief of the bewildered technicians who had worked frantically to rectify the mysterious crash. Those same technicians would now begin searching for its cause and perhaps stumble upon the faint trace of an alien signal coming from the uncharted forests. But that mattered little now. There was already a sense that they had made it, and each allowed themselves to relax a little and enjoy the ride. All that remained was open road ahead, until there came a bleeping from the cockpit.

'We got company,' shouted Mack. 'Two vessels coming this way.'

'Can we outrun them?' asked the King.

'If we try to outrun them we will create an incident where there need not be one. Let me handle it. I know all the men who sail these waters.'

The boats came into view and Mack cut the motor.

'Handle it,' warned the King. 'Or I will.' Without uttering another word, he stripped off his clothes and dived silently into the sea.

'Where has he gone?' asked the Professor, shocked and dismayed at being left to endure this encounter with only Mack there to protect him. He scanned the water surrounding the boat and could see no sign of him.

'I wouldn't worry about that boy,' said Mack, as they bobbed up and down on the choppy mid-channel waves. 'I know killers when I see them. They were my business. And that boy is as cold as they come.'

The first of the boats pulled up along their starboard side while the second stopped a little distance off. Ropes were thrown from the first boat to Mack's and the two were pulled tightly together. The Professor looked upon the leathery faces of these seafarers and decided that these were no fishermen. It was the oldest of the crew of three that stepped aboard and shook hands with Mack as he glanced around his vessel. He had greasy dark grey hair that curtained his weather-beaten face and his light-blue eyes gave him a wolf-like demeanour. His left leg limped slightly when he walked and he shuffled uneasily on it when he stood still. The Professor thought he detected a little disappointment on his face when Mack first presented himself.

'Should have known it was you,' he sneered. 'The waters are quiet these days. It has been a long time since we had your boys out here ripping it up.'

'Those were the days.'

The wolf-like eyes of the old seafarer settled upon the battered and bandaged figure of the Professor, and Mack seemed keen to present his accolades. 'This man is the most highly esteemed expert on defence systems in all of the Free world,' he announced. 'He works for the Company, teaching at their Academy.'

The old seafarer was impressed and nodded as he listened. 'And what would a retired man like you need with such expertise?'

'A man like me is never retired,' responded Mack, 'just more selective with his time. There is a small job I have to do that requires a man with his skills.'

'Will you be needing a little extra security on this job?'

'It's not that kind of job. There may be something for you when I get back though. Something that will bring us both a few credits.'

But these empty words fell upon distracted ears and the old seafarer walked to the back of the boat and picked up the King's fur jacket from the pile of clothes he had left there.

'That belongs to the third member of our group,' claimed Mack in a boastful manner. 'He went for a swim when we stopped. A man of nobility, and who it was that brought me this job. The King of Hexlon.'

'The King of Hexlon is dead.'

'But his son lives.'

The old seafarer laughed and dismissed Mack's tale with a grunt.

This seemed to enrage Mack, who turned their computer to face him. 'How else would I have this?'

'What is it?'

'Only an hour ago did we shut down the Company's system,' bellowed Mack, demonstrating its power with a few keystrokes. 'We have access to their most secured sites and have the power to take down any defence system we please. It is the Shadow-disk.'

The old seafarer inspected the screen more closely and shook his head in amazement as Mack traversed through the restricted realm of cyberspace. 'You could take over the Free world with such a system!' he said with cool excitement. 'You could make yourself rich beyond belief!'

'Our mission does not involve monetary gain.'

The old seafarer sighed. 'I'm afraid that ours does,' he said, producing a pistol from his belt.

'That was a mistake, old friend.'

Two shots rang out and his shipmates fell dead. The old seafarer looked around to see where the shots had come from and his eyes narrowed upon the second boat. He could just about make out the single figure standing naked at its head with no sign of its crew behind him. There was a splash in the water nearby, as Mack cast an old anchor overboard and the seafarer's attention returned to the situation at hand. As he raised the pistol in Mack's direction, his one good leg was taken from him, caught in the rope that held the anchor, and he was helpless in following it overboard and all the way down to the bottom of the sea.

As Mack began hacking at the ropes that bound the old seafarer's boat to his, the King pulled alongside on the second boat and riddled the floor with bullets, through which the sea took hold. He did the same with the other once Mack had released them and looked around apprehensively. 'They may have been talking to others before they encountered us, or the radar of a nearby ship might notice three boats becoming one. We can take no chances. Full speed ahead to the wastelands.'

Each fell into a well of thought as they skimmed along the waves and let their imaginations race ahead of them.

Soon, the sulphurous air of the wastelands rang loud in their nostrils and the King rose from his seat. In the distance to his left, he could see the floating barrier of endless signs, warning travellers that the Paegonaeans' defence grid began from that point. On they travelled with this great barrier parallel to them until the red coastline rose from the horizon ahead. They then veered left and penetrated deep into the formerly protected zone before the water became discoloured and eventually turned to a thick sludge, whereupon the keel of their boat was held firm. They each hopped out and sunk knee-deep in the soft mire and began wading their way to the shore with large uneasy strides. Once there, they cleaned themselves off and sat for a moment, gathering their bearings before continuing on.

The festivities had grown steadily out there, with Ferris wheels and carnivals to entertain the gathering masses. Huge marquises had been erected to house them and the Trade-convoy had visited especially with enough provisions to sustain the crowds who had ventured beyond the perimeter of their world. The spirit of it all had wearied a little and the expectant patience of the pilgrims was being tested along the slow route of disillusion. It was this disillusionment that was now pushing many of them closer to the Paegonaean wall, looking for answers.

Families sat around campfires in the previously protected zone, singing songs or telling stories, while others walked around like nomads, in search of some elusive solace. The rickety and makeshift stages of the many preachers were now reinforced with more enduring materials and still they shouted with the same conviction. Some pleaded with the people to leave this place and prepare for a just and righteous defence of their homeland. Others called out and begged for donations to build monuments of repentance. Many were already under construction, as the people tried to communicate with those on the other side through whatever means they could. Some had even began to chip at the wall despite the guards that patrolled this area.

The three men made their way through the confused atmosphere. Only they knew that the defence grid would turn on again at midnight, and this they each contemplated as they looked at the faces around them. A baby wailed inconsolably in the distance and there was a constant rattle of coughs, as the unconditioned lungs of those from Fortress city breathed in the poisonous dust. The wall grew before them as they approached, stretching off in each direction and reaching ever higher into the sky.

'It's like a stadium for the Gods,' remarked the Professor. The ground seemed to tremble slightly as they walked the last stretch and there was a helpless feeling of humility in the vast and night-like shadow it cast. They each held out their hand upon finally arriving at their destination and touched the base of this great wall.

'So, where to now?' asked Mack.

'There should be some kind of way in around here,' the King responded. 'Spread out and search for it.'

After ten minutes of stamping about, the King stepped upon some hollow ground and he called to the others that he had found what they were looking for. He dropped to his knees and swept the dust from what appeared to be some kind of hatch. By the time they arrived, the King was already trying to pull the metal cover from its place, but without any success. Mack dropped to his knees beside him and groaned as he got the tips of his fingers beneath it, but their combined strength could lift it no further. The Professor joined them in their effort and, with the unrestrained might of all three, they managed to lift it clear from the shaft below. An echo reverberated through the long and narrow passageway and was lost in a cavern at the bottom.

The foundations of the great wall went deep underground and eventually gave way to a vast underground chamber that stretched off behind them. It took twenty minutes to climb down the ladder, and the King was first to step upon the metal platform at its base.

The rodents that inhabited this world of everlasting night sniffed the aromatic air and their hungry tummies rumbled at the prospect of fresh meat. Their beady little eyes drew near and gathered upon these huge upright creatures. The King looked around blindly and, with the flick of a match, the torch he held went up, and a collective screech resounded from the cavern.

What lay before them was hardly the red carpet they expected. A thin layer of water trickled down the gently sloping gradient of the cavern beyond and fell into the narrow channel that the platform they stood on crossed. Huge columns held the roof somewhere above them and there was an unpleasant odour in the stagnant air.

'What is this place?' asked the Professor.

'Judging from the water marks on those columns,' answered the King, 'I'd say that much of this was submerged until a day or two ago. It is a sewer. Stay close to the light and watch your step.'

Their feet splashed with every step as they made their way up through the empty cavern and held close together within the bubble of light from the torch. The hungry dwellers of this horrible world encroached upon them as their eyes grew more and more accustomed to the hellish light. The King swung the torch back and forth to fend off their advance when a thunderous thud struck the chamber. Before anyone could recompose themselves or question what it was, another struck, this time louder and more violent. Dirt was falling from the roof above them and the men halted and huddled close together. The ground quaked violently as the intermittent thuds became a constant barrage, like heavy drops of rain in the world of the tiniest insects.

'Midnight!' shouted the King, with the world around them shuddering, as though in the grip of a mighty earthquake.

Through the deafening blasts of untold destruction were the chilling shrieks of the defence grid that made the hairs of all three men stand on end. Thoughts of divine glory became stained with the devastation unfolding out there and haunted by the faces of those they had passed along the way. Hopes of forgiveness and peace would have gone in that instant and the mood of the Free world turn to panic and fear. The consistent rattle began to lessen into distinct thuds as the last of the survivors were mopped up. A deathly silence ensued.

The three men continued on in silence, downcast by false reasoning and the lives they could have saved. Their torch burned low and, from the deepening blackness, there appeared a dull grey ahead and they marched towards it with growing excitement.

'What is it? asked Mack.

'Foundations,' answered the King. 'Like those at the start of the sewer. There should be another wall right above us.'

A small archway through these foundations took them along a narrow corridor laid with bricks and lit with lights that ran along its ceiling. Cool fresh air rushed against them, as though the stuffy sewer was sucking it into her putrid lungs and the King was returned to thoughts of high honour. At last, the end was in sight with a ladder reaching out from the tunnel and into the fragrant darkness of Paegonaean night.

'We shall rest here for a few hours,' said the King, standing at the base of the ladder. 'We will need daylight to venture any further.'

– XI –

Paegona

A knee-high mist held over the countryside and birds were singing in its trees. The King peeked his head from the narrow shaft and scanned the landscape carefully before committing himself more fully. Once out and upon Paegonaean soil, the King took a few steps forward and drew in a deep breath of fresh air. His eyes slowly roamed the surrounding scenery in the vague hope that something extraordinary was there to be found. A wall of equal magnitude to that which enclosed the Free world stood a short distance behind and arched indiscernibly along its curved perimeter. Cattle grazed undisturbed and the birds remained on their perches as the men pulled themselves from the shaft. This place seemed no different from any other wild pasture, but for the unnatural twilight of the rising sun which had yet to clear the wall behind.

'We have bypassed the outer ring,' explained the King.

During the war, the Paegonaeans' entire war machine was restricted to the area held between the outermost wall and that before it. As the front line was pushed forward this set distance again, another wall was built, and their armies moved into this new sector. This was how their worldwide conquest progressed.

Beyond the narrow channel of pasture, running parallel to the wall behind them, lay a forest of tall but youthful trees. Mountaintops rose high above it in the distance and their promise enticed the King to venture further into this land. 'There seems to be nothing out here for us. We will find better opportunities to make ourselves known at the other side of this forest.'

What a strange and wonderful woodland they found it to be once they entered into its fold. It was as though everything around them came alive in acknowledgement of their presence. Flowers seemed to turn and greet them and a whispering breeze carried their delicate fragrance. Both Mack and the Professor walked on, so deeply entranced by their environment that they had not noticed the King fall behind with unusual distraction. His agitated air forced him to stop altogether and he called out for the other two to listen. Mack and the Professor stopped and attuned their ears to their surroundings, but could hear only the rustling of the leaves.

The King seemed a world apart from his colleagues as they started off again through the undergrowth. There were ephemeral noises floating in the air; indistinct whispers that lay just beyond his comprehension. He spun around to catch each new breath as it spoke, as though invisible fairies buzzed about him, and his head muddled and grew dizzy. The voices were joyous and excited, but still the King could not understand them. Then, a more familiar voice shouted to him and the mysterious apparitions fell quiet.

'There is something up ahead!' Mack informed him.

He led the King along the wild course of undergrowth and they joined with the Professor who had crouched behind some bushes. More and more sunlight was breaking through the thinning cover above as the forest abated up ahead and gave way to a vast open space beyond. It was then that the King spotted the little wooden shack, huddling amidst the failing trees in the shallow depths of the forest. Even with the binoculars, there was little to be discerned from this building. It was only large enough for the simple existence of a single man and there was some sort of vehicle parked behind it. The King set down the binoculars, breathed in deeply and closed his eyes, as though entering into meditation, and walked off to investigate upon reopening them.

There was nothing unusual about the little hut itself; planks of wood nailed together in unadorned fashion, most probably by the hermit who now lived there. A simple stone barbecue sat in front of it, between two tree-stumps positioned at each end. The final stretch of forest became an orchard as the King approached the little shack, with trees of all kind bearing fruit around him. He could tell that there was no one home as he walked up the path and pushed the door open gently. There was nothing inside but for a neat little bed and a table, upon which, sat an odd collection of stones. He left the room undisturbed and went around the back, where his eyes grew in wonderment upon beholding the curious machine that sat there. With no wheels to support or move it, the tractor-like vehicle seemed to hover several inches above the ground. The design was sleek and pioneering, perhaps a little out of place in this rustic landscape. The King then returned to the group with the news of what he had seen.

'Do not be afraid,' he said, as they continued on together. 'There is no one around here. We are quite alone.'

No one spoke as they stepped from the forest into the vast meadow beyond. They were each struck dumb upon beholding the glorious and unspoilt realm of nature that stretched on in every direction for as far as the eye could see. It was as though anything could have been possible at that moment; from an ambling herd of dinosaurs emerging from behind a cluster of trees to the landing of a spacecraft packed full with heavenly warriors. Rather than seeming ancient or advanced, this world seemed somehow remote from time and humankind. The men wondered how such natural beauty could be possible so near to the scorched world outside, and had this land not once been scorched itself as the front line of the defence grid rolled across it. Mack pointed out another little shack some way down, snuggled in the forest with the same tractor-like vehicle parked next to it.

Each sweep of the horizon brought new pleasures to the eye, but there was no sign of life anywhere. They ventured out a little further into this earthly paradise and found themselves captivated by each of its individual aspects. Everything had been meticulously choreographed and carefully tended by the discerning eye of the people who lived in the little shacks all around this area. But where were these workers now?

The King walked deeper into the warm sun-lit glade and pointed to a faint billow of smoke, rising from behind some trees in the distance. Its plume grew darker and reached further into the azure sky and the three men watched it develop with tingling anticipation. Whatever it was that lay beyond those trees was now their new destination, and the men gathered themselves for its journey.

'I shall go ahead alone,' announced the King, and then turned towards his colleagues. 'You will stay here by the edge of the forest and await my return.'

'How are we to protect you if you leave us behind?' said Mack, obviously bothered by this command.

'I need no protection from these people.'

'But, why leave us here?'

'They will hear you coming,' the King answered smoothly, wilting Mack's testing ego with the natural authority of its delivery. 'I do not wish to startle them.'

His defiance faded into an uneasy submission and Mack sat down on the grass in defeat as the King took off with a sprint through the meadow. He soon disappeared from their view amidst the beauty of this Edenic world and did not stop running until he reached the cluster of trees, at the other side of which, lay his concealed destination. Strange sensations raced through his body as he silently pulled himself through its cultivated undergrowth. Again the whispers stirred.

The ghostly voices grew steadily as he approached and became more distinct. *What was that?* said one as it passed. *They are close,* said another. A smell of roasted meat filled the King's nostrils as he slithered the final distance through the forest floor and pulled apart some bushes.

Six men in robes of black sat on two logs facing one another with a fire roaring between them. His attention was quickly drawn upon a curious craft that hovered close to the ground some distance beyond and the King rose to his feet to view it more clearly. It was entirely black in colour and of an egg-shaped design with no discernible front or back to it. His eyes returned to the six men before him, all now watching him intently, and he emerged from the forest with his hands raised. A door on the craft, where before there had been none, slid open, and a seventh man emerged and made his way down an unfolding platform. Captivated by the craft's graceful movement, the King lowered his hands and asked who they were.

All six of the men remained seated as the seventh made his way between the logs on which they sat. 'We are the Knights of the Innermost Circle,' he answered in a strong yet accentless voice. 'It is our duty to escort you to the heart of our land, where your mission will be explained in full.'

'Where?'

'To the Innermost Circle, of course.'

The King was shown aboard the craft and was seated with buckles fastening around him. Its impenetrable black exterior was, from the inside, almost all transparent window but for that beneath his feet and was tinted by varying degrees to counter the brightness of the sun. The King was excited by the prospect of flying in such an innovative piece of machinery, though he struggled with its concept against all that he knew of aviation. The remaining Knights bustled aboard and filled the seats around him, leaving those on each side of him empty.

There was not a sound as the craft launched itself into the sky with such an imperceptible motion that the King would have thought them still on the ground had the skyline outside not shifted. Within an instant, they arrived at the edge of the forest and the craft lowered itself slowly upon the meadow below.

Mack watched with unbelieving eyes as it suddenly appeared overhead, while the Professor fled back into the woods. As it touched on the ground, the door slid open and the King showed himself and shouted that their transport had arrived. Despite their initial shock and natural apprehension, both men finally boarded and took their seats in this strange vehicle. Again, the craft seemed to leap effortlessly into the sky and they were soon rising high above the grand forest, revealing its vast system of lakes and meadows.

'I had no idea the world could be so beautiful,' muttered the Professor.

'Our land has returned to a natural state in preparation for what is to come,' responded the leader of the Knights. 'Now, we wait, so that we may rebuild as instructed.'

'Instructed?' asked the Professor. 'By whom?'

The Knight pointed towards the ceiling of the craft and his eyes followed on beyond. 'By them.'

Before the Professor could enquire further, Mack began to struggle in his harness and gawped out the window. 'What is that?' he shouted.

Without looking out or acknowledging the slender obelisk-type construction, much taller than the tallest tower in Fortress city, the same Knight continued. 'We call them Structures, for the message from our great descendants, by which we received their design, contained no specific name for them. There are thousands of these Structures across our land, all equally spaced apart. A long metallic chime, made from the same composition of materials, hangs within each of them, and all are the exact same size, shape and weight, so that when one is struck, they will each resonate sympathetically with its neighbours. Once our world is complete, their unified note shall be heard through the ages and herald a new era of enlightenment. That day will soon be upon us,' he added, glancing towards the King.

They passed many more of these Structures and the cities from which they sprang. Had it not been for the cities at the base of each of these Structures, one may have assumed this land to be deserted altogether of humankind. There were no highways linking neighbouring cities together or planes in the sky shuttling between those more distant. It was indeed a primitive scene, but it somehow held a sense of great and unprecedented advancement. Mack and the Professor watched the wonders of this world pass beneath them while the King stared ahead blankly, a slight smile curling the ends of his mouth.

Their journey continued with increasing speed, zipping over wall after wall on their journey deep into the heart of the Paegonaean Empire. Each new sector, or Ring, as the Knight referred to them, proved more beautiful than the last, as those who lived there demonstrated their solidarity and harmony by creating a landscape worthy of this new world; each differing only slightly from the others, as though they served a different purpose. These walls then grew smaller in a gradual state of deconstruction until they were nothing more than the celebrated ruins of the Innermost Circle.

Whatever hope they had of landing shortly, however, was to be continually postponed, as the craft showed no sign of slowing down. How fast they were travelling was difficult to judge, but they had been in the air for over four hours when the leader of the Knights leaned forward to speak. 'We are now approaching the first forest,' he said. 'The first village lies at its heart.'

All eyes turned to the eternal countryside below and the thick forest that sprung up from it. So immense was this forest that it consumed the entire landscape and there were several of the hallowed Structures poking from its leafy surface.

'There are people down there,' shouted the Professor, as the craft began to slow and lower slightly. 'There must be thousands of them.' They seemed like ants from this height, rummaging about on the forest floor and waving from the branches of its tallest trees. There were wooden houses there too, cradling amongst these branches and gradually merging together to form a sprawling city of tree-dwellers. The Professor then looked along the top of the never-ending forest with still no sign of the first village and softly muttered. 'There must be millions of them.'

A Structure rose steadily from the forest just ahead and the craft descended even further overhead the wooden city. They could then see the large clearing from which it rose; a hill with a reservoir atop it, the overflow of which fed the streams down its sides and the pools and lakes around its base. Houses dotted the landscape here and there and huddled more tightly around the base of the Structure that rose from the corner of the clearing; a stone-throw from the surrounding forest. All of the villagers had come out to watch the arrival of their foretold guests. The craft hovered overhead for some time, as though carefully choosing its spot, before descending upon a stretch of ground near some fields of corn and wheat, some way from the more residential area at the base of the Structure.

The villagers began clapping as the door of the craft slid open and the three figures emerged. The Professor hobbled down the platform on his crutch and, upon reaching the bottom, brushed the luscious grass of this village with his hand. Mack and the King joined him moments later and the three men stood there as the clapping fell into a deep and profound silence.

The Structures they passed on their journey had delighted from the air, but their magnitude could only truly be appreciated when standing near one and watching it reach high into the sky above. They were made from strange metallic bricks and each contained a spiralling staircase that wound around the chime it held, all the way to the top. There were around a hundred small lodgings built around it.

As no one approached from the still-silent crowd, the men took a moment longer to take in all around them and breathe in the essence of this sacred place. A large totem pole stood behind them and had been carved into the broad form of a Neanderthal. If this was south of the village, then to the east and west stood two more totems with distinct shaping to both of them. Though both were distant, the three men could clearly see that the one to the west took the form of their evolutionary contemporary; lean with eyes of hopeful glory, while the figure to the east was shaped more disproportionately. Its eyes were huge and elliptical on a head grown large with the knowledge of our universe and a body grown small with technological advancement.

'It is the progression of man,' explained a villager, as he walked towards them, draped in a flowing white robe. 'For the foreseeable future, at least.' This villager then pointed to the tightly packed posts that ran between these totems and marked the perimeter of their village. On each of these posts was an engraving that progressively marked the increments of evolution between each of the celebrated stages. They noticed immediately that these posts continued on from the totems east and west to join with a northern totem hidden somewhere behind the hill. What strange half-breed would be represented there, they wondered.

'My name is Ohan, the gatherer,' announced the villager. 'I have been chosen to welcome you to our village and show you to your lodgings.'

There was not a whisper in the air as the three men were led through the parted sea of onlookers. Each of these villagers had a role in this society and all were busy in the overall maintenance of their isolated community. In the crop fields that separated the main concentration of the village from the landing-site, farmers leaned upon their rakes and spades and watched as the outsiders were led by. Those in the village itself were more diversely employed, with occupations ranging from entertainers and storytellers to teachers, public speakers, healers and any other post that their little society required. All of these villagers, from the very oldest to the smallest infants, were dressed in the same white robes. Women stood in groups alongside the banks of the hill's streams and watched in the same silent manner as everyone else. Beside them were weaved baskets stacked high with soiled robes while those just washed were stacked in others. The noise from the surrounding forest rang dimly all around.

'You have nothing to fear from those beyond our village,' said Ohan. 'They have been gathering in the forest since the beginning. It was here that our visionary father lived; the man who wrote the book, which has since become our Bible, that prompted the people of the old world to rise against their oppressors and begin us on our sacred journey. He wrote everything that was to be done for the revolution and his assassination was a catalyst in the great war. Then came the message from our descendants when our crusade was almost complete, vindicating his every command and earning him the title of visionary father. His bloodline still flows today through the veins of his great grandson; a man we call the Descendant. It is this man, his wife and daughter that you are here to meet.' Ohan then turned towards the King and asked. 'You are familiar with the prophecies?'

The King shook his head. 'I heard them long ago when I was a child and vaguely recollect them.'

Ohan looked back to the hill they climbed and smiled. 'Then you have much to learn.'

A strong mid-afternoon sun shone down on them and the air was thick with nature's fragrance. Ohan took the time to explain that the four totems and interlinking posts were relatively new and that they were the only such markings in all of their land. 'As the path before us becomes clear,' he said, 'our world shall become a shrine to the idols of righteousness and truth.'

It seemed that they were now walking more directly towards two houses of identical construction, only a metre and a half apart, about halfway up the hill. The relationship between these little bungalows was further tightened by the fact that they shared a wooden table just before them. For the first time on their steep trek, the men stopped and turned to take in the view, now that their altitude had risen above the canopy of the surrounding forest. All that any civilisation needs to flourish is water and nature, and both were in abundance there. The ancient forest seemed infinite and impassable and created a sense that this little village was a world all of its own.

A beautiful woman in the middle years of life appeared from the little house to the left and looked upon the approaching figures with a haughty air. Her form was slender and flowing beneath her robe of white and there was something about her deep-blue eyes that the King found vaguely familiar. Flowers adorned her long golden hair with two plaited strands hanging just before her ears. She took off with a quick step and nodded curtly as she passed them and did not look back as she descended the hill into the village.

'She is the wife of the Descendant,' said Ohan, 'a woman known as the Queen. Though she comes from no royal lineage herself, it is her daughter, and the role that this young woman will play in the future of our world that has earned her this title. Do you remember what it was from your childhood story?' Ohan asked of the King.

The King's eyes narrowed into thought before shaking his head that he did not know.

'Do not worry,' said Ohan. 'It will come to you soon, I am sure.'

Ohan opened the door to the one-roomed abode and showed the guests inside, explaining that this house had just recently been built for the coming of age of the Descendant's daughter. For the duration of their stay, however, she had agreed to return to her parents' house next door and asked only that they make themselves at home. There was a bed for each of them and a wardrobe stocked with fresh linen and the village's white robes.

After Ohan dismissed himself from their presence, the King gave his men the simple order of bathing and to prepare for the evening ahead. This they did and, upon their return, lay down on their beds to relax.

'This land is strange,' said Mack.

'It is nothing like I expected,' claimed the Professor. 'These are highly exceptional people. They do not seem to talk amongst themselves. They just smile and continue with their work. Everyone is happy.'

Mack shook his head, as though universal contentment could only be bad news. 'We may be sacrificed to some God yet.'

The King did not take part in the conversation. His mind instead rattled through its archives for the old rhyme that now bore such importance. It had often been told and retold when he was a child being lowered into the depths of sleep by the Priest's soothing voice, but never had it been repeated through the years that followed. *A king, a wise man and a thief, to decide the fate of mankind.* Fragments came back to him in the form of an outstanding word here and there, sometimes leading on to a fractional sentence. Uncovering this rhyme would be key to understanding why they were there and what was expected of them now.

A knock at the door startled the men from their sleep and slowly they rose from their beds. By the time the King opened the door, he found the figure that had knocked wandering amidst a small patch of flowers nearby. He looked up from the close scrutiny he bestowed upon each bud and blossom and a smile broke across his face as he walked towards the King. 'I do apologise for waking you,' he began. 'I confess to being a little impatient when I am excited.' His eyes seemed to glow with incandescent shades as they studied the contours of the King's bruised face. 'My name is Joseph, the Descendant,' he resumed. 'It is with the greatest honour that we welcome you to our land. Our people have waited many years for this day and hope that you share in the excitement you bring. Ohan, the gatherer, has already answered your initial questions, but many more have filled your heads since then, I am sure. Consider me your servant in this regard.'

Mack appeared at the door and yawned. 'What is it you want us to do?' he asked.

The Descendant simply explained that all would become clear soon. Two families had been chosen through a random selection to dine with the Professor and Mack that evening, while the King would join with the Descendant and his family. The Professor would join the Somerville family in the village and Mack would dine with the Treore family near one of the orchards.

'And how do we find these families?' asked Mack.

The Descendant responded as he turned and took the King under his arm. 'They will find you.'

And with that, the Professor and Mack were given liberty to roam as they wished and both disappeared off down the hill.

'You understand why you are here?' asked the Descendant as they began walking.

The King drew a long and slow breath. 'There are voices in the air that whisper. I cannot tell what they say exactly but know they all look forward to something great. It is like I can hear the thoughts of the world around me and it is sometimes very confusing.'

At that, the Descendant nodded sympathetically. 'The transition to our world will be difficult for your colleagues, but you are one of us. You carry our blood and therefore share in our vision. You have nothing to fear from these *voices*.'

They sat at the shared table outside their houses and continued talking for some time about the different worlds they came from. Mid-afternoon passed through late afternoon and soon they were entering into early evening; the lengthening shadow of the Structure slowly sweeping along its course, like that which points the passing hours on a sundial. Fires were being lit in the village and there was a sudden rise in activity all around with the dull murmur of conversation rising from the collective silence. Those tables and benches that had lain vacant amongst the houses of this community were now filling with its people, as preparations for dinner got underway. Horses pulling carts laden with fresh meat and sacks filled with fruit and vegetables stopped by each of these tables and their ware perused and selected by those who sat there. Soon, the air was heavy with the smell of cooking food and its moments of silence rich with thought.

A few of these carts arrived at the base of the hill and began their laboured journey up it, zigzagging between the tables of gathered families and friends. One made its way towards the home of the Descendant and he invited the King to choose the meat. They waited till the fire beneath the grill burned low enough before laying the strips of beef upon it. A weathered metal pot was filled with water and into this went a selection of vegetables before being placed on the grill beside the meat.

The door to the Descendant's house opened quietly and his wife stepped out from behind it. Each step of her approach was so graceful that it had something of a ghostly disposition. Her eyes inspected the meat and vegetables before she sat down next to the King and nodded salutorily in the direction of both men. This woman did not seem to have much to say for herself, thought the King, though her presence reminded him of the reason he was there that night. She smiled when spoken to and answered with brevity in a mild voice.

With the sun now falling to their right, as though into the midst of the great surrounding forest, the fires of the village rose to replenish its diminishing reign. The shadow cast by the great Structure now stretched along the forest to their left before disappearing altogether amidst the darkness of night. A silence resumed as the villagers began to eat, when a sudden commotion caught the King's attention at the far edge of the village. Seven girls appeared from the forest and made their way along a path through a medley of benches. They were like the petals of a single rose, distributing themselves one by one upon their families until only one remained and made her way up the hill.

Her beauty set her above anything the King had ever seen before and he found himself rising to his feet as she came near. Both the Descendant and his wife smiled at one another before returning their gaze upon the acquainting couple.

'I present to you, my daughter,' said the Descendant proudly. 'The future Queen of our enlightened land.'

The King stood and reached out his hand. As the couple shook, the King found himself drawn to her gaze and something of the old prophecy arose from the depths of his memory. There was something about a Princess in the second half of it... *A woman of direct lineage... would join with the king, and together they would...*

'What exciting times these are,' said the Descendant, interrupting the King's train of thought. 'Here we are, in the very chalice of existence, as the gates of Heaven begin to open, seated with those who hold the key. From a dark age we have emerged to find ourselves upon this peaceful plateau; the threshold of unknown majesty and enlightenment. And it is you, our dear entrusted King, who is at the very centre of all to come. To you, sir,' he toasted, raising a small glass of mushroom wine.

The King graciously accepted.

Once they began to eat, the conversation became less formal

'So, how do you like it here?' was the Princess's first question.

The King smiled towards her and then to the surrounding area. 'I have often dreamt of such a place, and now that I am here, I feel as though... I have finally come home.'

This sparked another formal address from the Descendant, to which the King tried to attune himself, but found his attention drawn helplessly to the young woman across from him. She was very young, he thought, and the Descendant changed the conversation accordingly.

'To keep within the guidelines of the prophecy, we understood that we had to have a daughter after your birth. We had some trouble conceiving however, until just over sixteen years ago, our daughter was born, carrying with her the light of our land.'

The young woman brushed aside her father's remark and turned towards the King. 'Tell us how you received those bruises to your face.'

'It seemed that one of the men who now accompany me had been misinformed as to my arrival and mistook me for an enemy.'

'He attacked you?' asked the Descendant.

'He took down the craft I was piloting with a missile. I was forced to evacuate in mid-air and sustained the injuries you see falling to the ground.'

'A missile!' cried the young woman. 'But you could have been killed!'

'I narrowly escaped.'

'I'm sure you escaped with honours,' laughed the Descendant. 'Your exploits are well known in our land. You are something of an anomaly. You belong to neither world fully, and in this lies your power. Our people look towards you as a saviour. We know everything about you.'

Not everything, the King hoped.

'Do not worry, sacred warrior, your life has been tended by the greatest writers of our land with the single intent of earning you a place in the hearts of our people.' His voice then lowered into a more explanatory tone. 'The price of everlasting peace is indeed a costly one, though once it has been paid in full, it need never be further supplemented. But we are not there yet, and when our people understood what lay ahead, many reacted against it. It seemed that this impending bloodshed could not be tolerated by the serene mind and the very thought of it was enough to taint the purity of our people and lead us from the righteous path. This presented us with a very particular dilemma. However, a possible solution was found in the literature of my great grandfather, and was to become one of the prophecies we speak of today. We did everything in our power to effect the conditions he wrote of and left what we could not alter to providence. It was then that we contacted your father and gave him what he needed to set up his Kingdom. In life, we sometimes make what we assume, at the time, to be mistakes, but whether they are detrimental or conducive to the grander scheme can only be known with hindsight. Our fathers talked as we do now, and the brave King before you set forth on the mission that we now ask of you. The only female relative of age in my great grandfather's bloodline was a distant cousin, and there were whispers at the time that all was not right. This was confirmed when your father failed in his mission, but he was successful, however, in starting off a chain of events which have led us here today, around which, the conditions of the prophecy have aligned perfectly. It is without doubt that you shall be successful in your mission,' said the Descendant, and then added, glancing towards his daughter. 'In both of them.'

Once their evening meals had finished, the younger members of the village excused themselves and dispersed from their familial gatherings to meet with friends and endeavour upon a range of activities. Some made their way out to the surrounding forest and joined in the festivities to be found there, while others stayed within their immediate communities and arranged games with their neighbours. Courting couples mingled through the mixing crowd, meeting with others and conversing with friends before disappearing, hand in hand, into the flowering night on walks along love's path. Young children joined growing crowds around the village's story-tellers and entertainers and gave gasps of intrigue and delight through the collective silence of their engagement. Whilst all this was going on around them, the older members of this village remained where they were or joined others at tables nearby and shared steaming mixtures of potent herbs.

'Would you like to see the old stone ring?' asked the Princess, upon watching the King swallow the last bite of his meal.

They walked off into the night holding hands, across the hill and down the other side. Before them emerged the totem of their evolutionary contemporary, illuminated by the fires that burned in a semi-circle around its base. People there danced and sang and howled to the moon in joy. The Princess stopped upon overlooking this scene and turned towards the King. He wanted more than anything just then to kiss her, but instead she came close to him and held him in a warm embrace. They then followed the course of a small river and left its side near the bottom of the hill and walked some distance to a secluded spot in the midst of a cluster of trees.

A set of moss-covered stones loosely marked the perimeter of a jagged circle and the Princess led her King to the very centre of it. 'These stones were placed here thousands of years ago,' she explained. 'No one knows why. What wonder it would have been to have lived such a mysterious existence!' she exclaimed, looking up at the night sky.

'Such mystery was the cause of all their wars,' answered the King. 'An unenlightened world still needs its Gods, and these they created in their own image. These Gods passed through the generations and sent vast numbers in each of them to fight brutal wars against those who claimed another. Be content, my sweet betrothed, that the imagination is to wither with enlightenment and restrict itself with sacred fact.'

The two embraced once more amid the old stone ring. As they returned home that night, they talked of their lives and the preparation they had undergone for the events that lay ahead. The King bid the Princess goodnight in the garden near the two houses and, after she had closed the door to her parents' house, he wandered off into the night, too thrilled by love to have it subdued by sleep.

– XII –

Worlds Gone and Worlds to Come

The King awoke with his limbs splayed limply amongst the branches of the tree that had cradled him through the night. A breeze swept through the small patch of forest where he now found himself, gently rustling the leaves around him as he struggled upright and watched the people of this strange and wondrous land go about their business. They emerged from their homes and were swept along in a marching tide towards a small forest some distance away, into which they disappeared. Others were emerging from the same patch of forest, having already availed of what lay within its fold, and the opposing groups mingled with a sociable silence. The King's eyes grew heavy as he watched them and, though he was sure he had not fallen asleep, a strange dream-like vision grew from the village, like roots reaching into the sky.

As the trance that held him deepened, an almighty Palace of grey brick sprawled out before him; monumental in its ambition and magnificent in its intricacies. Huge towers reached high into the cloud-filled sky with bridges and raised passageways connecting all as one. Gardens of exquisite beauty lay upon every tier and thick foliage adorned all and poked from every crevice, as though man and nature had come to a truce in its claim of this creation. It unfurled equally in all directions until this sprawling Temple-like construction was the size of a massive city and had consumed the entire landscape and beyond. Flags of white fluttered upon every tower, as though in recognition of some celestial event. Curious whorls then appeared in the sky, where they slowly turned and pulled the surrounding blue of our atmosphere into the darkness of some unknown dimension. From these portals emerged crafts of a distant design that slowed and lowered themselves all over the expansive city. The people below did not seem to mind them, and the King felt as though a caveman upon beholding the indifference of modern man with a sky full of small aircrafts. Instead, these people gathered steadily around the base of the tallest tower, at the very centre of this thriving metropolis. His vision then focussed, by direction of this crowd, upon a balcony on this tower's highest turret, where his young suitor waved ceremoniously to the jubilant crowd below. She was a little older now, and her beauty had only grown stronger with age. Evermore whorls broke in the tranquil sky between the city's innumerable spires and more of these strange crafts entered this realm and set themselves down to partake in the unspecified celebration. The Princess, now the reigning Queen of this land, watched from her tower as the evolutionary blend of humans gathered before her as one; many of whom had travelled back unprecedented distances through time just to be there on this special day. By the beautiful Queen's side stood a boy in the midst of his teenage years, and it was he who stepped forward to speak. As the vision fragmented and its shards began to fade, the King was left with an immense awareness of his own nobility.

How long this vision had detained him, he was unsure, but morning was blossoming more fully and the struggling sun now rose along its arching dominion. His focus returned to the world before him and he noticed now that the villagers wandered about more freely and many were setting about their chores. A couple passed by the edge of the forest in which he lay, walking arm in arm with their children following closely behind and, for the first time in his life, the King felt the sharp pang of loneliness that had before been the very constitution of his existence. Thoughts of the Princess made him climb down from the tree and he pondered the extent of this lust that had taken him. Out in the brightness of the mid-morning sun, the King looked around and wandered off towards an inviting orchard that lay near the very perimeter of the village. He summoned the power of all his senses to recreate every aspect of the Princess in his mind, when he saw a young woman of similar form standing amidst the orchard's fruit-filled trees. It became clear, as he approached, that this was indeed the young woman he was searching for, and he crouched behind a felled and overgrown log so that he may view her undisturbed nature.

The Princess stood on tiptoes with an arm outstretched, offering seeds to the birds in the leaves above whilst whistling softly. A robin watched her carefully and edged towards the tip of a branch before fluttering down towards her. She opened her hand and the tiny bird perched on the tips of her fingers and pecked until the last of the seeds were gone. It then seemed to study her face before venturing further up her arm with almost imperceptible little bounds, whereupon reaching the midway ruffle between her elbow and shoulder, it turned suddenly in the direction of the approaching King and flew off.

'You frightened him,' she said softly, turning to face the King.

The muffled clamour of the crowd beyond the perimeter of the village seemed to lull at that moment, as though to capture all that passed between them. The Princess leaned forward and kissed him. The silence continued as the young Princess withdrew only far enough to gaze into the depths of the King's barbarian eyes, and she whispered. 'You are falling in love with me.'

The King shied slightly from her scrutinising eyes before she placed her hand upon his cheek and reassured him. 'It is okay,' she smiled. 'Our falling in love is as important as the task that our people have asked of you. But infinitely easier, I should hope.'

'All has become clear to me,' said the King softly, a dour sadness seizing his mighty heart. Only now that he had something to leave behind did this affect him so wretchedly. 'I have seen the future and I am not there.'

The Princess bowed her head in helpless sorrow before resuming. 'But our son shall live on. You will always be by my side when he is born and you will reign through him.' She kissed him again and both gave themselves fully to the embrace that followed. At that moment, the surrounding forest seemed to erupt in joy and the noise they created rose to a thunderous celebration. Nothing more needed to be said, and the royal couple began to walk in the direction of the towering Structure and through the main concentration of the village, held tightly in the others' grasp.

Most of the houses were now empty, as everyone had been employed in a variety of tasks in preparation for the ceremony this evening. Those there only seemed to be passing and quickly rushed off once they had got what they needed. Some way from the Structure that dominated the village lay a sacred area where no houses had been built, and this was the focal point of everyone's attention. There had started a loud chorus of banging, as carpenters hammered lengths of wood together into benches. Gardeners trod softly through the surrounding gardens, selecting the most fully blossomed and radiant flowers, to be arranged later by those responsible for the displays that would decorate the event. Farmers worked their plots and made sure the village would have all it needed for the subsequent banquet. Those who found themselves with an idle hour spent it carrying wood from the forest, and this they piled high in the village's sacred area.

The Princess squeezed the King's arm tightly when she saw the preparations, and those who passed the betrothed couple stopped and bowed before them; a custom never before seen in this land. They each understood what was to come of this royal alliance and already its sense of hierarchy came instinctually to them.

Once they had satisfied themselves that all was well underway, the Princess led the King back across the village to that small forest where he had watched the people come and go before his vision. The undergrowth through it had been compacted into a solid surface and they held each others' hand as they walked amongst its trees. A group of children filled baskets with the fallen fruit that had been poked free by their colleagues in the branches above. These baskets were then quickly couriered through the forest to the area held in its midst, to where the young couple now walked.

There was a sound of water falling up ahead, punctuated with the occasional splash and the sounds of laughter and loud conversation. The sound grew louder as they approached and beyond the last row of trees lay a pool, into which poured the river that flowed down the hill to form a waterfall of intense natural beauty. Children played around the edge of the pool while others bathed beneath the cascading water or swam from bank to bank. Those who entered took off their robes and discarded them in one of several large sacks that lined the perimeter of the pool, between which were tables laid with selections of fruit. The Princess lifted off her robe with one motion and dived into the cool water. She emerged just before the waterfall and motioned for the King to come and join her.

The surrounding embankment had been set with stone and the King was surprised, as he waded in, to find that its deepening floor had also been tiled with flat rocks. Once the level of the water reached his navel, he dived underneath and glided beneath the roar of the waterfall to find the Princess waiting on the other side. A more private world existed there behind the translucent screen of cascading water and the Princess pressed the King against some rocks with her body.

The Descendant and his wife stood by the bank and watched as the two eventually emerged. The Royal couple swam back to the edge of the pool in perfect unison and were handed two fresh robes by a rotund little woman, who then dutifully curtseyed before them. A smile broke across the Descendant's face upon witnessing this and he turned to his wife and said. 'It has begun already.'

When the King and the Princess had dried and pulled on their fresh robes, they walked towards her parents. The Queen pulled a strand of hair from her daughter's face and looked lovingly at her for some time before embracing her tightly. While still holding her daughter, she glanced towards her suitor and commented almost tearfully. 'You look so well together.'

The Descendant took the King under his arm and suggested that the two of them take a walk through the forest and around the lake that lay beyond. They set off in this manner; the upper torso of the highly evolved totem towering above the trees to their right as they followed alongside the stream that ran from the pool to the lake.

'I saw it all today,' said the King, as they began along its banking. 'The future... The Empire to come. I saw it before me like it was already there.'

The Descendant nodded and began. 'The old world's perception of time was of the smallest measurement passing on to the next and so on. But time is a continuum that spans the abyss of eternity, existing in the past and the future as it does in the present. With knowledge comes the expansion of perception, and ultimate knowledge, theoretically, would be to see and understand this continuum in its entirety, bestowing divine-like enlightenment to those who possessed it. Though ultimate knowledge lies some way off, it is not uncommon for we Paegonaeans to glimpse the future of the path we are on, as one would recall a memory from their past. This is an honour granted to the peacefully-evolved mind. My great grandfather was the first to see the future and he documented what he saw in his novel, which inspired everything and gave us the prophecies we hold today. He saw all of this,' said the Descendant, waving his hand to summarize all that lay around them.

'Society has radically changed since his day,' he continued, just as the distant half-breed totem at the head of the village came into view. 'He had been born into the final stages of a monetary system that had thrived on war and disharmony for so long that it had convinced the people that lasting global peace was an impossible dream. Only a crooked civilisation can be built upon the foundations of a monetary system. There is greed inherent in it, and it will always be tilted to favour its architects. Success and ethics come into conflict in such a system, therefore, one struggles to maintain a coherent set of standards by which to live, creating a chaotic and confused society. The pursuit of money was its lifeblood; so much so, that it was the only thing that made sense. To have a lot meant contentment, luxuries and status, while having little meant hunger, fear and denunciation. And so, man became competitive and self-conscious and he evolved accordingly. Employment was essential for those who wished to fulfil the natural ambition of doing well and providing for one's family, and so, the people were forced to work in the factories of those who garnered the world's wealth for themselves. This cycle of consumerism is the very engine of the monetary system and it spins and spins until the masses are left with nothing and the elite have it all. This elite then grew oppressive with the power they gained and their establishment was to be maintained at all costs. Revolutionary technologies, cleaner and more efficient ways of doing things, were suppressed so that those who grew rich yesterday in the established fields would continue to grow rich tomorrow. The products they produced in their factories were designed to last only a handful of months, as long-lasting and durable products would need only to be bought once and would not require a service industry, which employed even more consumers. They poisoned our planet with unnecessary waste in the name of their own profit, and by this method, kept the system recycling. But this system, like everything about it, was built to gradually collapse. Once the elite had everything, they no longer needed their factories and workhouses. The puppet governments of the old world fell to reveal a darker world of slavery. Those in debt or on social benefit schemes were forced into hard labour, building the palaces for their new masters. Even education cost money, and its price rose according to the wishes of the elite so that more and more of the masses would remain ignorant and know nothing of the world around them. The price of food and commodities then soared so high that the people had to sell whatever pittance they had left just to survive. They had become the peasantry in a new world order, where the sons and daughters of the greedy elite were to be the new royalty.'

'Then what happened?'

'There was a famine amidst the anarchy, designed and instigated by the elite to lower the number of the peasantry and weaken their collective will. Mankind was growing weaker and weaker, accepting everything that was brought upon them without fighting back or demanding more. But, with their cities rife with disease and destruction, there were some who took to the countryside and returned to the eternal and abundant essence of nature. These people were the forefathers of the Paegonaean regime, from whom we are descended. It was in the forests of our world that the resistance against the old world formed. A worldwide revolution then began with people taking to the streets of the elite's cities in protest of the horrendous fate that had been brought upon them and they demanded a better future for all. Curfews were imposed across the globe and measures taken to suppress any further level of uprising. The people responded with unreserved attacks on official buildings, strengthening the resolve of the elite for tighter security and a harsher regime imposed upon the subjugated people. Meanwhile, the communes of the countryside were growing strong for the war they now saw as inevitable. Lies and false allegations were disseminated by the ruling power to convince their weak and demoralized citizens of the treachery of this resistance and justify the atrocities their armies were about to commit. But the resistance had been better prepared than they thought and great losses were recorded on both sides throughout the world. Cities were won back in some places while vast expanses of forests and their inhabitants lay smouldering in others; the world now divided more clearly. A shaky truce was brokered.

'It was during this time of relative tranquillity that work began on the first circular city; the design of which had been outlined by my great grandfather in his celebrated novel. It was to be a clean and efficient metropolis that would serve as a prototype for those that followed. People came from all over and united under this common goal, travelling thousands of miles to help in its creation and resources were procured from wherever they could be found. Problems arose and were solved, as the fine details of such a city were decided upon, and it took the million-strong workforce just over five years to complete. It was named Paegona, and many more of these circular cities were to appear across the resistant territory in the years that followed. The technical advances uncovered from such an undertaking armed us with a new range of technology and our cities were superior in every way to those of the old world. High efficiency labour automation coupled with scientifically managed resources allowed for a near fluid, near scarcity-less environment, which could be operated by only a small fraction of its citizens. With all that one needed readily available to everyone, there was no longer any reason to hoard or steal items, as there was no longer a market in which to trade them. If someone wanted to play tennis, for example, they would visit the recreational area outside the city and visit one of many courts. There, they would borrow a set of rackets made from the finest and longest-lasting materials, play their game, and return them once they had finished. There were no laws to prevent anyone from taking them home, of course, but the citizens of Paegona soon learned that there was little point transporting them and taking up room in their living space when a set would be made available when they next needed them.

'What was more astonishing was the evolution of our people. Mental illnesses, long-thought to be the symptoms of an imperfect society, began to diminish and ultimately grew extinct within three generations. From as early as this time, the first shards of enlightenment were recorded, and this was the split from our cousin-man of the old world that set us upon the path we now tread. We began to dominate all sporting activities and our music, art and poetry was unprecedented.

Something beautiful had been uncovered, and the order was given for more cities.'

'These cities must have been a great burden to build?'

'The first were, but those that followed simply clicked into place once their constituent parts had been assembled.'

'How so?'

'The hub of each of these circular cities was what we called a Central Database of Resources; a system something like a library of all technical knowledge with a fully automated manufacturing centre which was like the hands of the library's brain. When a citizen wanted something that was not readily available to all, they simply went on-line and connected with the CDR and searched for functionality, and only when a product was requested was it put together and delivered through an automated subterranean delivery system. This central system combined all our technical knowledge with catalogues of every resource at its disposal to make the most efficient construction decisions. If a resource grew scarce at any one time, the CDR simply adjusted production methods and informed the manufacturing centre of the next best material or combination of materials. Everything was overseen by a small group of our citizens known as Technicians. These were posts of honour allotted to the experts of their particular fields. If someone were to go to the CDR and input an acceptable resolution to a newly-arisen problem, they were then asked to become part of the technical team relevant to the idea. The CDR was constantly revolving with those who wished to partake in the system, like an election of the willing, in a society that was always seeking to improve. As there was no such thing as money in this society, they received no pay for their services other than bearing the fruits of a new way of life. Jobs like bankers, lawyers, accountants, politicians, advertisers and peacekeepers had become obsolete, as well as the cybernation of other jobs from factory workers to the medical profession. Doctors were replaced with optical scanners, connected directly to the CDR, which then informed the automated surgery devices, which then completed the subsequent operation more precisely than the human surgeons they replaced. When the minds of our people had been freed from the daily grind and stress of the monetary system, we began moving into an uncharted realm of pre-enlightenment. And once a city was running smoothly, its CDR was then programmed to create the components for another, and soon we had cities rolling off our conveyor belts.'

'But how did this world of high technology evolve into what is now?'

'That world was merely a step in the crossover process; a halfway point between the old world and the new. War was coming, everyone could see it, and the reward for victory was to be everlasting peace. By now, of course, we had established ourselves as the Paegonaean Empire. We programmed the CDR of every city to fuel this war effort, and within months we had a military superior to those who stood against us and a generation of men and women willing to lay down their lives for the generations to come. The sacrifice of those who died during this dark campaign will always be remembered through the beauty and tranquillity of the world today. By the time we had perfected the defence grid, the war had already been won, and we prepared for final victory. It was then that our satellites received the message that was to change the course of life as we knew it. Those who had sent it claimed to be descendants of Earth from a time in the future when the physics of time travel had been mastered. They immediately advised us on postponing the annihilation of what remained of the old world, and instead, suggested that we build the wall around it and get on with things without them. Their message also included some hints of technology and the blueprints for the Structures you see about our land, which they spoke of as a test of our readiness to receive further instructions. These Structures sapped us of resources and the cities fell so that they could be constructed, and our world then returned to the more natural state you see about you today. This was our test.'

'All that remains now is my mission,' said the King gravely.

The Descendant nodded. 'If you can see beyond it, you have already achieved it.'

It was now midday and the Descendant excused himself from the King's company, explaining that he had much to do before this evening, and left him there by the edge of the lake. The King thought of the Priest as he stood there and imagined what he would say to him if he were there now. What would he make of all this?

All was now in the final stages of preparation for the ceremony tonight. Last minute touches were being added to the large stage which had just been lifted into position and now stood proudly with long rows of benches around it to seat the entire village. The King mingled amidst the medley of employment, savouring the cordial ambience that hung in the air. A little old woman approached with a steaming bowl of stew in her cupped hands. She held out the bowl for the King to take and he accepted this offering and returned her kindness with a gentle smile. Its flavoursome aroma instantly aroused the hunger that had lain dormant beneath the reflections that had consumed his mind that day. He then found a quiet corner to enjoy his meal and spent the rest of that afternoon on a solitary wander around the village.

With the sun now setting amidst a haze of red and purple that darkened the gilded clouds, the King thought it time to return to his abode. Youthful cries of playful delight grew distant as he ascended the steep hill towards the two houses that sat side by side. Smoke chugged from chimneys upon every house he passed, as those situated within prepared for the ceremony that evening. Upon coming into view of the two houses, he noticed that candles had been lit in both of them. Someone moved around in the house to the left while the light in his own remained constant. There was a presence inside that was neither Mack nor the Professor, yet it was no stranger, and the King approached undaunted by it.

He skirted the premises with the intention of gaining some intelligence before entering. A figure lay veiled in the linen of his bed and slept with the soundness of a lifeless slumber, yet the King knew who it was in that instant. With a soundless manoeuvre, he first lifted his legs through the window and set his stealthy feet upon the floor and stalked the dormant body with skilled steps. He placed a hand upon the grey-haired head and his slumbering master responded immediately. His disturbed countenance softened into a smile upon beholding his young ward.

'Have I been gone from my land so long?' asked the Priest of himself, as he rose from the bed and shook from him the final shackles of his sleep.

'Perhaps you have trained me better than you think.'

The Priest looked proudly upon his protégé. 'It has not been a week since I saw you last, yet you look like an entirely different young man from he who left the Palace.'

'Much has happened since then.'

The Priest rose to his feet and pulled a robe over his head and let it fall around him. 'It is good to see you,' he began. 'I hope you understand now the importance of your sheltered existence. Your preparation was my only concern and it left little time for enjoying life. But now that you are here, what do you make of your homeland?'

'If you wish for me to draw parallels between the land outside and here, I cannot. They are two worlds entirely, separated by that outside wall as though it were light-years of space.'

'Things have changed out there,' warned the Priest quickly. 'Those beyond now know of your existence and suspect your allegiance to the Paegonaeans. Your mission will not be so easy. They do not know what to expect, but they are preparing themselves. After the deaths of those killed by the defence grid two nights ago, most in the Free world believe that a war is coming. As great an army as they can muster is being raised at this minute and their system has tightened drastically. But you will strike at them like a pin through their heart. I suggest you rest and meditate upon what is to come.' His tone then softened and his smile returned. 'They inform me that you have already met with the Princess and the two of you have become very close.'

The King's cheeks reddened and he nodded in the affirmative.

But the Priest was unperturbed. 'The prophecies speak of a child by your union; someone very important to the future of this world. I suggest you also meditate upon that.'

The King had been meditating upon their union since he first laid eyes on the Princess, and he answered softly that they will have a boy.

'Then you have seen the future?'

'I have seen and heard many things since I stepped upon this enchanted land. Not only have I seen my own destiny, but the destiny of this world. Have no fear, all will be well soon enough.'

A wave of relief washed over the Priest and he nodded into the fist he held poised at his mouth. 'Good,' he repeated.

They talked for some time in the mutual confidence of friendship that their master and pupil relationship had till now forbidden. What a delightful young man the King had turned out to be, thought the Priest. His personality had blossomed in only a few short days after years of repression and strict lifestyle. Outside the house, a conversation between two approaching voices could be heard and the King rose to his feet with excitement. 'I have made two friends since you last saw me,' he told the Priest, 'and I now look forward to introducing you to them.'

Mack entered first, followed by the Professor, both startled by the presence of this new stranger. As the King made the introductions between them, the Professor smiled affably and reached out his hand, telling the Priest that the King had spoke most highly of him. Mack then stepped forward and bowed before this old man with the utmost respect and remarked that he must be a formidable and wise master to have raised such a warrior as the King. All of this praise was received with humble gratitude, though it seemed that the Priest wished to dismiss himself and the King from their company so that he could converse with him some more in the privacy of their absence. Both stayed where they were as the Priest led the King outside and walked several paces ahead of him.

'How do you feel?' asked the Priest.

'Nervous,' answered the King.

'This is natural. Focus on the future and let your instinct become your guide. My days of teaching are behind you. The voice of your brave father speaks through me and I say to you now that I am proud as a father to have had such a son.' He continued walking, still several steps ahead of the King, until he had reached that point in the hill whereupon every further step unveiled more of the gathering at its base.

Two huge fires burned at either side of the stage and the rows of seating had been filled. Those who remained gathered along unequal rows up the incline of the grassy hill. Never before had an event been so anticipated, and it was not just those seated around this stage who shared in it, but those in the surrounding forest and beyond.

Nerves began to rattle more solidly in the belly of the King as he took his position by the Priest's side. 'Rest easy, my boy,' the Priest told him, taking their first steps down the hill. 'Today you earn a wife.'

The late-evening air was warm and pleasant, carrying the ambrosial fragrance from the vast displays of flowers that had been arranged with such perfection down the hill and enveloping the ceremonious scene. Mack and the Professor followed behind at a distance and slid quietly into the back row of the surrounding benches. The Priest walked the King up the aisle and left him standing all alone on the stage, as he took his seat at the front row. The brightly burning fires on either side of the King and those surrounding the seated area blinded him to the faces of the congregation between. The general noise of rustling and whispers then fell so quiet that the scribbles of those employed to document the occasion were the only disturbance in the tranquil air. Slowly, as these scribbles began to stop one by one, a strange ensemble of music began to play that dipped and bobbed above the silence and the King felt his mind drift along with its rhythm to a place of deep repose. There was a sudden rustle amongst the crowd, as thoughts of the Princess swept through their collective mind. They turned in their rows and stared up the aisle into the darkness beyond the torch-lit perimeter.

She appeared by her father's side, as perfect and as beautiful as the Princess of a peaceful land should be, and began her measured march up the aisle. Her father nodded to those he passed while the Princess held the gaze of her betrothed.

An ancient little man took his position just before the couple and raised his hands for the congregation to be silent. Wrinkles formed like waves lapping on the bays of his large eyes and his long white hair was bound in a ponytail with ringlets of flowers. He produced two candles and gave one to the King and one to his bride and directed both to light them on the fire he then offered them. This they did and, upon his further instruction, both turned to light the candle of the person who had accompanied them up the aisle. Once they had been lit, these men then lit the candles of those beside and behind them, and soon the entire congregation was illuminated under the flickering sea of burning light. The ancient little man waited until it reached up the hill and all present held a burning candle in their hand before he began.

'When two people, bound by love, come to an altar to be married, we are reminded of the love in our own lives and how this binds us as one. Love is the attracting force of our universe, and only when we are united can we move forward with any meaningful progression. Our world has been built on love and its abundance lies all around us. We stand on the threshold of everlasting peace, and here before us are two halves of the one key that will unlock its door. It is our honour, here today, to unite this couple as one.' The minister then produced a sacred knife and asked for the right hand of both of them. With a clean slice along each palm, he clasped both their hands together, whereupon the blood from both mingled and dripped upon a rock below. 'I now ask you all to join in meditation.' He closed his eyes and raised his hands just inches from the crown of both of them.

Thoughts flickered through the King's mind as he closed his eyes and he felt as though his skull was lifting away or becoming thinner. These thoughts muddled into an unintelligible melange, but through it all he could hear the voice of the Princess call out to him. His head began to hurt, as though flashes of lightening were unleashing themselves upon his brain. As he opened his eyes, the pain subsided with no lingering effect and the Princess whispered gently that he need not be afraid. He found that he now knew everything about her and she everything about him. As he turned and looked out upon the crowd, he found that he also knew everything about those there as well. Everything was as one. There were no secrets in this world, no lies or deceit. Only there, in that enchanted land, could such a system of universal trust exist, and he was now a part of it. Without having to be told, they both leaned in and kissed and the crowd clapped joyously at this concluding act of their union. Mack and the Professor, both of whom had watched the strange ritual with equal bewilderment, slunk off amidst the dispersing crowd to discuss the strange event between them.

With the celebrations about to begin, the Princess led the King up the hill and away from the jubilation below. She raced on as hard as she could, pulling her husband by the hand as he followed. Her relentless pace began to falter about halfway up and she walked the remainder of the hill under the protective arm of her beloved. At the top of the hill sat the reservoir that gathered the rains that fed the streams from which this little civilisation was built. This height escaped much of the noise from below and there was not another being anywhere near them now. The King was led to the slanted bough of an old tree that reached out over the water, where the Princess had often sat alone with thoughts of this very day. And there, they sat, hand in hand, looking out upon the shimmering body of water with the moon's bright reflection on every ripple.

A chill fell early the following morning and woke the Princess from her sleep, and she found herself alone in the secluded spot where her husband and she had spent their first night together. She rose slowly and shivered a little beneath her immaculate robe that had now been dampened by the morning dew. There was a splashing noise coming from the midst of the reservoir and, on the first attempt to pull herself to her feet, the Princess noticed something else more interesting. She lay back down again and placed a hand upon her stomach. The splashing grew louder as the King swam towards the shore and pulled himself out of the water.

'What is it?' he asked, upon beholding his wife's distraction.

'I can feel it,' she said with a soft tone of excitement. 'My body is changing.'

The King struggled to understand her meaning and knelt down beside her and placed his hand on top of her own. Their eyes met and both understood at that moment. The Princess was pregnant. How he knew this he did not know, only now the future seemed more certain. They sat there for some time in silent triumph before making their way down the hill to share their good news.

The celebrations had lasted well into the morning and villagers were awakening everywhere and rising with dulled heads. Though Mack had already wakened, he was not yet ready to open his eyes, but instead enjoyed the cool and fragrant breeze. Something tickled the end of his nose and he swiped at it lazily. The family with whom he had eaten the night before all stood around him and now watched with delight at the sight of this rare little butterfly perching on the tip of their guest's nose. It struggled to maintain its balance and finally positioned itself with some comfort when Mack raised his hand and crushed it in his fist. He then opened his eyes and looked up at the clear blue sky and sat upright, taking in the flowered meadow in which he now found himself and wondered how he had gotten there.

'You drunk a little too much mushroom wine and danced out here naked,' explained the father. 'You slept well?'

Mack grunted and rubbed his eyes. 'Where are the King and the Professor?'

'The King will be with the Princess, I should imagine, and your friend has already been summoned for your trip.'

'Our trip?' said Mack, his mind clearing somewhat from the mist that had descended upon it last night. 'Where are we going?'

'To see the beauty of our land for yourselves.'

– XIII –

The Villages of Ervey

The mountain of Ervey rose high into the Paegonaean sky in the forty-third Ring; forty-three walls from the blissful hub of the Innermost Circle; situated somewhere in the continent that those of the old world called Europe. There had been many episodes of great importance during the war, and the capture of this mountain, to be renamed Ervey in the hands of the Paegonaeans, was among the greatest of them. These were the days before the awesome might of the defence grid had been put into operation and the front line of the Paegonaeans' conquest advanced by the relentless push of her army. The strategic importance of this mountain was not lost upon those who stood against the growing might of the Paegonaean regime, and they had justly entrenched themselves to defend it.

As the armies of the old world and new clashed in ferocious skirmishes all over the mountain, the CDR of the circular city that lay just behind it was programmed to assist in the effort of its capture by supplying everything needed for the assault. It took just over a year for the forces of the new order to push the enemy from their positions and install themselves on the mountain, whereupon they set up all manner of cannons and artillery. The flat land beyond was rich with enemy camps and garrisons, all of which were evacuated once the bombing began. With the CDR of the city at its base now producing a continual stream of more powerful and more accurate shells, the failing resistance was forced to make a total retreat to the land across the sea that now lies at the foot of the forty-forth wall.

Once this wall was built and the war pushed beyond it, the Paegonaeans had then to decide in what way this land would serve them. Nutrients and minerals conducive to the growing of their sacred crop were detected in the mountain's fertile soil and, from these social roots, there emerged a civilisation built upon its harvesting, packaging and distribution. Another circular city was built on the flat land before it, charged with overseeing and streamlining this production. This it did until some years after the war when a more primitive way of life began to prevail and the city itself gave way to the Structure that replaced it. What had once been the domain of specifically designed computers and machinery was now the task of the folk who inhabited the villages of the mountain. No longer were the fields traversed by sophisticated contraptions planting seeds with metal probes whilst supervising the individual growth of each and warning of potential problems. This equipment, and all like it, had now been broken down into its base components and used in the great Structures with all that remained thereafter stored for the day when they would have to rebuild and fulfil their divine instructions.

The rich forest that covered the mountain now looked like the intermittent patches of a quilt, broken as it was with the fields for growing crops and the villages where those who worked on them lived. Life was quiet up there in those peaks, but today there were unusual whispers that broke the rich silence and excited the torpid air.

The little school that served the children from the villages of Edenreagh, Slaughtmanus and Tamnaherin was the highest building on the mountain, with the exception, of course, of any little shacks the harvesters in the fields above may have constructed to shelter from the elements. Its three classrooms and assembly hall had been built from the wood of the surrounding forest and the glass for its windows had been delivered from the eighty-ninth ring, where the sand, soda and lime used in its production were in abundance.

Miss Carrington and her class of young pupils sat silently upon some rocks at the foot of the path that wound up through the playground to the front door of the school. Seventeen in all, including their teacher; all wearing the customary white robes of the land, listening peacefully to the harmonious and abounding wind as it swept through the trees just ahead of them.

In the midst of the rising forest floor that led from the back of the school to the harvest fields above, Mr Benson was walking with the school's middle class, all in single file along a narrow trodden path. They did so in silence, speaking only when their teacher had put to them a question or presented the class with a topic to be openly discussed.

The oldest group of children sat in their classroom with old Mr Depport explaining a complex diagram that he had drawn upon the blackboard. They had just spent the earlier part of that morning learning of their world's short history and were now becoming prepared in the art of construction and engineering.

But all through the air were ripples of unrest that disrupted the serenity in which they lived. Something was coming, everyone felt it and, though no one knew for sure who or what it was, there were those willing to speculate that it was the prophesised trio. More and more of this speculation crept into the air, adding heat to the simmering anticipation of these secluded mountainfolk. Yet it seemed that most were unwilling to speak of it aloud. This new level of consciousness; which all now accepted as instinctively as those before them did the ability to speak and listen, was still relatively undeveloped, and could only be trusted fully with the support of the other senses.

Chatter arose from the back rows of Mr Depport's classroom, who had to remind his pupils that there were to be no whispers during his lessons. Mr Benson had twice stopped his class's ramble to climb to the highest branches of a tall tree, where he scanned the horizon for anything out of the ordinary. The pupils below observed his demeanour with bated breath and let out a collective groan as he returned to the ground and resumed with their walk. Miss Carrington, a most intuitive and according young woman, twitched uncharacteristically in the gentle wind and tried more than once to shake her head free of these affecting thoughts. The usual tranquillity and clarity that she instilled in her pupils was today like a muddled fog of thoughts, evident in their incessant fidgeting and detachment. When Mrs Kirk, the overseer of the school, rang the bell just before lunchtime for an early close of the school-day, there was an unusual roar of excitement as the children made for home.

Queues quickly formed at the back of the school and up the three tallest trees; at the tops of which were the zip-lines that connected the school to the constituent villages of its community. Off they went through the treetops, one by one, as the queues behind waited eagerly. Others made their way to the stables, just past where Miss Carrington and her class had been meditating, and distributed themselves on the bicycles and horses that had been left there that morning. Many pupils, however, enjoyed the walk through the orchards that lay beyond and the simple pleasures of the winding path that siphoned the children to their villages in turn. They first passed Edenreagh, and the departing group waved farewell as they disappeared through the forest, along the lane that led to their village. After some further twists and turns, those that remained then passed by Tamnaherin and their group further dwindled so that only those from Slaughtmanus were left.

As each of the pupils approached their small mountaintop villages on this particular day, they found the ordinarily calm air distorted somehow, polluted with the thoughts of a great number of people. A strange and unusual scene below had brought the inhabitants of each village to the cliff on which they sat and all were peering over the edge with a mix of bemusement and wonder. The noise in the air grew louder as they approached.

Never had any of them seen such a large number of people making their way up the mountainside. They appeared through the forests and fields below and funnelled along the winding pathway, shaking the ground with their endless march. The retiring people of Slaughtmanus, Tamnaherin and Edenreagh watched as this vast movement passed by their villages, up along the steep path that their children walked each morning on their way to school. It was there, at the school, where the marching crowd stopped and began seating themselves in rows along its playground and surrounding forest, whereupon they lifted their eyes to the sky.

The hours passed into early evening and bowls of stew were distributed to the hungry and expectant crowd from various points. Large pots bubbled with fires lit beneath them while children ran to and fro with ingredients. A sudden murmur of activity awoke the crowd from their somnolent patience and quietened its whispered conversations. Some took to their feet and pointed towards a speck on the horizon while some of the more intuitive began celebrating their arrival. Any doubt that may have persisted as to the foresight of the prophecies was dispelled in that instance and everything they had been led to believe was confirmed. The mist of ambiguity lifted upon grand visions of the future, and most had become so enraptured in them that the craft had already landed by the time they came to.

A mighty roar went up as the door of the craft opened and the entire mountain seemed to quake, as though awakening from a long and profound slumber. The sight of the craft alone was enough to stir emotions uncommon in these people, as the mythical Knights were rarely observed so closely, only ever before zooming lights in the sky high above them. One peeked out his head as the craft's platform unfolded itself to the ground and the roaring crowd peered back eagerly for their first glimpse of the outsiders. Mack emerged from the craft and made his way down the platform when he was suddenly stopped by the sharp drop in the rapturous applause. A distant sneeze and a cough here and there were heard through this silence and the Professor followed more gingerly. They stood next to one another upon stepping onto the soft ground of the mountain, as though a pair condemned, and shuddered fearfully when the craft that had brought them took off with an unearthly bound. Those in front stared silently at the bemused duo for a few seconds before turning and making their way back through the crowd, revealing newer waves of spectators, who, in turn, followed the procedure of those before them.

Three hours passed in this manner before the last of the crowd pushed their way through the surrounding forest to view them. As the crowd frittered into nothing, a strange old figure approached the two men. He had once, presumably, been a tall man before his back had begun to stoop and he now carried his slumped and withered frame with the aid of a large wooden staff. His long shabby hair was as white as snow, as were his wild bushy eyebrows and long pointed beard. There was a lifelessness in his eyes that would have suggested blindness, though he seemed to see both men clearly as he approached.

'Welcome to our land and to our villages,' he said in a long and weary drawl upon reaching them. 'My name is Goshaden, and I am the village elder for Edenreagh and head of the council for the tri-village community.'

The whitened pupils of his inexpressive eyes seemed to catch nothing as they swayed back and forth between them, and Mack, duly curious, raised his hand before them and waved.

'The power of my eyes have withered with age,' he claimed. 'This world around me has faded and exists now only in my mind, yet my other senses have grown sharper in compensation.' The old man then turned and hobbled off in such a way that neither Mack nor the

Professor could doubt that he wanted them to follow him. They exchanged dubious glances before obeying his request, somewhat confused by the excitement of entering into the unknown reaches of such a mysterious new world.

The air up there was as sweet as in the other regions they had been to, though the fragrance in these desolate heights held the bold currents of wilder tones from a wonderful new collection of flowers and plants. All was contained within the same choreography that seemed somehow to extend to everything; from the passing of a horse-pulled cart loaded with barrels of milk to the flock of swirling children that passed them along the way. There was a surreal relationship in everything that their senses laid upon, which gave the dream-like experience of déjà vu.

A shadow crept slowly behind them, eclipsing much of the forest, as something large passed overhead. Both men looked to the sky while the old man hobbled on. There, amongst the clouds high above them, moving silently along, was what looked like a gigantic train with an endless procession of huge containers behind it, each staying afloat by the workings of some unseen technology. This vehicle would become a forerunner to the huge industrial spacecrafts that their future generations would use to transport waste to the refuse planets of their galactic System. This craft went on and on and on until it stretched the length of the sky and released one of the containers from its long convoy, which then floated down upon their horizon.

'That is the inter-ring delivery system,' said the old man, still hobbling on and planting his staff firmly in the gravel with every step. 'We receive a drop every three days or so with all that has been requested since the last one. It is our duty to return each empty container filled with the crop that our soil produces along with other small quantities of goods produced here. Everything is then taken to the first Ring, just outside the Innermost Circle, where those there are charged with the sorting out of requests and with loading the containers accordingly. It is the most advanced piece of technology we have with our protective defence grid coming second. Some day soon, these, too, will no longer be needed and our world shall flourish from the essence of purity, rich in the wisdom of enlightenment.'

They watched as a similar container lifted off into the air and inaugurated itself effortlessly into the ranks of this train. By the time they resumed their trek, the old man had disappeared along the winding path; the course of which he walked as though each corner had been imprinted on his mind like a map.

Down the narrow lane the old man now led them, first off the main route from the school, there appeared ahead of them another stable, inside which they could hear the rustling of the animals it housed. Bicycles were lined along the front; most slotted in rather raggedly in their young riders' haste earlier that day. It was not long ago that such stables, there in the forty-third Ring, were used in conjunction with palm-scan technology. Every animal and bicycle had then been logged onto a central computer and this system updated when one was taken from one stable and deposited at another. This technology withered in the same way it did everywhere and was now obsolete throughout the Rings. No longer were favourite horses kept by one person or some stables overflowing while others lay empty. The crooked frame of the old man straightened slightly as he passed by this building and pointed a long and slender finger to the village beyond. 'Edenreagh.'

A large old chestnut tree split the path around its trunk, forming the gateway to this small community. The path then formed an avenue with ten houses on either side, surrounded entirely by forest but for the cliff along the far side. Everything there held that same sense of coordination as everywhere else. Nothing seemed out of place, even with some of its villagers scrubbing this and that while others worked on at their assigned chores. Perfecting adornments hung along doorframes and windows and the Paegonaean pride was no less alive in these heights than in the first village of the Innermost Circle. Beautifully crafted tables and benches lay along the path between the opposite rows of housing, and it was there that the villagers came together each night to dine with their neighbours.

Four women rolled dough into huge balls on one of these tables and flattened them out into metals trays. These were then laid aside for a group of young girls to carry off somewhere else. At the far end of the path, a single tree silhouetted against the blue sky and beneath its shade sat a man employed in the task of mending the sandals he took from a basket by his side. The rest just seemed to wander about from house to house and trek in and out of the woods; everyone taking much less interest in their guests now that they had already been acquainted. Bicycles lay scattered just before the surrounding forest, as the children climbed the laddered trunks of its trees to the sprawling tree-house suburbia held in its foliage. The impressive jungle metropolis that linked each of the villages down the mountainside had been built, maintained and improved upon by the children of each passing generation. It was there that Paegonaean youth was spent, working and playing alongside their peers in a unified engineering project.

The women continued to roll their dough as the old man passed them and placed his fumbling hand upon a water pump that sat at the very centre of the village. 'Our world is very different from that which you know,' he began, not yet turned to face them. 'Walk wherever you like and take in all around you. Enjoy everything with an open heart and an open mind. There shall be a gathering at the Bowl tonight which you are both, of course, welcome to attend.'

'The Bowl?' enquired the Professor.

'Every six villages on this mountain share a Bowl. It is a place where the people from each of them and beyond can come together and share with one another. There will be many people there tonight in anticipation of your attendance. In the meantime, you may take a seat here at this bench and food will be brought to you.' The old man then walked off with his hands lifted slightly before him and fumbled his way through the woods.

Mack sat down and rubbed his fingers along his forehead before pressing the temples of his skull in an effort to curb a throbbing headache. The Professor first gulped at some water and then sat down beside him. 'He did not ask any questions of us, where we came from, what we do. Not even our names.' He waited, without reward, for Mack to add his opinion, and then concluded himself more thoughtfully. 'This is indeed a strange world.'

Two bowls of stew were brought to them by two young girls with another girl following behind with a basket of warm bread. All was set upon the table and the two men began their meal. The headache had robbed Mack of his appetite and he picked at his stew with morose enthusiasm before giving up altogether and again placing his hands on his forehead.

A young maiden exited a house some distance down and her eyes seemed drawn to the ailing figure of Mack. She carried a weaved bag by her side and her white robe had been garnished by the sprig of some wild flower. The Professor watched her approach and followed the unbroken attention she bestowed upon Mack, who sat oblivious of her interest. She set her bag down on the table and produced from it a pestle and mortar, along with some herbs and portions of wild plants. Once everything had been placed in the little bowl, she began to crush all together until the mixture had formed an even consistency. She scooped almost all of it with three fingers and rubbed the paste along the neck of Mack's robe, leaving a heavy stain of yellowish green. Mack and the Professor looked on curiously as the young maiden wiped her hand of the last of it, further staining his robe with these streaks. With a smile that seemed full of promise, she gathered her things and wandered off up the lane from the village.

'What was that all about?' asked the Professor.

Mack watched her pass by the old chestnut tree and shook his head that he had no idea. He wobbled slightly as he stood up and a wave of irrepressible tiredness washed over him. After explaining this to the Professor, Mack stumbled from the table and wandered to a house just opposite. As he staggered up the lane through its small garden, the front door was opened by a mother with a small child in her arms. Mack pushed past her with as much decorum as his failing system could muster and up the stairs to collapse on the first bed he could find. This left the Professor all alone in this strange new world and he finished his meal whilst appreciating the beauty of this peaceful day.

A horn sounded through the silence and the surrounding forest seemed to vibrate. Moments later, the first of a stampede of children emerged from its shadow and converged upon the village in full sprint. The large pack of runners gradually dissipated into a hopeful few in what seemed like a race to the water pump. A beautiful young woman emerged from her house and walked slowly towards their finishing post, just as the winner rushed by, followed closely by the boy in second place. Those who came after looked somewhat dejected in their defeat and dispersed to their homes or back through the forest to their villages. The victor hurried off to a nearby shed while the young woman took the runner-up under her arm and rhymed off a list of produce that the village would need for the Bowl that evening. She finished the list just as the victor arrived by their side with a large wooden wheelbarrow, and the two set off on their way to the local depository.

'Would you like to join us on a walk?' one of the boys asked the Professor.

The Professor consented with a pleasant smile and readied himself to follow them. Though still unable to walk without the aid of a crutch, his injuries were healing much quicker than he expected. The aches and pains that had ravaged his body since the crash had diminished greatly and his blackened eyes were now little more than light-bluish marks that would continue to fade through the course of the day. There was something rejuvenating in the air that filled the lungs with a spiritual joy and invigorated every muscle.

They passed by fields of cattle, grain and crop, and continued down the gravel path with people coming this way and that, carrying baskets filled with everything from cherries and plums to fresh robes and pots. The thick forest ebbed and flowed on either side and one of the boys strayed into its depths and was gone for more than ten minutes before eventually re-emerging again just ahead of them.

'The village of Trillick is through there,' the young boy explained. 'My friend lives there and I spend much time with her family. We are to be married once we are old enough and live by the sea in the next Ring, where the primary produce is seafood.'

'It seems that you have everything worked out,' replied the Professor.

The boy continued to explain everything they passed with the same youthful zeal; the village each diverging path led to, the history of some old building or where the best apples and oranges were to be found. A group of cyclists then passed through the forest to their right and both boys ran to the edge to watch.

'There is a track through the forest,' explained the same boy, 'that runs from the crop fields above our school right down to the storage and preparation facilities at the base of the mountain. I am still too young to attempt it, but my older brother holds the record for the fastest time. He now lives in the thirty-second Ring, where bicycles are manufactured. There are tracks there that only the bravest and most skilful riders dare attempt, which is why they requested him. Ask me where any product is manufactured,' he added bravely.

The Professor shrugged. 'Books?'

'That's easy. Paper is manufactured in the vast rainforests of the sixty-forth and sixty-fifth Ring and distributed throughout our land. All completed manuscripts are sent to the fiftieth ring, where they are bound and pressed and then distributed according to their demand.'

'Vehicles?'

The boy thought for a moment and answered somewhat falteringly. 'Trains and monorails? They were once assembled in a Ring that has since become part of the Innermost Circle, and so, there are no more in our world. However, the cable cars you see up and down the mountainside are made in the twelfth Ring. Or is it now the eleventh? Our cable cars are being used at the minute to transport all the crop to the base of the mountain, where it will be made ready for distribution. That is our speciality.'

'Pots and pans?' asked the Professor.

'Metal is forged in the... One hundred and twenty-first ring. We shall have pots and pans for some time yet. They say the houses there are made from silver and gold. It is as good as any other method of storage, though I must admit that I prefer to be housed in wood. When something made of metal breaks, it is returned there and fixed.'

'And how do you return these items?'

'Each Ring has a central depository, through which we receive and return these products. Those who become part of the Innermost Circle give up the right to these deliveries, as life there has been reduced to perfection, and so, need only the land around them to progress. We hope that some day soon we shall join this way of life.

Walls are now falling faster than ever and soon our entire world shall be at perfect peace.'

The Professor marvelled at hearing one so young speak of everlasting peace and patted the boy affectionately on the head.

At the bottom of a steep hill, the path veered sharply to the left and rose gently to an area with some benches overlooking much of the mountainside. An elderly couple sat silently at one end with some youths chatting amongst themselves at the other. Water fell from the height of the stone wall behind it and streamed through the area with a small wooden bridge leading over it. The sun was now setting, taking with it impressive swirls of orange and red and dimming the world around them. Forest flowed all the way down the mountain with villages and meadows dotting its complexion. Chimneys chugged smoke as the villagers came home from their daily chores or from the open fields where they played sports, exercised or meditated in large groups before their evening meal. There was a lake, only a short distance down the mountain, and the Professor noticed that the water was crystal clear. He looked upon the entire scene and was captivated by its simplicity.

As he stood there looking out, the Professor's heart was filled with a joy so strong that he clasped his chest and was suddenly overcome with emotion. Tears came to his eyes and a choking sensation to his throat. His heart began to beat faster and harder and he felt as though it was all too much for him and would somehow suffocate him where he stood. He then fell to his knees and wept without reserve, venting, at last, the strange sensation that had been building in him since stepping foot upon this land.

'Shall we go on?' asked the boy, obviously unaffected by the Professor's unprompted outburst. 'The depository lies just beyond those trees.'

The boy who pushed the wheelbarrow rushed on ahead of them and disappeared through the winding corridor of trees. Paths through the thick forest from other places converged upon their own and the steady flow of traffic began to build. This widening path then opened onto a meadow, the perimeter of which was lit with burning torches, with a large barn set at its centre. There were no windows in this building, but it had twelve open entrances with a small crowd gathered at each of them. Computerised boards hung from the roof at each of these entrances with precise accounts of what was stocked inside. By the end of next winter, these would be gone, and by the end of the following year, this technology would no longer be produced or repaired, when the sector charged with this task became part of the Innermost Circle. Youngsters with empty wheelbarrows lined the queues, while the hunters and producers of all types of foods carried their deliveries. This flow of produce was monitored by a central computer; weighing and tagging incoming goods and then deducting them as they left the premises. Though this system was no longer necessary in assisting efficient and fair distribution, there or in any of the other Rings further out, every step forward into perfection must be taken prudently.

Inside, their young accomplice was casting an expert eye over a table laid with pots of jam and honey. The wheelbarrow he pushed had been loaded high with all that had been requested and now the boy was indulging in a few luxuries. There were tables with biscuits and shortcakes, milk and cheese, fruit juices and wines, all manner of meat and vegetables, as well as those there to carry the more particular requests of this isolated pocket of their community to the central depository. The atmosphere was much livelier there and the Professor felt a relaxation fall upon him as he listened to the bustle of their conversations. Through the melee of wheelbarrows and those with large sacks slung over their shoulders, he caught sight of the young boy with the delivery for their village trundling along towards him.

Outside again, people laughed and joked and presented their children to the families of potential suitors. Already there were groups playing instruments with gathering crowds around them, many of whom would spend the rest of the evening there.

As they entered onto the path leading back up through the forest, a man upon a horse-drawn cart was lighting the last of the torches that lined either side. The two boys now took it in turns to push the heavy load back up the steep hill with the torches flickering in the fresh forest breeze. Tender notes of music wafted through the air and entranced the Professor so deeply that he would later struggle to recall most of this arduous journey. He broke from its trance at a fork in the path and watched his young guides walk up to the left while the path to the right seemed to call to him. It rose gently around a narrow bend and the Professor followed it through the forest. An unusual and rhythmic thud grew louder as he progressed and seemed as though a beacon through the darkness. Louder and louder it grew until the source of this drumming lay at the top of a steep set of stone steps. He could hear voices and laughter as he walked up those steps, all through the hypnotic beat of the drum and, upon reaching the top, felt a wave of exuberance whoosh against him.

A statuesque male stood upon a podium and beat the drum before him with heavy strikes from both hands; its rhythm rolling over the canopy of the underlying forest and to the villages that lay in its depths. The floor of this area had been laid with sawdust, and twenty cooking stations served food along its curved perimeter with benches placed before each of them for the revellers to sit and eat. A large cave led into the side of the mountain and many teenagers and young adults were walking in and out and milling around its threshold. Between this cave and the surrounding eating posts were a series of tables and benches, where the old men and women of the villages gathered and smoked on their pipes. There was little doubt that this was the Bowl of which the old blind man had spoken.

Mack spotted his abandoned partner immediately and made his way through the crowd to meet with his fellow outworlder, obviously refreshed after his remedial sleep. His eyes sparkled with renewed strength and there seemed to be no lingering effects from the headache that had so afflicted him earlier that day.

'You are feeling better?' the Professor enquired.

Mack nodded. 'I awoke not more than an hour ago after having had the most wonderful sleep.' He then took the Professor by the arm and led him through the benches to one of the sizzling cooking posts.

Steaks were being fried by an old woman under the close observation of those around her. She explained every ingredient she added and talked tenderly of flavours and textures. Mack and the Professor joined the small queue that stretched before her and, one by one, each received a single slab of meat which they took to the benches and began to eat. The deep and rejuvenating sleep, rendered by the young maiden's medicine, had left Mack feeling starved and he requested the last two steaks to accompany that which had been given to him, leaving the man and woman who remained in the queue behind to wait until the next batch had been cooked.

Men and women waded through the benches with huge pots of vegetables, scooping ladlefuls onto plates as and when requested by those there. The Professor savoured each bite of his meal and commended the old woman who had prepared the meat with a gentle nod and smile. It seemed, however, that Mack's ravenous hunger had been a false one, and he threw over half of his dish into the forest and patted his stomach to proclaim that he was full. As they sipped at some tea, Goshaden, the village elder, fumbled his way towards them and invited the two men to join some friends of his at a table nearer the cave.

The two men duly accepted and, once the old man had gone out of earshot, Mack commented. 'I don't think the old man is as blind as he lets on.'

All of the men at Goshaden's table had long beards and everything about them was reminiscent of a gathering of sorcerers. Each held a pipe in their hand which they loaded with dashes of their sacred crop that lay in a porcelain dish in the centre of their table. Goshaden gave both their own pipe as they sat down amongst them and the contents of the porcelain dish was offered to them with a wave of his hand. Once the two men had obliged, a lit taper was held out for both so that they may enjoy its smoke. The Professor choked immediately on its potency and took more measured draws thereafter, while Mack drew from his pipe with the experience of one accustomed to the practice.

'What do you think of our world?' asked one of the group.

'It is so beautiful,' answered the Professor, 'that I admit I have trouble maintaining an image of it in my head.'

'I agree with my friend that it is indeed a beautiful world,' interposed Mack more boldly, 'but it is of a very primitive nature. Upon hearing of this mission, I expected to find great cities built from an advanced technology within the walls of your land and the sky rich with vehicles like that in which we came here today.'

The men smiled as they drew on their pipes and one spoke for the rest of them. 'You are disappointed with our lack of progress?'

'Progress comes in many forms,' added another.

'Technology has helped man evolve from the animals we once were into the complex beings we have become, and has now prepared us for the great silence of our time,' another commented.

'We listen and wait,' explained Goshaden, who then leaned forward to speak more directly to their guests. 'I hope you enjoy your smoke. Our leaves are the finest of all on the mountain.'

'In all of the land,' exacted another, to which he received a round of gruffled commendation.

The world seemed to slow around them as they smoked, and a universe of possibilities opened above them for all to ponder. Their wandering minds seemed to trespass and cross with those around them, as though entering into a collective pool of thought. Images of flowered fields were conjured in the mind of the Professor, with the turrets of majestic castles rising high amongst them. A sun hovered close above this scene, much larger than usual with other moons and planets in its orbit, and he realised that this was no earthly scene. Each of these moons and planets seemed only a short distance from one another, with crafts jetting through the sky between them. The more he relaxed, the more the dream grew, and all those around him but Mack seemed to share in every detail of it. Instead, the notorious thief was taken along a solitary path.

Mack recognised instantly the poisoned red dust of the wastelands and the mountains in the distance that surrounded Fortress city. This peaceful scene was suddenly disrupted by a flash that turned all around him white, revealing as it faded, a huge puff of smoke mushrooming above the city. Another flash went off, engulfing the world in its sheer white veil and the ground shook more vigorously than with the first. More and more of these explosions went off with untold destruction unfolding around him and he awoke from this daydream with a gasp. He rose from the table hastily and pushed his way through the crowd with uneasy steps and disappeared down a path through the forest to the east of the Bowl. The Professor excused himself from the disrupted air of their group and raced down the path after him as fast as his injuries would allow.

A wooden balcony lay at the bottom of the path, reaching across a gap in another path that lay horizontal to it, forming a T-junction that overlooked the dark forest beyond. It was there that he found Mack, looking out with unseeing eyes to the sentiments within himself.

'What's wrong?' asked the Professor.

Mack breathed in deeply. 'I saw something just now, something terrible. It may have been some illusion of the mind, but I saw it as clearly as though I was there in the midst of it all. I fear that we have been brought here to sacrifice our brothers in the world outside. There will be no final war, no battle for the righteous to emerge as true victors, just a quick and apocalyptic extermination with us there to pull its trigger.'

Both men stood side by side in silence, lost in separate worlds of thought. 'It is late,' whispered the Professor finally. 'Let us find somewhere warm to rest for the night. Tomorrow will be another day.'

They awoke the following morning buried in the hay of the stable where they had passed the night. Horses rustled in the compartments on either side of them and voices rang out in the distance. The Professor walked outside after shaking the hay from his robe, leaving Mack where he lay undisturbed. His injured foot had improved measurably during the night and he tested his weight on it without the support of his crutch and figured that he would no longer need it after today. A mother and father passed by with their children following behind them.

'Good morning,' said the father.

'Good morning,' returned the Professor.

'I hope that last night was not too much for you, and that you both enjoyed your visit to our humble peaks.'

'Where are we?' asked Mack, interrupting their pleasantries as he staggered beyond the frame of the stable and winced under the morning sun.

The mother answered immediately that they were between the villages of Beragh and Ardmore, and that the path ahead would take them to the base of the mountain. There, they would meet with the King again aboard a craft that would take them to the Outermost Ring for the final leg of their journey. Mack looked down the path with a lazy resignation when one of the children suggested that they could do it in a fraction of the time, and with much less effort, if they found two bicycles.

They had only to walk for five minutes before coming across a small bicycle-stand. Two pristine bicycles had just been left back by a young man and woman who then disappeared off into the forest. Both Mack and the Professor took the bikes and began their descent cautiously, for it had been a while since either had cycled, and never had they undertaken such a demanding route as that which now lay before them. But they soon found their momentum and worked out their way to the bottom by keeping to the paths with the steepest downhill gradient. At the end of every lane along this course was a crowd of excited onlookers, many of whom were on bicycles themselves and joined the growing cortege behind their guests. Children cheered from the branches of the trees and from the wooden bridges that reached overhead between the forests on either side.

The forest that had held them so tightly began to spread out and fell back behind them as the path opened onto a large meadow, much larger than any they had passed thus far; so large in fact that it seemed to separate that above from that below. Mack cast a glance behind him as the crowd that followed poured endlessly from the upper forest. Families rose from their picnics to watch the spectacle and stood their ground as the human avalanche slalomed past them and approached the forest of the lower reaches. An awaiting crowd formed distinct channels and funnelled the massive throng of oncoming cyclists into its narrow lanes.

They were again engulfed with trees and the bright sun struggled through their foliage to reach them.

Villages in this new sector were much larger, perhaps twice the size of those further up and more people waited on bicycles by the end of their lanes. The path widened as it eventually began to level out, and to their left and right they could see huge wooden factories, fed by conveyor belts through their rooftop ports with loads of the sacred crop. Once treated and packaged, it was then taken to the storage warehouses further down, where it would await to be transported to the central depository for delivery. These storage warehouses stretched on and on, containing not only their primary product, but all other materials and resources that would remain there until the day they were needed.

Beyond these warehouses was flat countryside with fields of green and yellow, all tended by the clusters of villages that sprung from their midst. The Professor looked around and was amazed to see the horde of cyclists that followed still emerging from the forest. On they cycled towards a Structure ahead of them, around which, the villages grew closer and finally merged into a city-like formation. Somewhere within this suburbia was the central depository for the forty-third Ring and employment there was split between it and the maintenance of the Structure. The people who lived there had come out from their houses and ushered the more leisurely approach of their illustrious guests through their streets and alleyways, ending with a huge crowd gathered around a podium, hastily erected for their arrival. The cheers of the crowd were almost deafening as Mack and the Professor climbed off their bikes and ascended the steps to the top. And, just like when they arrived at the school at the top of the mountain, the crowd fell into a deep and profound silence.

Only when a craft appeared in the sky above them moments later did their chatter resume. It hovered above the city for some minutes before lowering itself gently. Once it was upon solid ground, the door opened and the King jumped from it and ran up the steps to complete the foretold alliance. The three men waved at the crowd as they descended the steps together and were ushered inside the waiting craft. And with that, they were lifted up into the air and whizzed off across the land for the final episode of their stay.

– XIV –

The Outermost Ring

The wall that separated the peaceful rings of the Paegonaean Empire with its Outermost Ring rose steadily from the horizon as their craft approached, and, in an instant, the world beneath them turned from the varying shades of nature to an endless expanse of inescapable grey. Only the reflective solar panels of the power-conversion plant that hugged along the other side of this wall offered any break in its dull and monotonous complexion.

A congruent lattice of motorway formed the upper crust of this stratified Ring with the top floor of the city's tallest tower blocks poking from its canopy at the four corners of every grid. From each of these towers ran a series of smaller towers, each reaching five storeys less in height as they descended towards the centre of the square they rose from, with the carriageways and platforms that run between them forming the subsequent levels in this metropolis.

The occupants of the craft looked out in captivated silence as they descended through the first of these narrowing caverns and into the shadowy depths of this new world. It was Mack who was most deeply touched by the first sight of life out there: a select group of soldiers training on a small platform between the tallest towers where they lived. The soldiers grew younger as they descended further through the floors of the constricting network of tower blocks and passageways, and their groups grew steadily larger until they numbered near a thousand on every platform, doubling from there on with every floor. All wore robes of grey and their heads were shaved without exception. It seemed that nature was to play no part whatsoever in this society and had been banished in all its forms with the same effort that their brethren in the Rings beyond had sought to celebrate it. The gloomy atmosphere of the subdued human spirit hung in the air like a stagnant heat and fed hungrily on any glimpse of life that glimmered from the souls it had quelled.

There was no great ceremony to greet them there as they stepped down from the craft and took in their surroundings from the ground floor. Sporadic bursts of gunfire sounded from the tiers above them while the unified shouts of those in training echoed from the darkened recesses all around. The effect of this world was of disorientation and displacement on the three visitors, who had just travelled across many time-zones to get there and now found themselves submerged in its unusual twilight. It was with utter relish that Mack licked his eyes along the levels of this garrison, while the Professor's sheltered imagination could only liken the surrounding infrastructure to a city-sized car park. A man approached, flanked by two others who walked a few paces behind him; all three camouflaged by their robes against the grey backdrop of their world. The eyes of the two that followed stared straight ahead with focussed and unbroken concentration while those of the man who led them sparkled with reverence as they settled upon the King.

'Welcome to the Outermost Ring,' he began. 'My name is Commander Cornelle, leader of the 30th to the 39th Battalion of the Paegonaean army. I have been charged personally with briefing you on your mission. You will reconvene at this spot tomorrow morning at 0530, where you will then be taken to the far side of the Ring, where transport to the outside awaits. Follow me, please.'

Cornelle and his escorts led the three men from the midst of the four small towers that surrounded them, along a maze of narrow pathways and through an assortment of buildings that offered no distinction from those before or after. Even the squads of young boys they passed, all marching in strict formation, looked as though they may have been cloned from one another; neutered of all distinguishing features and subjected to the same diet and regime.

'Our world here must seem foreign from the inner Rings,' said Cornelle, as he strode onwards. 'However, I assure you that any question you ask out here shall be answered with the same honesty and candour as anywhere else in our land.'

'Why is there no colour here?' blurted the Professor. 'Why only the same shade of grey?'

'It focuses the troops,' he responded quickly. 'Grey bridles the imagination and suppresses free-thought.'

Mack considered his unskilled management of the young men he had trained into bounty hunters and the money and hours that could have been saved by shaving their heads and painting everything around them grey.

'We have some training fields up ahead,' said the Commander, leading them through the last of the buildings for now.

They walked from the dark captivity of the buildings' alleyways to a large open space with a sky of overlapping lanes and carriageways above. A seemingly infinite ocean of boys and girls, aged only four or five, stood in regimented rows, punching and kicking the air before them with perfect synchronicity. As the men were led up a thin column between this young army, Mack inspected each new row with an appreciative passing of the eye.

'They begin training here,' said the Commander. 'Their number shall dwindle as they progress through our ranks, as the cogs of our system are oiled by the blood of the weak.'

An appropriate demonstration was brought to their attention as the communal warm-up ended and the boys and girls settled into groups around their instructors. The instructor of the group they stopped to watch was not more than twenty, and this important position would have been highly revered amongst his peers on the levels above. He read aloud two numbers from a notebook and the corresponding boys stood up. Both were skinny little things, but a hunger took their eyes as they locked upon their opponent. With a blow from the instructor's whistle, the two boys lunged at one another and began grappling and punching with all their youthful might, both showing neither fear nor mercy. The brutal duel ended with a crack to one of the boys' ribs and the instructor dutifully ticked his notebook before tending the defeated child. In an unacceptable lapse of concentration, one of the youngsters in the group turned his attention from the lesson before him and glanced at the Commander and his entourage. Another boy jumped to his feet and shouted. The distracted boy was immediately disciplined with heavy blows from the group and the instructor again ticked his notebook.

Every one of these young soldiers worked themselves to exhaustion in all aspects of their training, with their only goal in life to be initiated into the upper ranks of their army. Each new session was yet another competition with those around them. They jogged on the spot till their legs grew heavy and could no longer be lifted from the ground. They did push up after push up with mean determination until only they remained or completed star jumps till their growing muscles could offer no more than a feeble flailing. Every exercise had a leader within the group itself; being he or she who held the record for most completed, and would be replaced by another when this record had been surpassed. Competition amongst them was rife, but never did they let this spill out in any other way than in their own personal performance. Loyal and focussed warriors, what a price he would have got for any one of them, thought Mack.

'This is how they spend their days?' said the Professor flatly, skimming his eyes across the sea of youth. 'How can they be happy?'

'Happiness is relative,' Cornelle responded. 'These young men and women have been educated in honouring strength, bravery and loyalty above all else. To become the strongest and bravest of their unit is, for them, happiness. But I understand what you mean, and for that, they have the many Coliseums that our system has to offer.'

'Coliseums?' asked the King.

The Commander turned to face him. 'We may visit one later, if you like.'

The rattle of traffic from the lanes overhead grew louder as they approached a cluster of buildings that surrounded one of the towers in the infrastructure's rising sequence. Again they were led through a system of alleyways and courtyards, where the youthful elite trained in their special units under the supervision of their masters. It was a strange sight to behold a child of four or five fire a weapon with such controlled ease, but to hit with such accuracy the targets that had been positioned for them was something else. A sudden jolt of horror struck the Professor upon regarding the characters on the targets they shot at; men, women and children were all represented, many of whom were portrayed in a state of terrified retreat. None from these groups looked up from their tasks as the Commander passed by with the three outsiders in their robes of white.

The building they approached appeared no different from any other and, upon entering, the men found that the dull grey world outside had pervaded its interior. They found no signs or symbols to explain what was done there, but detected the faint scent of hot food lingering in the air. Rows of seats to hold one thousand young soldiers lay empty before what appeared to be a kitchen and a serving area. The three men had not eaten during their long journey and their morning appetites had now turned to afternoon hunger. A frail little woman carried a large steaming pot to the service area and ladled a thick grey mixture into each of their bowls. Her timorous eyes awakened as the King passed by and she spoke with a slight tremor in her voice. 'You are from the outside?'

The King only nodded, peering deeply into the woman's fearful eyes, and she reacted by shielding them from him and scurrying off to the kitchen, as though fearful she would break down and cry. The King's eyes then dropped to the thick grey gruel that had maintained its ladle-like shape in his bowl and returned to the Commander and his friends. The two private guards who had flanked the Commander through the streets of their city had remained by the door outside, where not a word passed between them. Many questions were asked of their Commander however, as the outsiders ate their insipid meals, and conversations blossomed from the answers they received.

'Why,' asked Mack with a mouthful of gruel, obviously enjoying the hot mixture of oats, 'are there no signposts or directions about this place? Everywhere looks the same. How do your people know where they are going?'

'The soldiers here learn to find subtle characteristics in their surroundings and use them to navigate through our Ring. They will soon find themselves in a foreign world outside our walls, where they must establish themselves quickly if they are to carry out their task efficiently. Also, should the unthinkable happen and our outer wall be breached, the invaders would not have the advantage of directions through the layers of our city. This is also the reason why all of our heavy artillery is stored at highly secured locations; in case they are turned around and used against our inner wall. Every precaution against such a breach has been taken.'

The gruel they ate was a hearty feed that filled each of the hungry men and they scooped the last of it as they finished talking. To the back of the room was a staircase which they followed to the third floor of the building. The Commander then led them down a corridor with several doors leading off from it. They continued to the very end of this corridor, where the Commander carefully removed a grey tile from the wall. He placed his hand upon the scanner it revealed and there was a slight rumbling from the wall to their left as a hidden door slid open.

Darkness was pushed up along the staircase as the lights above it lit, and the secret floor to which they were led then illuminated and presented itself. Desks were arranged along its windowless perimeter and screens hung above them displaying different scenes from cameras around the district. Beneath these screens were large control panels and chairs for those who oversaw their operation. The room was now empty of all personnel so that the Commander could speak with their guests alone. In the centre of the room was a large table with three chairs tucked below and the screens nearby had been turned to face those who sat there.

'You all know why you are here,' began the Commander, 'so I will get straight down to business. We do not presume to know more than your Highness in the land where he was raised, but with the importance of such a mission, we took it upon ourselves to lighten the load of your burden.' With his opening delivered, the Commander turned his attention to the screens around them. He pressed a button upon a small handheld controller and these screens went blank momentarily before returning to colour with a map of what they called the Outside.

Mack immediately rose to his feet and examined the accuracy of the interpretation on one of the screens by tracing his finger steadily along the ridge of a familiar mountain and, upon satisfying himself with its accuracy, he returned to his seat without a word.

'We have ways of... planting things where we want out there,' resumed the Commander. 'Twelve devices have been delivered to strategic locations around the central metropolis known as Fortress city and its surrounding wasteland. Each of these devices need to be armed before they can be detonated for a synchronised attack. This will mean entering a ten digit code on each device, and arming all twelve of them before detonation would amount to a total eradication of the Outside. This devastation shall depreciate accordingly with the less you arm. Nevertheless, the devastation from only those in key areas would be sufficient to destroy any form of organised resistance.'

The screens around them then flashed with a red circle emanating from each of the twelve locations and the men got to their feet to examine the blasts more fully. There were no names of towns or villages on these maps, only the topography of the land. Mount Hexlon rose beneath the radius of one of these blasts and the King located its epicentre somewhere within the walls of his city. The Professor touched the centre of one of the screens, where the emanating radii of four blasts set at the corners of Fortress city overlapped upon it.

The Commander smiled towards the King and his men. 'Each of the devices are located in remote and isolated areas but for a few. You will be given the codes for each of the devices along with the coordinates of their locations. Our destiny lies in your hands.'

Hours rolled by as the location of each device and surrounding security were explained in fine detail. Having nothing to add or question, the Professor's interest began to wane. It was becoming increasingly clear that his role in this mission was to be a ceremonial extra in the fulfilment of a prophecy he knew nothing about. Mack would occasionally put forward a comment, though it was more in an effort to highlight his presence than elicit any new or overlooked information. It was to the King that the Commander directed his discourse, and he focussed more upon him as the details of the plan became more minute.

When the brief was over, the men rose from their chairs and were led down the staircase to the building below. Day had passed into night during their internment in the windowless chamber and the world outside was now as black as the most barren stretch of wasteland at this hour. There were no streetlights or torches to assist the swarms of young soldiers, who were now making their way from the training fields to the surrounding towers for their evening meal. The Commander looked from the windows with his acclimatised eyes and, without breaking his stride along the corridor, said. 'You have seen the lower end of our army, but you have yet to see the older ranks. There is a Coliseum nearby and the first of the spectacles shall be starting soon.'

They were led outside and climbed into a waiting vehicle. Once the crowd of hungry young soldiers dissipated from around them, the Commander took off through the empty streets and entered upon a road that coiled around a supporting column to the next level of the city. How he could see or where they were going, the outsiders did not know, as the vehicle they travelled in had neither headlights nor digital-layout technology. Only a fluorescent marker that ran along the edge of the roads and separated the lanes on the carriageways stood out from the darkness. They ascended high into the widening system of roads between the taller towers of the city, on their way to one of its Coliseums.

Through the grid of criss-crossing motorway that formed the top level of this world, one in every ten of the caverns below had been left without towers descending into its depths. These were the Coliseums. The surrounding platforms formed the stands of its stadium, where spectators from every level gathered to share in the entertainment below. A dim and fading light reached out through the darkness, and this the men focussed upon as their vehicle pulled off from the carriageway and approached more directly. By the sides of the road they now travelled along, the footpaths were thick with the warrior-like citizens of this world, all now gravitating towards the nightly shows at the Coliseum.

The night air was warm as they stepped out of their parked vehicle and a dull clamour arose from below, as though a sports game was being played with the surrounding crowd cheering their teams. There were rattles of crowd-pleasing gunfire and an occasional explosion would shake the ground as the four men shuffled along with the marching crowd. They took their seats among the surrounding sea of grey robes and turned their eyes to the apocalyptic arena below.

Shells of buildings formed a staggered horizon and selected soldiers applied their skills more directly amongst its rubble. There was no partition between the cheering crowd and the action-packed spectacle so that everyone could share fully in the atmosphere. They had arrived just in time to watch an unlucky few on the ground fight the bitter end of an unfair battle. These soldiers protected themselves with bullet-proof shields as they tried to move on those who fired down on them from above. Occasionally, a mortar would explode and take with it the side of a building or launch a group of soldiers into the air, receiving a shrill cry of delight from the bloodthirsty spectators. Medics ducked and weaved their way through the battle to tend the wounded soldiers. High above the arena, so that those on all tiers could see, were several large screens, along which rolled endless streams of numbers and the current status of each of the soldiers below. These screens then began to count down from one hundred in unison, and the fighting intensified before the buzzer that ended it all sounded. Not a single shot was fired after and their objectives were forgotten as they crawled from their positions and cleared the arena. There was a brief intermission as the stewards prepared for the next show and the crowd lapsed into silence in eager anticipation of what was to follow.

Sixteen sullen-looking men and women were then led onto the stage, bound to one another by the links of a single chain. They were unlocked from their bondage into the limited liberty of the arena, each taking in their surroundings with great attention. The buzzer then sounded and the screens above began to count down from one hundred, the dropping figure echoed by the crowd. Off the sixteen ran in all directions, scouring every nook and cranny of this created world for somewhere to hide. By the time the countdown reached zero and the buzzer again sounded, all had disappeared from view.

'The weak of our system,' explained the Commander.

Upon the second buzzer, soldiers of all ages flooded the arena and immediately began hunting those who had hid moments earlier. A gunshot rang out as the first of the sixteen were found, followed seconds later by another being thrown from the heights of one of the battle-worn buildings. The soldiers searched high and low, executing those they found as the countdown ticked down from five hundred. Fifteen had been found, according to the screens, by the time the buzzer sounded for the end of the event. The searching soldiers left the arena in a shared sense of disappointment, while the stewards entered and pulled a shaking little girl from the depths of a septic tank. She was led from the arena under the adulation of the clapping crowd and everyone cheered her resilience. Another batch of soldiers took their positions in the arena, ready to participate in another battle, but the Professor had seen enough, and he urged his group to return to their accommodation.

There was little talk amongst them as they drove back down through the dark and winding channels of the city to its ground level. The spectacle at the Coliseum had left no doubt in the minds of the three men as to the horror that awaited the survivors of their attack. When the subject was broached, the Commander responded that they should therefore ensure all twelve devices were armed before detonation. 'Those who remain will be hunted and exterminated in much the same manner you have just witnessed.'

'And, of course,' added the King, 'Paegonaean history will honour your men as the noble soldiers who overcame the last of the cruel and savage beasts from which they evolved. But surely the fate of your men are as decided as those you hunt. The future holds no place for your mercenary men and women.'

'Death is no longer feared by our people,' said Cornelle. 'These people merely know when it will come to them and they give their lives gladly in the service of something greater. It is those who live and die without ever having had such a cause that you should pity.'

They returned to the mess hall in time for supper and the Commander quitted his guests at the door with a reminder to meet the following morning. Inside, the young boys formed a queue around the large room as they were each served their supper and ate in a collective silence, broken only by the scraping of their plates. Now, without the Commander to guide them through the customs of this world, the three guests followed the lead of the boys and did not speak as they ate. Once they had finished, each of the youngsters arose from their tables and walked outside, lifting off their grey robes and placing them in one of several large hampers outside a building across the street, into which they now huddled.

Water fell from taps above their heads and was carried away in drains beneath their feet. Soap hung from strings with an arm-length between each, to be shared by those within its reach. A row of mirrors surrounded the showering room, where large containers dispensed toothpaste. Clean robes were lifted out of hampers as they left through the other side of the building. The King and his men each took a robe after showering and walked back to the mess hall and up the stairs to the first floor of this building.

Tightly-packed rows of single beds stretched its entirety with a small locker beside each of them to hold the few possessions of each young soldier. The King and his men found their quarters up some steps in a partitioned room, where three beds had been laid. There was a light shuffling from the room as the lights began to go out and was followed by a silence that lasted all through the night.

Morning was announced by the sounding of an alarm that came from the speakers around the room and lights above flickered on. Up got the young soldiers and they immediately marched down the stairs as they pulled on their robes and ventured out into the cold morning to begin their day. It was still dark outside and the King and his men awoke more hesitantly, struggling against the warmth and comfort of their beds. After pulling on their robes, they followed the King through the city's alleyways to the spot where the craft had landed the day before. There, they sat without speaking, their thoughts communing around their mission and the day ahead.

A truck pulled up and they were waved aboard by its driver. Morning had yet to break upon the layers above and the men watched blearily as the same habits were acted out across the city, with the waking masses queuing to get washed and fed in the districts they passed through. A dormant Coliseum in the distance broke the monotony of their journey and reminded each of them of what lay ahead.

They stopped a short distance from the final wall, next to a small windowless building no bigger than an outhouse. Beside it stood the Commander, again escorted by his two guards. A smile broke across his face as the three men approached in the grey robes of the Paegonaean army. He stepped from before the door of this tiny building and ushered them down a narrow set of stairs within. At the bottom of these steps was a platform, which ran alongside a track that extended through a dark tunnel beyond. Upon this track was a flatbed carriage, on which sat a sleek little vehicle with seats inside for three.

'All that remains is to wish you every success,' said the Commander, as the men climbed inside. 'This carriage will take you beyond the reach of our defence grid and the vehicle has enough charge to last you three days. Its on-board computer shall direct you to each of the devices.' He looked at the three men earnestly as the vehicle sealed around them and saluted each of them in turn as the carriage began moving. They gathered speed as they rolled along the slight gradient of the dark tunnel and, three hours later, splashed underwater, where the vehicle disconnected from the carriage and its motor roared to life.

– XV –

The Decision

Sunlight streamed in from above and orange beads of muddy water ran down the vehicle's frame as it emerged from the murky pool. The vehicle's digital-layout came to life as they struggled up the slippery embankment and connected with the wastelands' system. There were no vehicles in the immediate vicinity that could have picked them up on their radars, nor any wayward travellers or campers lurking nearby to watch them emerge from the marsh with their own eyes. The once-proud trees that surrounded this ancient spring were now withered corpses, and the water source on which they subsisted now poisoned mud. Once they had pulled themselves free from it and rolled onto more solid ground, the King got out of the vehicle and lifted a pair of binoculars to his eyes. A huge convoy rolled along on its way out into the depths of the wastelands, only recognisable from such a distance by the sheer number of vehicles of which it consisted. After lowering the binoculars, the King tapped on the window of their vehicle and asked the Professor to find out what was going on.

The Professor tapped his commands on the vehicle's keyboard and awaited their results. 'Heavy artillery and military vehicles from almost every registered security firm,' he answered. 'They seem to be arranging themselves around the walls of Hexlon and lining before the perimeter of the defence grid.'

'They are preparing for battle,' replied the King in a slow drawl that descended into thought. Something was amiss. 'Search the radio for any news.'

Mack switched on the radio and began searching the airwaves through a mesh of voices giving orders and the occasional whirl of music when he happened upon the dramatic jingle of a morning news report.

'The siege of Hexlon has ended,' announced a female newscaster, followed by another short jingle, after which, she continued. 'Despite sparse pockets of resistance throughout the city from those who have remained loyal to Hexlon and the Company, the Free World Coalition claim to have, at last, taken control of the level one fortress. Two days ago, the dissident group, led by Company rebels and senior elements of the Techtorian guards, stormed the city of Hexlon and the Company's military base at Tyra after accusing them of putting their establishment before the threat they now faced and maintaining too casual a response towards the Paegonaeans. A pre-emptive strike against their wall has always been regarded as unacceptable by the Company, and they have maintained this stance despite growing opposition. With the annihilation of the thousands who were caught in the prohibited zone when the defence grid went back on-line without warning, many now feel that a retaliatory strike is needed. Opinion polls are showing that the rebel group have over seventy percent of public support and are pulling together the disillusioned ranks of security firms from all over the Free world into one unified army. Hexlon has always been suspected of sympathy towards the Paegonaean regime, and now it seems that the Company are being accused of putting profit before the safety of its citizens. A spokesperson for the newly established group reassured reporters at a press conference, only minutes ago, that with the level one fortress behind their new army, any ground or air assault against them shall be met with significant resistance. With whatever tentative semblance of peace now gone, it seems that war has become inevitable. Whatever the outcome, we advise all of our listeners to take necessary precautions and look out for one another in the days ahead. Good luck to all of us.'

Mack turned off the radio and watched the King's downcast features for any sign of hope. It seemed that there was none, for the King's usually-impassive eyes glimmered with dismay and his voice was somewhat disheartened when he spoke. 'That changes things significantly.'

A raw and uncomfortable silence arose as the King wandered off and kicked at the dust. 'We now face an active and united force,' he began, 'and so, we will need weapons. Set coordinates for Hexlon. There is a bunker just beyond their outer marker where we can get all we need. I will tell you when we are near it.'

Despite the dour expressions that had seized both Mack and the Professor, the King quickly resumed his optimism as he climbed into the vehicle and reassured his companions that they would indeed fulfil their mission yet. They smiled uneasily in return and the wheels of their vehicle then spun, raising two fountains of dust behind them as they took off through the wastelands.

Having been forced from the trodden path that acted as a motorway through the soft dust by the endless push of military vehicles on their way to Hexlon and beyond, the team were forced through the little communes and villages that dared not stray too far from it. The thick wheels and speed of their vehicle proved enough for them to pass over the treacherous ground without faltering, and it was there that they best observed the uncertain mood of the Free world. Those villages that had not already been evacuated were in the process of doing so now, as essentials and cherished items were loaded onto all kinds of vehicles. FWC trucks lurked in the background with the intention of assuming the vacated villages as their bases. As the team travelled further into the wastelands, the more adapted these villages became; transformed from humble homes and workplaces to armoured posts with small missile defence systems overlooking the vast plain before them. The guards in these stations huddled around radios for any precious word of their situation and feverishly contacted all those who may have been privy to some morsel of information. But there was an ominous feeling that hung thick in the silent air.

'It really is a pity,' said Mack in a slightly bitter tone. 'It seems to me that both sides are evenly met and a battle between them should decide the future. There is no greater feeling than fighting for your homeland. These people would go to their death gladly having tasted such honour and their lives vindicated in the final glory of battle.' He paused for a thoughtful moment and resumed again more personally. 'I have a son, as you know. He lives with some of the other boys in an encampment in the east. They have been waiting for a battle like this all their lives and it would be a shame if they were to perish before the invasion began. Would it be possible to contact them... and them alone... tell them of what is to come and where they would be safe? What difference would a handful of men make against such an army as we have seen beyond the wall? Perhaps they could even help us locate the devices and immediately half our workload?'

'No,' said the King with such immediacy that it defied any level of retort.

Mack sighed silently and thought of the opportunity being robbed of his former students. What he would have given to be standing before them now on the steps of his academy. Fragments of the rousing address he would deliver flowed through his mind alongside the battle-hungry faces of his boys, crying out for blood and glory. How he loved to hear them whoop and cheer at the success of one of their missions, and this was how he saw them now. A strange smile curled the ends of his mouth as the close of his reverie drew near.

Up ahead, the mountain of Hexlon rose steadily and lifted the flat horizon further into the blue sky. Outside the city walls, in the red dust beyond, were encamped the mass of security vehicles, hoping that they would soon receive some direction from the newly-established FWC leadership within.

'The bunker is near,' said the King, quite out of the blue. He gave the Professor the coordinates, who dutifully inputted the data into the digital-layout, and a path appeared on the screen to a point just ahead.

For those lost, outcast or unfortunate souls who found themselves out there in that barren stretch of soft dust, there was nothing in the surrounding landscape to suggest any hint of deliverance. These mysterious bunkers, however, had entered into folklore; their existence whispered among certain circles, and there were stories of travellers stumbling upon these treasure-troves. Whether these tales were true or not, the King found every bunker he had visited fully stocked and secured. As the path on the digital-layout came to an end, the cruiser's motor began to slow and the King climbed out once it had stopped. A haunting silence was held at bay by the crossing winds as he stood there.

'It is around here somewhere,' he said, stamping about in the dust, searching for hollow ground below. Once he had located it and confirmed its presence by tracing the bunker's outline, he skimmed around it once more and unearthed a wire that was connected to a tiny retinal scanner. He wasted no time in placing it to his eye and he blinked several times so that a correct reading could be taken. The Professor climbed out of the vehicle and approached, watching all in silence from a few feet behind the King. There was a thud and a loud sucking noise, as though the underground bunker had just depressurised, and the ground began shifting backwards, pouring the overlying red dust into the darkened chamber it concealed.

'Incredible!' mouthed the Professor, as the rising dust caught in the mid-morning sun and formed a fading screen over the contents it held.

Fourteen stone steps ran down from the edge, where both men now stood, and the King ventured down them with a hand covering his mouth and nose. The Professor began choking as he followed him down and they waited at the bottom for the dust to settle and afford them both a more thorough perusal. There were guns of all descriptions shelved on rows on either side, from those that could be concealed in the palm of a hand to those that rested upon a muscled shoulder. There were things there that the Professor could have no clue as to their purpose, as well as body armour and medical kits marked with the treatment of every injury that could befall a stricken warrior. He could hear the clink through the dust ahead as the King filled a backpack with all that they would need.

The sound of the idling motor above poked sharply through the whistling wind and was followed by the shriek of cogs being forced upon one another against their will. Terror struck the Professor like a thunderbolt, and he made it to the top of the steps just as their vehicle spluttered by. He chased after it as though his life depended on it and locked eyes with Mack, who stared almost fearfully through the window behind him. His escape then gained some measure of fluidity and the vehicle pulled away from the Professor's grasp.

'Treacherous dog!' shouted the Professor, before falling to his knees and weeping aloud. 'All is lost!' he repeated. All is lost!'

It was obvious that he was heading for Hexlon. The full extent of this defeat fell upon the Professor like a shower of bricks and he wept as his imagined glory turned cold and bitter and grey. In the midst of this turmoil, the King pushed an old motorbike up the steps from the bunker and fired up its motor.

'That dog is gone!' shouted the Professor, pointing to the dust trail leading off towards Hexlon. 'He has everything! We are defeated!'

There was no turning back after that.

There were no excuses or explanations that could now conciliate his former accomplices, who he had just left stranded in the middle of the wasteland desert. He had chosen and must now remain true to his decision. Mack's heart raced with an excitement that he had not felt in years. The Professor's eyes, however, had been branded into his mind and held their look of deep reproach, now serving as the conscience he had lived his life without. At the touch of a few buttons, the digital-layout flashed with the location of the twelve devices and he memorised each of their coordinates and codes by a system of mnemonics. Such information was more real than all the credit in the Company's monetary system and, along with inside intelligence of the Paegonaeans' Outermost Ring, Mack was now in a very powerful position indeed. Before reaching Hexlon's outer marker, he ripped out the vehicle's on-board computer and buried it in the dust where no one would ever find it. He would need to act quickly if he was to impose himself in this mess. The sight of the disorderly army that surrounded the walls of Hexlon somehow heightened his lofty aspirations, but he would first have to negotiate his way through them if he was to be allowed near the upper echelons of power.

There had been little news to excite these troops; held at bay outside the city walls by the politics of those who now claimed leadership. They had been lured with the promise of joining the ranks of a new and unified army, but instead found only chaos and confusion. A power struggle was unfolding amongst the representatives within, as old rivalries and alliances were resurrected and corrupted the flow of information. And so, the rabble sat in the shade of the city walls, trying to establish contact with those who might know something and making alliances of their own. Overthrow, it seemed, was the easy part.

Their wavering attention soon found focus upon the mud-encrusted vehicle that was hurtling towards them.

All were instantly united in the vague hope that the occupant of this vehicle brought with him news of some kind. There were no tags on the vehicle, however, and its panels bore no markings to claim which group it represented. A warning shot was fired, followed several seconds later by another two that took out its front tyres and the head of the vehicle dug itself sharply into the dust. It was immediately seized upon and surrounded by twelve men on horseback with weapons pointed towards the dazed driver as he climbed out of the crumpled wreck.

The group that now detained him wore the uniform of the Dryson Cats; a group who protected no land or region, but worked as outside contractors for those with grievances against their keepers. However, they were more known nowadays for their diplomacy. The leader of the group stepped forward and looked this stranger up and down. 'State your name and business.'

'I have information that must be delivered to the holders of Hexlon city,' said Mack, wiping a trickle of blood from his forehead.

'What kind of information?' the guard asked more keenly.

'Information regarding the Paegonaeans and their attack.'

His words were met with silence and the guns slowly dropped from around him.

'What do you know?'

'I know of a plot to detonate twelve devices already positioned around the Free world, one of which lies within the walls of Hexlon. I have the coordinates of each of these devices and will only speak to the highest in command. Now, do you wish to detain me further and have those who survive know that it was the Dryson Cats who let the apocalypse come about?'

'How do you know all this?'

'You have been told all you need to know. Now let me through.'

The guard took a step back and summed all that he had just learned in his head. If this man spoke the truth then there could be no further wasting of his time. However, he could never let such a promising asset simply slip through his fingers, to be profited by someone else further along the chain of command. This would be their ticket in.

'I will make some calls,' he said, signalling to one of his men who stood by with a radio. 'But we have some conditions of our own.'

Mack nodded that he continue.

'You will be taken into our custody. Those at the gates shall be informed that we will hand you over in exchange for being stationed inside the walls with a direct line to the Palace. Accept these demands and you shall pass. Refuse, and let the apocalypse be on your head.'

Mack agreed without wasting a second and was pulled onto the back of a truck, where he was forced to his knees by several armed guards. The leader of the Dryson Cats walked just ahead of the truck and fired several shots into the air, ending the rambling of the crowd. 'Make way!' he shouted. 'We have a prisoner who has information about an attack! He claims that there is a bomb in the city and we are escorting him inside! Stand back, for he is our prisoner!'

The sea of bodies drifted apart into a corridor that led right through to the eastern gate of the city and vehicles of all types were moved out of their way. They made it halfway when a stout and elderly man stepped before their vehicle. 'And who is this man?' he shouted. 'Is he not one of your own who you have bound as your prisoner so that you may deceive this crowd?'

'We answer to no one out here! There is a bomb somewhere in the city and we alone know its coordinates. Once inside, we shall pass on what we learn! But first you must step aside!'

A murmur of mixed response arose and the suspicious guard yielded from his questioning and stepped back into the crowd. There was pushing and shoving as those around scrambled to get a look at this prisoner. Some vented their frustration by throwing supplies of food and empty water bottles at the truck and their prisoner. Word was passed from ear to ear inside and a group of officials were summoned to the city's gates and watched the men approach.

The stench of its battle had been well contained by the city walls and, once beyond them, the true devastation of Hexlon was revealed. Rows of buildings lay smouldering and plumes of smoke withered in the air. It had been mostly Techtorians alongside guards from a few other security firms who did most of the fighting and, now that the battle was over, it would be them alone who rebuilt the conquered city.

Upon his delivery to the awaiting officials, Mack was quickly ushered aboard another truck. After some explanation of the conditions he had before agreed to, he was joined by four of the Dryson Cats.

'Where is the device?' asked one of the so-called officials. His uniform belonged to the upper ranks of the Techtorian guards and his long ginger hair was matted with blood and dust. It did not seem as though his ragged patience would hold out to ask another time, but Mack knew that he needed to be recognised as an equal rather than a prisoner if he was to begin his ascent to the top.

'Take off these shackles,' he demanded.

His request was immediately met.

'I shall take you to the device on the condition that *I* deliver the coordinates of the eleven that remain to those in command myself.'

A silent vote of acquiescing nods from his colleagues gave the guard the backing to agree to this substantial demand. 'The Dryson Cats shall go no further than the fortress, where they will be stationed with a direct line set up between them and those of their group who remain outside. Only Techtorian guards are allowed to the Palace at this time, and I shall personally escort you there.' The guard then added in a quiet whisper. 'Should your bomb be a hoax, you shall be executed by order of the new leadership for wasting her time and resources.'

The dawdling pace of the truck exploded into haste and a siren set wailing once Mack had given the coordinates of the first device. It raced along the devastated streets of Hexlon with curious and battle-worn guards looking on from the sides. Many jumped in vehicles of their own as it passed and followed the speeding truck in the hope that something worthwhile was about to reveal itself. When they reached their destination, Mack was pushed from the back of the truck and the guards looked around the empty alleyway for anything out of the ordinary. Those involved in the search turned up nothing, and Mack felt a chill run along his spine as his status slowly slipped back to condemnation. Only now did he consider that these bombs may have been a ploy to expose his treacherous nature. A manhole was lifted some distance up the alleyway and a guard climbed down into the sewer below and shone a torch through the dark cavern. With this their last hope, everyone gathered around the top of it and someone shouted down if he saw anything.

'It stinks,' returned the voice. 'There's nothing down here.'

Reproving and hungry eyes found Mack and a nod was given to the two guards behind to move in and seize him.

'Wait!' shouted the guard from the sewer. 'There is some kind of shaft here and the plate used to seal it seems newly fitted. Throw me down something to wedge it off.'

Tools were fetched and lowered down and the suspicion centring on Mack eased momentarily.

'Woh!'

'What is it?' shouted the gathering above.

'I don't know, but it has flashing lights and does not look like it belongs down here.'

A ripple of excitement passed through the crowd that had gathered behind the cordoned area and whispers spread in every direction beyond. Everyone in the city was now converging upon the head of this narrow alleyway and even those outside were jumping with anticipation. Those with expertise in diffusing such devices were asked to come forward and, within fifteen minutes, a team of three men from the outside were pushed through the crowd.

'State your profession,' shouted the ginger-headed Techtorian guard, as the men made their way down the alleyway.

'We worked for the Company until three days ago and were stationed at Tyra, where we were charged with diffusing such devices found in the wastelands.'

'What are your demands?'

'That we be allowed to pick our own team and resume this post under the Free World Coalition.'

'Agreed,' said the guard quickly, and the three men climbed down the ladder to tend the device that held them all hostage.

With his men now occupied by the demands of the team below and the crowd captivated by the scene they created, the Techtorian guard took Mack by the arm and led him aboard the truck. Its motor started seconds later and the Dryson Cats jumped on before it took off. Again, the siren began to wail and a passage was cleared for them through the crowd that now stretched along what remained of the city, all the way to the fortress.

'How do you know about all of this?' asked the Techtorian guard in a friendlier tone.

'I will tell you when we are on our way to the Palace.'

This was enough to satisfy the guard for now and he fell back into his seat and looked out towards the mountain before them.

Those at the fortress gates had already been informed of the news and the racing truck was waved inside without further delay. There were many guards within the compound and they all waited in hope as they watched the men climb out. Mack, however, had been forbidden to speak to anyone but the guard who now led him through the lower reaches of the fortress. Instead, the men who had gathered there were ordered to show the four Dryson Cats to their new station and acquaint them with their duties. No one dared challenge this concerted show of authority for fear that it came directly from whoever it was in charge. The path was then cleared for Mack and his escort to pass through the warehouses that held the cablecar within their spread.

They climbed the ladder to the cablecar stall, where they were met by a representative from the provisional leadership. He commended the guard for a job well done and then turned to Mack and shook his hand before welcoming both to the Free World Coalition's new headquarters.

'Fighting at the Company's base at Tyra is ongoing,' he added, as the doors of the cablecar were closed behind them. 'But we expect victory soon and then we will have total control of the Free world's defence network.'

After outlaying some details requested by the representative as to the operation involving the device found in the city, the Techtorian guard reminded Mack of the promise he had made in the truck.

He began as they were hoisted into the air. 'I was contacted by the King of Hexlon and another some days ago and was asked to escort them beyond the wall into Paegonaean territory. There, I learned of the plot against us and now bring this information to you. What remains of this tale will await the attention of those in the Palace.'

'You wish to exchange this information for money?' asked the guard.

Mack shook his head.

'For power?' asked the representative.

Mack nodded with a crooked smile.

'How do we know that the device you led us to was not planted by yourself in order to gain our confidence?' asked the Techtorian guard.

'One has only to think of the effort necessary in building a bomb and having it delivered to know that it could not have been done without drawing some attention. No, the bomb you found was constructed in the Paegonaeans' Outermost Ring; where their army is stationed and poised for their attack.'

'You have seen this land?'

Mack again nodded, and both men looked to one another and marvelled at this immense slice of fortune.

They ascended through the jagged course of mount Hexlon, with the true cost of their coup evident in the blackened city below. All three maintained a respectful silence as they looked down upon this devastation until the fine wisps of cloud began to cover it from view. When they emerged through the canopy they formed into the restricted world above, the representative again spoke with another question. 'So you have met with the King of Hexlon?'

'I have,' answered Mack. 'A very honourable and brave young man and a formidable warrior. I left him and the other I mentioned out in the wastelands and have already informed the Dryson Cats as to their location. It is imperative that they be captured immediately.'

Again they lapsed into silence as the spires of the secret Palace rose high into the sky amongst the peaks of its mountain. The Techtorian guard gasped as it revealed itself and the representative commented that it was indeed an awesome sight to behold. Mack thought of the King when he saw it and again felt the eyes of the Professor burrow deeper into his soul. The splendour of the surrounding gardens came into view as the cablecar pulled onto the docking station, and Mack stepped out as though he had finally come home. They were met by three guards, who led the way up the winding path, through the forest and between the narrow corridor of trees to the Palace. It was obvious that there had been no battle up there. Everything was still perfectly intact; every flower and brick lay just as it had, undisturbed beside its neighbour.

As the great doors opened and the decadent domain of the King laid before him, Mack stepped onto its red carpet and was immediately filled with the importance in which the previous tenant had lived his life. Those who had gathered in small groups here and there turned from the papers they discussed and watched as he was led up the stairs to a room in the Palace's top floor. By its double doors stood a guard at each side with instructions to admit only them. A silence rushed through the room as the three men entered.

'So this is him?' asked one of the men, as he made his way towards them, beholding Mack with an undecided mixture of gratitude and distrust.

Mack dismissed his attention and wandered past him in full appreciation of his surroundings. Screens lay all around the room, on which those with privileged lines of communication exchanged their scraps of information with those in command. A table had been placed in the centre of the room with a detailed model of the Free world, encased by the great wall that surrounded it. These men had spent the day speculating on every eventuality and moving around the model armies in response to each of them. With the arrival of this stranger came the hope of more solid information and he now held the room in silence as he finished his perusal of their operation.

'Who is in charge here?' he asked.

There was a shuffle of unease as those in the room looked to one another and then to the person they thought most highly ranked.

'We have very little time,' announced Mack. 'I need to speak with those in charge before I detail our plan of attack.'

Three men stepped forward. They gave their names and each followed by stating their rank as Director of their respective firms.

'You have two problems,' Mack began. 'The first is a lack of information regarding the enemy, and the second is a lack of leadership. I am here to propose a solution that will help you with both. It is true that I have been to the Paegonaean territory beyond our wall, and there, I learned of their plot. I have the coordinates of the remaining eleven devices and inside information regarding the layout of their territory and defence grid. Using this knowledge, I have devised a plan that will ensure the best chance of victory; but to do so, I will need your army under my command.'

A gasp of incredulity escaped from those in the room and the smallest of the three Directors stepped forward and spat scornfully. 'Who do you think you are, making such demands? What gives you the right to demand leadership?'

'You need someone unaffiliated with the security firms, now individually defunct and unified under a new order,' began Mack nonchalantly. 'I have seen the enemy's base and the power source of their defence grid. Once we have diffused the eleven devices they have planted around our land, my plan is to destroy this power source and breach the wall.'

'And if we refuse?' asked the same small man.

'Then you refuse the details I alone possess.'

'Extortion!' he cried aloud, pulling a sidearm from its holster. 'You shall give us the coordinates of the remaining devices or be executed here and now for withholding vital information!'

'I don't think you will,' replied Mack, wandering off around the room again, as though now appealing to those who sat in the background. 'You have zero chance of success without this information. Kill me and you kill everyone. This is a formidable army we face, gentlemen. Our only chance is to take down the defence grid and storm their territory.' He then returned his eyes to the small Director who had dared to question the authority he proposed. 'You are no leader for what lies ahead. *I* shall lead this army to victory.'

'You have seen the other side?' asked someone else.

'What is it like?' asked another.

'It is very picturesque,' Mack answered. 'Their world is divided into rings by great walls. Only their Outermost Ring holds any military capability. Once we have gained this territory, we would be free to penetrate further into their peaceful realm with little or no resistance.'

'What about the defence grid?' asked one of the other two Directors.

'Along the back wall of their Outermost Ring, there runs a continuous field of solar panels. These are the source of the defence grid's power. I propose that we fire every missile we have in their direction in the hope that we can cause enough disruption to bring it down altogether. It is uncertain, but it is our only chance.'

'You have seen these solar panels?'

'I know exactly how far beyond the outer wall they are. Once the defence grid goes down, we breach this wall here, here and here,' he said, utilising the model that lay before him. 'Now, I suggest that we find the bombs they have planted about our land quickly so that we may begin our attack.'

Even the doubtful Director could not help but admire the firmness and directness of this plan. They now had targets in the solar panels and objectives in diffusing the remaining bombs. All they needed was the location of each of them and they could begin their attack. Having already entreated to their sense of survival, Mack now confirmed their allegiance by indulging their avarice. 'I am confident of victory, and positions of wealth and power for every man in this room. We, gentlemen, shall decide the future of mankind.'

He was inaugurated with a handshake from each of the three Directors and the room began to clap their new and undisputed leader. The coordinates of each device were given and the lines of communication flowed. A wave of purpose rolled through the city and vehicles were sent off in every direction under the orders of the new regime. Confirmation that the first of the devices had been diffused came in shortly after, and they watched upon a screen as they began to disappear. With only a few remaining, the new ruler of Hexlon set about his strategy for the immediate expansion of his realm. Missile launchers were summoned and slowly made their way to the front line and their trajectories were set. He watched his army assemble and arrange themselves into formation on the surrounding screens, only waiting to hear that the last of the bombs had been diffused before giving the order to fire.

A radio crackled to life and was presented to the new leader of this army with a bow. 'It is for you, sir.'

Mack lifted the radio to his mouth and spoke. 'Hello?'

High upon a mountain, windswept from the miles they had covered at high speed, sat the remaining two members of the team. A cold shiver passed through the Professor upon hearing Mack's voice again.

'The die has been cast,' said the dethroned King. 'The vote is two against one.'

Mack's response was uncharacteristically hesitant. 'Is that you?' There was no reply and he continued in his usual tone. 'I knew you would get away. Where are you?' Again there was no reply. 'I suppose I can't ask you that now? Well, your mission is over. We are awaiting confirmation on the last of the devices as we speak and our troops have been mobilised to the front line. The fate of the world does not rest with you any longer. War shall decide what is to come.' He waited a little longer this time, but there was still no reply; no one was on the other end.

The eyes of the room stared at Mack, who sat motionless and silent for a moment before jumping from his chair. 'Hasten our attack!' he shouted. 'We move now!'

A siren began to sound through the fortress at that point and those in the room looked around in confusion. The screens, upon which they had watched the progress of their mission, went off momentarily and resumed again seconds later, all now with the number ten upon them. Before anyone could question this turn of events, the number on the screens turned to nine. Someone had triggered the fortress's self-destruct sequence and a panicked evacuation ensued.

The sky that rested upon the dull red horizon flashed white and the great explosion carried through the wastelands and reached the mountaintop on which they sat as a gentle breeze.

'You knew he would betray us?' asked the Professor.

The King nodded and smiled. '*The thief would forsake all to become king for a day.*'

'But they have found the bombs. We are defeated.'

'Mack's actions have been known long before he knew them himself,' answered the King. 'The bombs were a decoy. Our destination is the Company's military compound at Tyra. There, we must take control of the missile defence system and use it to launch our attack.'

– XVI –

The last chapter

The destruction of Hexlon was instantaneous and absolute. Bricks and mortar rained down on the city and all were caught in the thick and choking mist that descended upon them. Those who watched from the surrounding villages and encampments felt a lonesome chill as they tried in vain to establish contact with anyone who had survived. The vague promise of a grand assault upon the surrounding wall went up with the roaring ball of flame in the distance. No longer were they the outstretched arms of a unified army, but isolated pockets of resistance strewn amongst the wasteland dunes.

Those further back retreated to the defence of their last stronghold at Tyra, on the border of Fortress city, where the battle for control still raged. The lower half of the famed military installation was now firmly in the hands of the Free World Coalition; their troops now occupying its network of bases and tenements. The upper half, situated high amongst the peaks, was still being defended by those loyal to the Company. These faithful soldiers had insulated themselves from the invading force below by sabotaging all links and passageways between them. It was there that the controls for the Company's missile defence system was situated, and it was this that they now protected. Many had worked all their lives for the Company and trusted their superiors more than this ragged army below. They would never relinquish control of the missiles to them. It would be them who used the necessary force when it was called for, but not before. Besides, if the rumours were true, these FWC invaders had just blown themselves up at Hexlon.

A tall but flimsy wire gate was all that separated the growing crowd outside from the FWC in the lower reaches. There was a constant chorus of gunfire from the battles up and down the mountain and, every now and then, a mortar would explode and debris would come crashing down upon the FWC's base. This beleaguered force now faced opposition from two opposing fronts; from those defending their position in the peaks above and from the civilian mob demanding protection in the base's rumoured bunkers. Warning shots were becoming less and less effective as those outside grew increasingly desperate. Frightened and angry cries at those who held the line against them rang out with more hostility as the day progressed. With the impending arrival of those who had pulled back from the safety of the demolished city of Hexlon, it was clear that the meagre force who held this thin line would soon be overcome. The King watched all through his binoculars, waiting for the time to move.

They climbed upon their motorbike and slowly descended the hilltop, discussing, as they did, the plan that would gain them access to the mountaintop base. In the distance were trucks and vehicles of all types converging upon the base from the wastelands, and they drove alongside them and eased their bike amongst their ragged convoy.

'I have studied the blueprints of both the lower and upper military base thoroughly and know the dimensions of every room and passageway,' said the King. 'There are several ways through to the hub in the upper compound, and there we will have access to the Company's missiles. However, security will be much tighter now and we will have to negotiate our way through the force that holds the lower part before convincing those at the top to hand over control of the defence system.'

'And how will we do that?'

'You are a highly esteemed employee of the Company and are considered an expert in the field of defence systems,' replied the King, as they ducked and weaved through the slowing convoy on their way towards the base. 'They are in a heightened state of alarm and uncertainty, and we will use this to our advantage. If we claim to have information regarding an imminent attack, they will have no option but to allow us through and hand over control. It will take bravery and imagination, two things you possess in abundance, my friend.'

The Professor gulped at this prospect. He knew that he was not a brave man, but he was no coward either. His frightened mind first filled with the obstacles they would face, but slowly cleared with thoughts of glory when he focussed upon the honour of their mission. The unification of Earth was now finally within the grasp of mankind and it was he who was charged with taking the final step. When they could go no further through the tightening crowd, they both jumped off the motorbike and made their way towards a truck, upon which stood a man who spoke with blistering zeal to the surrounding crowd.

'They take over our security and then deny us safety!' shouted the disillusioned guard, hoping to inspire the crowd to further insurrection. 'While they squabble for power amongst themselves, we are left outside to die like animals! I say we show them that we are no animals and take back our security for ourselves.'

His fiery words fanned the dormant embers of rage within each of them and the eager crowd began cheering so loudly that it sent a chill through the compound's fence and down the spine of every man behind it. Someone then broke from the crowd and climbed onto the back of the truck. After talking his way past the two men guarding the preacher, this man was allowed a quiet word in his ear.

'Wait!' the preacher shouted to the crowd, once this stranger had finished his whispered tale. 'There is someone here who brings word from the ruined city of Hexlon and claims to have information about what happened there!'

The microphone was handed to the Professor and the crowd fell silent to receive what he had to say. Bravery, thought the Professor, as he opened his mouth to speak. 'There shall be some here who recognise and know me, but for those who don't, let me explain. It was I who designed the Company's security system and I have worked at their Academy in the city for the past twelve years. After the Paegonaeans' defence grid went down, I discovered a latent signal within the codes that constitute our system. Upon further inspection, I traced the source of this signal beyond the wall that surrounds us to somewhere in the territory beyond. When I informed my superiors of these findings, I was put aboard a truck and taken to Hexlon. Upon my arrival there, I was taken to a cell, where I could tell no one of what I knew until my escape earlier today. This signal that I have found is how the Paegonaeans are manipulating our defences, and this they will use to destroy us, as they have done at Hexlon.'

The crowd fell into a deep silence, from which arose the murmurs of their disquietude.

'But how did you escape?' shouted someone from the crowd.

'I heard the siege from my quarters and was liberated by the guards who had taken the building in which I was being held. They mistook what I told them for the ramblings of a crazy fool and have paid the price for their dismissal.'

'What can we do to make sure that this does not happen here?'

'Our missile defence system must be taken offline immediately. It is in the hands of the enemy as we speak and our fate lies at their whim.'

This unsettling notion was just the right incentive for the panicky crowd to assist in any subsequent endeavour and elect the Professor as their new hope.

The FWC guards behind the wire fence looked on with increasing curiosity. Something was happening out there. Those who had chanced their lives trying to cross the wire that separated them had now pulled back and the protests they made fell silent. Like the swell of a tsunami, pulling the tide out to sea before unleashing its wrath with one deadly wave, the guards braced for what they thought would be the initial strike in an unstoppable insurrection. But instead, a path cleared between them, and those on both sides gesticulated to them that something or someone was coming through. The guards could do nothing but accept the delivery of this Trojan horse and they encircled the vehicle once it had passed through their gates.

'Who are you?' asked one of the guards inside.

The preacher, who had escorted them this far, spoke in place of the Professor in a hollow show of authority. 'This man has vital information regarding the missile defence system, and we, the people, demand that he be allowed through to resolve the crisis immediately.'

'What crisis?' asked the guard, turning to the Professor and urging him to speak.

'My boy,' he began. 'I have stumbled upon a plot that has seen me incarcerated for the past week and am now hunted by those who wish to destroy us. It is imperative that we take control of the missiles in the upper reaches of this base or we shall meet with the same fate as Hexlon.'

'We have not yet taken the upper reaches,' he said falteringly.

'Then I suggest you make peace right away or we shall all be united in death.'

A sudden awkwardness struck the guard, who turned with relief towards the approach of his superiors. All was explained to them in private discussion and they glanced throughout at the men requesting access to that which they themselves were fighting for.

'You know of a plot against us?' asked one of them.

'I do, and time is of the essence.'

A retinal scanner was produced and the Professor told to confirm his identity. When it was done, the superiors huddled around the screen of the device, awaiting the results. 'Head of systems at the Academy,' nodded one of them as they broke from their huddle. 'It says here that you have been missing for some days now and are wanted by the Company?'

'As I have told your colleague, the Company had me locked up so that I could tell no one of what I had found.

I only escaped by chance when your forces laid siege upon Hexlon. It is imperative that we move quickly and take the missile defence system offline.'

The superiors felt their authority dwindle in the presence of this knowledgeable newcomer. 'Who is your friend?' asked one of them, nodding towards the King, who had remained silent throughout.

'This young man has saved my life twice in the last four hours and was the only one at Hexlon to believe the tale that I now relate to you. There may be some of the conspiratorial element within and I have charged this guard with my personal protection. I shall go nowhere without him.'

'And what exactly is this conspiracy?' asked another.

'We do not have time to indulge in details,' the Professor replied quickly. 'There is a signal embedded in the Company's system that seems to be coming from the territory beyond the wall. Upon its discovery, there were attempts made to silence me and stop it from being exposed. Now, I beseech you; let us pass so that we may avert this disaster.'

No further word was spoken and a truck immediately summoned. The gate was closed after them as the Professor and the King were led further into the compound and awaited the arrival of their transport. Shelled buildings were being patched up whilst makeshift encampments housed the weary soldiers of this new army. Men in stretchers were being carried from the battles higher up the mountain and medics struggled to tend their heavy workload. The stench of death and its impending promise was everywhere.

'I can take you to our headquarters,' said the superior who had remained by their side. 'But it will be the decision of those loyal to the Company in the higher reaches whether you are allowed access to the defence system. Our advance is making progress, but I fear that it will be morning before we have control of what you seek.'

'By then we shall all be dust,' said the Professor.

A small transporter arrived for them and the Professor and the King climbed aboard with their new escort, who whispered their destination to its driver. They took off through the battle-damaged buildings of the lower compound with the soldiers of this new army running this way and that. Every now and then, a shower of heavy rocks would come crashing down the mountainside and fall like meteors upon all below.

The Professor cast his thoughts to those in the higher reaches in preparation of what was to come. He had the advantage of representing the Company at a time when their leadership had been evicted from power and hoped that those loyal servants above would see him as one of their own. There was also the fact that the news he brought had gained the confidence of those below and could put an end to the petty squabble between them and unite them with its knowledge. He cast a glance towards the King, who sat in deep meditation, revising the outlay of the upper reaches in his head and listing the ways they could get to the hub in order of probability and likelihood. They stopped outside a large building, relatively unscathed by the preceding battle and were hurriedly ushered through its corridors and led finally to the FWC headquarters.

'This is him,' said their escort as they entered the room.

All rose to their feet in anticipation of their new directives. There were thirteen men and women in total, all charged with the management of the various strands of their diverse operation.

'The Paegonaeans are in control of our missile system,' announced the Professor with such confidence that all were immediately rendered under his spell. 'They have manipulated the level one fortifications of Hexlon to destroy itself and, I fear, they are planning to use the missiles above in the ultimate destruction of the Free world.'

Horrified gasps from some were met with groans of defeat from others.

'Our only hope of survival is to take these missiles offline as quickly as we can.'

'How do we do that?' one of the men asked.

The Professor did not respond right away, but took a position at one of the computers and began to type his commands. 'We must first establish contact with those above and inform them of this plot.'

'Communications have been down for some time now,' another answered. 'There is no way of getting through to them.'

The others agreed that this was true, just as the Professor resurrected the downed communication feed between the two bases by entering a series of secret codes. A bewildered young guard appeared through the fuzz on the screen before him. 'Who is this?' he asked, with eyes squinting back at the Professor.

'Listen carefully. Our defences are being manipulated by a force outside of our realm and they are plotting to destroy us with the missiles you have in your possession.'

'Professor?' said the guard with deepening bewilderment, who then went on to explain. 'I was one of your students and graduated four years ago and have been posted out here since. What is this plot you speak of?'

The reception on the screen began to settle. 'There is a foreign signal in the system, by which those outside our realm are controlling our defences. This is why Hexlon now lies in ruins.'

The guard on the other end of the communication turned from the screen and conversed with someone else for a moment before returning with his answer. 'We can't see any impurities in the code, Professor.'

'The signal is too deeply embedded,' he answered. 'Any level of scanning available to us will be unable to pick it up. You need to isolate everything in the bottom bracket and listen for irregularities.'

'By ear?' asked the incredulous guard, knowing that there could only be a handful of people in all of the Free world with the ability to differentiate the signals of the system by listening to it.

'It is the only way.'

Again he turned from the screen to consult with those in the room. 'What is it exactly we are listening for?'

'Anything out of the ordinary. A systematic disruption in the flow.'

The guard then rose from his chair and returned moments later with a sheepish look upon his face. 'We're not entirely sure how to do that,' he said. 'Maybe you could help us find it?'

Even the King was impressed with his ingenuity. The Professor turned towards the men in the FWC headquarters and asked if they had a helicopter.

They all nodded, but one quickly added. 'There is too much fighting going on up the mountain. You would be shot down long before you reached the upper base.'

The Professor now addressed the guard on the screen before him. 'Can you tell your men to stand down and allow for my arrival? I can give you an assurance that those on this side will desist with their assault.'

After some consultation with those in the room, the guard responded with a bright beaming smile that he could, but to await his command before taking off. The two men were then led outside, where a helicopter was being prepped for the short journey. Gunshots rang out with decreasing regularity and eventually ceased fire altogether. Both the Professor and the King climbed aboard as the rotors began to whir. Moments later, one of the FWC guards came rushing out with authorisation to take off. As they lifted into the air, the Professor felt a wave of accomplishment rush through his bones and he looked towards the King beside him. 'I have done my part. Now, it is time to do yours.'

As the helicopter lifted into the air and began its ascent up the steep face of the mountain, one of the more meek members of the FWC leadership on the ground spoke with an innocent realisation that immediately soured their hopes into fear. 'Didn't the guard along with him look a little like the old King of Hexlon?'

By the time their suspicions were relayed through the line of communication the Professor had opened, the King had taken out the pilot of the helicopter and was approaching the landing site of the upper base.

The secured area that held the hub was sheltered deep beneath the rock of the mountain, with only the tip of its inner structure poking above the surface, with a drawbridge lowered to allow access to its depths. Defence from the air had been the principal focus of its design and it was said that the bunkers it contained could withstand any type of apocalypse. An assault from the air would be dealt with at the push of a button and the compound itself could be locked down so as to deny an assault up the mountainside.

'That's not good,' said the King, as the scene below presented itself through the trees that surrounded it.

'What is it?

The King nodded to the ground, where scores of soldiers were pouring across the building's drawbridge and taking positions around the landing site. It seemed that the hint of suspicion from below was enough to call for their detainment, at least until more sense could be made of their story. When asked how this affected them, the King responded by saying that his first four plans involved walking across the drawbridge and that they deviated respectively once safely inside. 'But, do not fear, there are other ways in, though we are forced now to reveal our intentions sooner than I had hoped.'

Three of the highest ranked Company officials and the guard who had authorised their arrival by agreeing to the ceasefire stood by the landing site and awaited the arrival of the helicopter. They were to detain both men and question them some more on the alleged signal before letting either of them near the controls.

But instead of watching the helicopter land just beside them, it descended amongst the trees ahead and disappeared from view. A siren sounded immediately and the order was given to retrieve the men without harm. The drawbridge began to close and the entrance to the cavernous world below was sealed.

The two men climbed out of the helicopter in a small clearing and the King went about his business. Whatever doubt the Professor had in the King's contingency plan was momentarily alleviated when he saw him kick the lid off an air-vent that reached down through the ground and into the bunkers below. The King first threw down his bag and then jumped down the vent himself, shouting for the Professor to follow him. Through the forest, the Professor could hear the measured convergence of the surrounding force and wasted no time in doing so.

The rotors on the helicopter still whirred as the Company guards moved in slowly with their weapons trained on their target. They could see the pilot sitting there and motioned for him to step out of the helicopter and place his hands behind his head. When he did not comply, they ventured a little further and reiterated their command with more urgency. Two of this team were then dispatched to open its doors and apprehend its occupants while the rest held their positions in preparation to fire. As the two men approached with cautious steps, those around them tightened their fingers upon the triggers of their weapons.

A mighty explosion ripped through the air and every one of the guards were sent tumbling backwards by the solid wall of fire and debris that emanated from it. There were dying groans in the air as they resurfaced into consciousness along with screams from those badly injured. The blast had been so loud that it had deafened those closest to it and alerted their entire force as to the whereabouts of the intruders. Helicopters were scrambled by the FWC and efforts made to assert their innocence in this affair, requesting that they be allowed to join forces in the apprehension of these individuals. The first of the downed guards with the presence of mind to report what had happened did so with a loud ringing in his ears. 'It was a trap!' he shouted. 'We have a large number of men down! No sign of the hostiles but they cannot be far! Get everyone over here now and comb the area!'

This message was relayed to all and the previous order to bring them in without harm rescinded. The request by the FWC to join in the search was rejected, though the line of communication between them remained open.

Through the network of ducts below crawled the King with the Professor close behind him. He had memorised this maze, amongst those of every such establishment in the Free world, during his lessons at the Palace and had fallen asleep on those nights to dreams of crawling through them. Upon reaching its end, the King kicked out an air purifier that obstructed their exit and it fell some distance before smashing on the floor. He jumped down into the large and dimly-lit bunker and held out his arms to catch the Professor. Emergency lighting illuminated the room in a shade so dull that they could just about make out the rows of seating towards the back of the bunker and the stores of tinned food and supplies. The first of those from beyond began to trickle in through the bunker's doors and they took their seats nervously, exchanging what little information they had.

Both men watched from their concealed position and, once the bunker had almost filled, they made their way through the doors and along a passageway that led up to the bottom floor of the main chamber. At the end of this passageway was a guard directing the dwindling flow of people into the bunker, and the Professor walked towards him and asked what was happening.

'Security has been breached,' he said. 'Go to the bunker and remain there until the threat has been neutralised.'

'But we must first secure the missiles' controls.'

'I can't allow anyone to go up there,' said the guard. 'There are others up there now doing just that.'

The King took him out with a flash of his knife and carried the lifeless body down the passageway to the bunker, as though helping an injured comrade and shouted for assistance. They quickly surrounded the fallen figure, as those first upon the scene checked his vitals and pronounced the man dead. The young man who had delivered his body now pushed shut the metal doors to the bunker and sealed it from the outside. He met with the Professor again on the bottom floor of the chamber and both looked up at the objective before them.

The narrow chamber that formed this inner sanctum had been built around the cylindrical hub of the missile defence system that reached up through its levels with platforms crossing to each floor. A spiralling staircase wound from the top to the bottom and connected with the platforms across every level with metal doors leading beyond. The hub itself was alive with flashing lights and screens with all manner of data rolling across them. On the middle floor, in the very centre of this hub, was the control room; a small inlet just large enough for five men to direct precision strikes to anywhere within the surrounding wall of their world. Though the compound had been locked down and all available personnel summoned in the search for the intruders outside, there was still a number of troops trapped within, concentrated mainly on the upper floors. It would not take long, however, before someone stumbled across the vent that the explosion from the helicopter had hereto concealed, and the entire army would then close in around them. The King fired the first of several shots and the Professor cowered at the sound of their echoing report.

A voice shouted from above. 'You are contained within this area and are outnumbered and outgunned! Surrender now and you shall not be killed!'

The King saw the head of the man who spoke through the mesh of overhanging passageways and railings and directed his rifle in his direction. With a single shot, the guard slumped to the floor and those around him opened fire. A fierce firefight ensued as the King began his ascent up through the floors. It was imperative that they reach the control room quickly and set the targets for their attack before reinforcements arrived. Bewildered technicians fell where they stood as the descending guards were forced to retreat back up through the chamber with the intensity and precision of the invader's attack. From the safety of the top floor, the guards reorganised themselves into two separate teams and slowly made their way down again, in the hope that one group may force their target into the line of fire of the other. But a well placed grenade thrown by the King wiped out one of the wings of this attack, and those at the other side were forced to retreat once more and formulate a new response with their diminishing resources. By the time the King and the Professor made it to the control room, sparks had begun to trace the outline of the sealed doors on every level.

'It will not be long before they are through!' shouted the King, still directing his fire to keep those above them at bay. 'Load the targets and get ready to fire!'

The Professor began entering the coordinates. 'The missiles must be prepped before I can launch them! This could take some time!'

As though in anticipation of this dilemma, the King quickly modified his command. 'Begin the preparation and download the controls onto your portable handset! Once we are breached there will be no holding those who enter back! There is a staircase one floor up that leads out to a helipad on a secluded part of the mountaintop! You will need to hack the system for there is a door sealing this exit! Make sure you open that door and that door alone!'

It did not take long before the Professor was inside the compound's security system. He perused the options of which door to open carefully and pushed the button to that which he had selected. A gust of fresh air filled the chamber. The desperation of their failing situation inspired the guards above with a kamikaze spirit. As the Professor began downloading the controls onto his handset, the guards pushed towards them with lessening regard for the sanctity of their own lives. Bullets now whizzed by with more regularity and pierced the hub that they had before tried to safeguard. An occasional body would fall through the chamber, bashing lifelessly against the platforms along the way and splat on the ground below. The King motioned for the Professor to move and covered his ascent up the stairs by spraying a hail of bullets upon the few remaining guards above. Sparks from the door opposite then subsided, having now traced the perimeter of its frame, and those on the other side banged against it. The King followed the Professor up the steps as the hull was breached.

'Have the controls downloaded yet?' shouted the King, as he knelt down beside him, opening fire on the force now storming the compound from every level.

'Thirty-four percent!' the Professor shouted back. 'Thirty-five!'

'We need more time! Go! I'll hold them off for as long as I can! Launch the missiles once the controls have downloaded!'

The King was hit as the Professor turned to run and he let out a roar of anger with his rifle firing brightly. With some hesitation, the Professor continued up the steps beyond. At the end of the tunnel lay a beautiful evening sky and he could hear the King shout for him to keep going. He ran out onto the blustery peaks and slowed to a crawl as he surveyed the land outside with a cautious eye. Grassy crags poked from the rocky surface with the helipad off in the distance. His first tentative steps gathered pace once assured that no guards lay in wait for him out there.

There were few places in all of the Free world where one could enjoy such a view. He could see the entire length of the wastelands to the thin grey horizon of the wall as the sun set beyond and was momentarily distracted in its appreciation. A strange noise disturbed him and he was suddenly forced to hasten on when he saw the blades of a rising helicopter. They opened fire upon spotting him and had just about reached him with the trail of their bullets when he fell down a hole and slapped his head off a rock. The Professor took his hand from his head to find it covered with dark red blood and looked at the screen of his handset with blurry eyes. The download had now reached eighty percent and he watched with fearful impatience as the meter slowly progressed. All above him was being ripped to shreds by the constant fire of the helicopter that held him pinned, when suddenly it turned its attention to another target. The Professor peeked out his head and saw the King running towards him, getting hit repeatedly by the bullets of the army that chased him. He fell down the hole to join with the Professor, somehow still alive and held together only by the will to see his mission through.

'Ninety-nine percent,' the Professor told him.

A weary smile broke across his face. 'Get ready.'

As they watched for the last hundredth of the controls to download and the system to initialise, a sniper in the peaks behind caught the King in his sights and was about to pull the trigger when something else caught his attention. Everything fell silent in that moment. Even the approaching army stopped in their tracks and looked to the sky in amazement. More and more were pointed out and all was forgotten in their mystery. The King looked up with the light of life fading fast within him to see the strange whorls from his vision slowly churning up high in the sky and the crafts that had travelled through them streaking the heavens as though a shower of shooting stars. The handset then bleeped that the controls were now ready, and the two men looked at one another before pushing the button to launch. There was a loud and powerful rumbling that seemed to shake the entire mountain as the first wave of missiles whooshed off to their targets.

David Blair was born in County Derry, Northern Ireland. He attended St. Columbs College and graduated from the University of Ulster with a Degree in English and French. The Paegonaean Story is his first book. You can follow the Paegonaean Story on Facebook and Twitter.

Breinigsville, PA USA
12 April 2011
259707BV00001B/3/P